MARY GRAY

MORE WILDSIDE CLASSICS

MARY GRAY

KATHARINE TYNAN

WILDSIDE PRESS

MARY GRAY

This edition published in 2006 by Wildside Press, LLC.
www.wildsidepress.com

CHAPTER I

WISTARIA TERRACE

The house where Mary Gray was born and grew towards womanhood was one of a squat line of mean little houses that hid themselves behind a great church. The roadway in front of the houses led only to the back entrance of the church. Over against the windows was the playground of the church schools, surrounded by a high wall that shut away field and sky from the front rooms of Wistaria Terrace.

The houses were drab and ugly, with untidy grass-plots in front. They presented an exterior of three windows and a narrow round-topped hall-door which was a confession of poverty in itself. Five out of six houses had a ramping plaster horse in the fanlight of the hall door, a fixture which went with the house and was immune from breakage because no one ever thought of cleaning the fanlights.

In the back gardens the family wash was put to dry. Some of the more enterprising inhabitants kept fowls; but there was not much enterprise in Wistaria Terrace.

Earlier inhabitants had planted the gardens with lilac and laburnum bushes, with gooseberries and currants. There were no flowers there that did not sow themselves year after year. They were damp, grubby places, but even there an imaginative child like Mary Gray could find suggestions of delight.

Mary's father, Walter Gray, was employed at a watchmaker's of repute. He spent all his working life with a magnifying glass in his eye, peering into the mechanism of watches, adjusting the delicate pivots and springs on which their lives moved. His occupation had perhaps encouraged in him a habit of introspection. Perhaps he found the human machine as worthy of interest as the works of watches and clocks. Anyhow, in his leisure moments, which were few, he would discuss curiously with Mary the hidden springs that kept the human machine in motion, the strange workings and convolutions of it. From the very early age when she began to be a comfort and a companion to her father, Mary had been accustomed to such speculations as would have written Walter Gray down a madman if he had shared them with the grown people about him rather than with a child.

Mary was the child of his romance, of his first marriage, which had lasted barely a year.

He never talked of her mother, even to Mary, though she had

vague memories of a time when he had not been so reticent. That was before the stepmother came, the stepmother whom, honestly, Walter Gray had married because his child was neglected. He had not anticipated, perhaps, the long string of children which was to result from the marriage, whose presence in the world was to make Mary's lot a more strenuous one than would have been the case if she had been a child alone.

Not that Mary grumbled about the stepbrothers and sisters. Year after year, from the time she could stagger under the weight of a baby, she had received a new burden for her arms, and had found enough love for each newcomer.

The second Mrs. Gray was a poor, puny, washed-out little rag of a woman, whose one distinction was the number of her children. They had always great appetites to be satisfied. As soon as they began to run about, the rapidity with which they wore out their boots and the knees of their trousers, and outgrew their frocks, was a subject upon which Mrs. Gray could expatiate for hours. Mary had a tender, strong pity from the earliest age for the down-at-heel, over-burdened stepmother, which lightened her own load, as did the vicarious, motherly love which came to her for each succeeding fat baby.

Mary was nurse and nursery-governess to all the family. Wistaria Terrace had one great recompense for its humble and hidden condition. It was within easy reach of the fields and the mountains. For an adventurous spirit the sea was not at an insuperable distance. Indeed, but for the high wall of the school playground, the lovely line of mountains had been well in view. As it was, many a day in summer Mary would carry off her train of children to the fields, with a humble refection of bread and butter and jam, and milk for their mid-day meal; and these occasions allowed Mrs. Gray a few hours of peace that were like a foretaste of Paradise.

She never grumbled, poor little woman, because her husband shared his thoughts with Mary and not with her. Whatever ambitions she had had to rise to her Walter's level — she had an immense opinion of his learning — had long been extinguished under the accumulation of toils and burdens that made up her daily life. She was fond of Mary, and leant on her strangely, considering their relative ages. For the rest, she toiled with indifferent success at household tasks, and was grateful for having a husband so absorbed in distant speculations that he was insensible of the near discomfort of a badly-cooked dinner or a buttonless shirt.

The gardens of the houses opened on a lane which was a sort of rubbish-shoot for the houses that gave upon it. Across the lane was a row of stabling belonging to far more important houses than Wistaria Terrace. Beyond the stables and stable yards were old gardens with shady stretches of turf and forest trees enclosed within their walls. Beyond the gardens rose the fine old-fashioned houses of the Mall, big Georgian houses that looked in front across the roadway at the line of elm-trees that bordered the canal. The green waters of the canal, winding placidly through its green channel, with the elm-trees reflected greenly in its green depths, had a suggestion of Holland.

The lane was something of an adventure to the children of Wistaria Terrace. There, any day, you might see a coachman curry-combing his satin-skinned horses, hissing between his teeth by way of encouragement, after the time-honoured custom. Or you might see a load of hay lifted up by a windlass into the loft above the stables. Or you might assist at the washing of a carriage. Sometimes the gate at the farther side of the stable was open, and a gardener would come through with a barrowful of rubbish to add to the accumulation already in the lane.

Through the open gateway the children would catch glimpses of Fairyland. A broad stretch of shining turf dappled with sun and shade. Tall snapdragons and lilies and sweet-williams and phlox in the garden-beds. A fruit tree or two, heavy with blossom or fruit.

Only old-fashioned people lived in the Mall nowadays, and the glimpses the children caught of the owners of those terrestrial paradises fitted in with the idea of fairyland. They were always old ladies and gentlemen, and they were old-fashioned in their attire, but very magnificent. There was one old lady who was the very Fairy God-mother of the stories. She was the one who had the magnificent mulberry-tree in her garden. One day in every year the children were called in to strip the tree of its fruit; and that was a great day for Wistaria Terrace.

The children were allowed to bring basins to carry away what they could not eat; and benevolent men-servants would ascend to the overweighted boughs of the tree by ladders and pick the fruit and load up the children's basins with it. Again, the apples would be distributed in their season. While the distribution went on, the old lady would stand at a window with her little white dog in her arms nodding her head in a well-pleased way. The children called her Lady Anne. They had no such personal acquaintance with the other gardens and their owners, so their thoughts were very full of Lady Anne and her garden.

When Mary was about fourteen she made the acquaintance of Lady Anne — her full name was Lady Anne Hamilton — and that was an event which had a considerable influence on her fortunes.

The meeting came about in this way.

Mary had gone marketing one day, and for once had deserted the shabby little row of shops which ran at the end of Wistaria Terrace, at right angles to it. She had gone out into the great main thoroughfare, the noise of which came dimly to Wistaria Terrace because of the huge mass of the church blocking up the way.

She had done her shopping and was on her way home, when, right in the track of the heavy tram as it came down the steep descent from the bridge over the canal, she saw a helpless bit of white fur, as it might well seem to anyone at a distance. The thing was almost motionless, or stirring so feebly that its movements were not apparent. Evidently the driver of the tram had not noticed it, or was not troubled to save its life, for he stood with the reins in his hand, glancing from side to side of the road for possible passengers as the tram swept down the long incline.

Mary never hesitated. The tram was almost upon the thing when she first saw it. "Why, it is Lady Anne's dog!" she cried, and launched herself out in the roadway to save it. She was just in time to pick up the blind, whimpering thing. The driver of the tram, seeing Mary in its path, put on the brakes sharply. The tram lumbered to a stoppage, but not before Mary had been flung down on her face and her arm broken by the hoof of the horse nearest her.

It was likely to be an uncommonly awkward thing for the Gray household, seeing that it was Mary's right arm that was injured. For one thing, it would involve the dispossession of that year's baby. For another, it would put Mrs. Gray's capable helper entirely out of action.

When Mary was picked up, and stood, wavering unsteadily, supported by someone in the crowd which had gathered, hearing, as from a great distance, the snarling and scolding of the tram-driver, who was afraid of finding himself in trouble, she still held the blind and whimpering dog in her uninjured arm.

She wanted to get away as quickly as possible from the crowd, but her head swam and her feet were uncertain. Then she heard a quiet voice behind her.

"Has there been an accident? I am a doctor," it said.

"A young woman trying to kill herself along of an old dog," said the tram-driver indignantly. "As though there wasn't enough trouble for a man already."

"Let me see," the doctor said, coming to Mary's side. "Ah, I can't make an examination here. Better come with me, my child. I am on my way to the hospital. My carriage is here."

"Not to hospital," said Mary faintly. "Let me go home; they

would be so frightened."

"I shan't detain you, I promise you. But this must be bandaged before you can go home. Ah, is this basket yours, too?"

Someone had handed up the basket from the tram-track, where it had lain disgorging cabbages and other articles of food.

"I will send you home as soon as I have seen to your arm," the doctor said, pushing her gently towards his carriage. "And the little dog — is he your own? I suppose he is, since you nearly gave your life for him?"

"He is not mine," said Mary faintly. "He belongs to Lady Anne — Lady Anne Hamilton. She lives at No. 8, The Mall. She will be distracted if she misses the little dog. She is so very fond of it."

"Ah! Lady Anne Hamilton. I have heard of her. We can leave the dog at home on our way. Come, child."

The Mall was quite close at hand. They drove there, and just as the carriage stopped at the gate of No. 8, which had a long strip of green front garden, overhung by trees through which you could discern the old red-brick house. Lady Anne herself came down the gravel path. Over her head was a little shawl of old lace; it was caught by a seed-pearl brooch with an amethyst centre. She was wearing a quilted red silk petticoat and a bunched sacque of black flowered silk. She had magnificent dark eyes and white hair. Under it her peaked little face was the colour of old ivory. She was calling to her dog, "Fifine, Fifine, where can you be?"

A respectable-looking elderly maid came hurrying after her.

"I've looked everywhere, my lady, and I cannot find the little thing," she said in a frightened voice.

Meanwhile, the doctor had got out of the carriage and had taken Fifine gently from Mary's lap. Now that Mary was coming to herself she began to discover that the doctor was young and kind-looking, but more careworn than his youth warranted. He opened the garden gate and went up to Lady Anne.

"Is this your little dog, madam?" he asked.

"My Fifine, my darling!" cried Lady Anne, embracing the trembling bit of wool. "You don't know what she is to me, sir. My little grandson" — the imperious old voice shook — "loved the dog. She was his pet. The child is dead. You understand —"

"Perfectly," said the doctor. "I, too — I know what loss is. The little dog strayed. She was found in the High Road. I am very glad to restore her to you; but pray do not thank me. There is a young girl in my carriage at the gate. She picked up your dog from under the wheels of a tramcar, and broke her arm, I fear, in doing it. I am on my way to the hospital, the House of Mercy, where I am doing work for a friend who is on holiday. I am taking her with me so that I may set the arm where I have all the appliances."

"She saved my Fifine? Heroic child! Let me thank her."

The old lady clutched her recovered treasure to her breast with fervour, then handed the dog over to the maid.

"Take me to see Fifine's preserver," she said in a commanding voice.

Mary was almost swooning with the pain of her arm. She heard Lady Anne's praises as though from a long distance off.

"Stay, doctor," the old lady said; "I cannot have her jolted over the paving-stones of the city to the Mercy. Bring her in here. We need not detain you very long. We can procure splints and bandages, all you require, from a chemist's shop. There is one just round the corner. What, do you say, child? They will be frightened about you at home! I shall send word. Be quiet now; you must let us do everything for you."

So the doctor assisted Mary into the old house behind the trees. Lady Anne walked the other side of her, pretending to assist Mary and really imagining that she did.

The splints and the bandages were on, and Mary had borne the pain well.

"I'm afraid I must go," said the doctor, looking at his watch. "I am half an hour behind my time. And where am I to visit my patient?"

"Where but here?" said Lady Anne with decision. "It is now half-past eleven. I have lunch at half-past one. Could you return to lunch, Dr. — ah, Dr. Carruthers. You are Dr. Carruthers, are you not? You took the big house at the corner of Magnolia Road a year ago?"

"Yes, I am Dr. Carruthers; and I shall be very pleased to return to lunch, Lady Anne. I don't think the little dog is any the worse for her experience."

His face was flushed as he stood with his hat in his hand, bowing and smiling. If only Lady Anne Hamilton would take him up! That big house at the corner of Magnolia Road had been a daring bid for fortune. So had the neat, single brougham, hired from a livery-stable. So had been the three smart maids. But so far Fortune had not favoured him. He was one of fifty or so waiters on Fortune. When people were ill in the smart suburban neighbourhood they liked to be attended by Dr. Pownall, who always drove a pair of hundred guinea horses. None of your hired broughams for them.

"You are paying too big a rent for a young man," said Lady Anne. "You can't have made it or anything like made it. Pownall grows careless. The last time I sent for him he kept me two hours waiting. When I had him to Stewart, my maid, he was in a hurry to be gone. Pownall has too much to do — too much by half."

Her eyes rested thoughtfully on the agitated Dr. Carruthers.

"You shall tell me all about it when you come back to lunch," she said; "and I should like to call on your wife."

CHAPTER II

THE WALL BETWEEN

"The child has brought us luck — luck at last, Mildred," Dr. Carruthers was saying, a few hours later. "When I lifted her in my arms she was as light as a feather. A poor little shabby, overworked thing, all eyes, and too big a forehead. Her boots were broken, and I noticed that her fingers were rough with hard work."

He was walking up and down his wife's drawing-room in a tremendous state of excitement, while she smiled at him from the sofa.

"It is wonderful, coming just now, too, when I had made up my mind that we couldn't keep afloat here much longer, and had resolved to give up this house at the September quarter and retire into a dingier part of the town. Once it is known that I am Lady Anne Hamilton's medical man the snobs of the neighbourhood will all be sending for me."

"Poor Dr. Pownall!" said Mrs. Carruthers, laughing softly.

"Oh, Pownall is all right. They say he's immensely wealthy. He can retire now and enjoy his money. If the public did not go back on him he'd be a dead man in five or six years. He does the work of twenty men. I pity the others, the poor devils who are waiting on fortune as I have waited."

"There is no fear of Lady Anne disappointing you?" she asked, in a hesitating voice. She did not like to seem to throw cold water on his joyful mood.

"There is no fear," he answered, standing midway of the room with its three large windows. "She is coming to see you, Milly. If I have failed in anything you will succeed. You will see me at the top of the tree yet. You will have cause to be proud of me."

"I am always proud of you. Kit," she said, in a low, impassioned voice.

Meanwhile, Lady Anne herself had made a pilgrimage to Wistaria Terrace in the hour preceding the luncheon hour. She had left Mary in a deep chair in the big drawing-room. Outside were the boughs of trees. From the windows you could surprise the secrets of the birds if you would. The room was very spacious, with chairs and sofas round the walls, a great mirror at either end, a paper on its walls which pretended to be panels wreathed in roses. The ceiling had a gay picture of gods and goddesses reclining in a flowery mead. The mantelpiece was Carrara marble, curiously inlaid with coloured wreaths. There was a fire in the brass grate, although it was summer weather. The proximity of the trees and the natural climate of the place meant damp. The fire sparkled in the brass dogs and the brass jambs of the fireplace. The skin of a tiger stretched itself along the floor. The terrible teeth grinned almost at Mary's feet.

The child was sick and faint from the pain of having her arm set. She lay in the deep sofa, covered with red damask, amid a bewildering softness of cushions and rugs, and wondered what Lady Anne was saying to Mamie. Mamie was Mrs. Gray. From the first Mary had not called her Mother. Her name was Matilda, and Mamie was a sort of compromise.

Meanwhile, Lady Anne had gone out by her garden, through the stable, and into the lane at the back. There was a little door open in the opposite wall; beyond it was a shabby trellis with scarlet-runners clambering upon it.

Lady Anne peeped within. A disheartened-looking woman was hanging a child's frock on the line which was stretched from wall to wall. Three children, ranging in age from two to five, were sitting on the grass plot. Two were playing with white stones. The third was surveying its own small feet with great interest, sucking at a fat thumb as though it conveyed some delicious nourishment.

"Do I speak to Mrs. Gray?" asked Lady Anne, advancing. She had a sunshade over her head, a deep-fringed thing with a folding handle. She had bought it in Paris in the days of the Second Empire.

Mrs. Gray stared at the stranger within her gates, whom she knew by sight. There was some perturbation in her face. She had been worried about the unusual duration of Mary's absence. Mary had not come back with the market basket which contained the children's dinner. At one o'clock the four elder ones would be upon her, ravening. What on earth had become of Mary? The poor woman had not realised how much she depended on Mary, since Mary was always present and always willing to take the burdens off her stepmother's thin, stooped shoulders on to her own.

Now she caught sight of the market-basket. One of Lady Anne's white-capped maids had come in and deposited it quietly.

"Mary?" she gasped. "What has become of Mary?"

"Pray don't frighten yourself," said Lady Anne. "I have a message from Mary. She is at my house. As a matter of fact, she met with an accident. There — don't go so pale. It is only a matter of time. Her arm is broken. She got it broken in saving the life of my little Maltese, who had strayed out and had got in the way of the tram. I always said that those trams should not be allowed. The tracks are so very unpleasant — dangerous even, for the carriages of gentlefolk. There is far too much traffic allowed on the public highways nowadays, far too much. People ought to walk if they cannot keep carriages."

She broke off abruptly and looked at the three small children.

"These are yours?" she asked. "They seem very close together in age."

"A year and a half, three years, four years and three months," said Mrs. Gray, forgetting in her special cause for pride her awe of Lady Anne.

"Dear me, I should have thought they were all twins," said the old lady. "How very remarkable! Have you any more?"

"Four at school. The eldest is nine. You see, they came so quickly, my lady. Only for Mary I don't know how I should have reared them."

"H'm! Mary is very stunted. It struck me that she would have been tall if she had had a chance. Those heavy babies, doubtless. Well, I am going to keep Mary for a while. How will you do without her?"

Mrs. Gray's faded eyes filled with tears.

"I can't imagine, my lady. You see, we have never kept a servant. When I lived at home with my Mamma we always had three. Mr. Gray has literary attainments, my lady. He is not practical."

"I can send you an excellent charwoman," Lady Anne broke in, "for the present. I will see what is to be done about Mary. The child has rendered me an inestimable service. I must do something for her in return. By the way, she is not your daughter?"

"My stepdaughter."

"Ah, I thought so. Well, the charwoman shall come in at once. She can cook. Later on, we shall see — we shall see."

"By the way," said Lady Anne, coming back with a rustle of silks while Mrs. Gray yet stood in bewilderment, holding the baby's frock in her limp fingers. "By the way, Mary is very anxious about her father — how he will take her accident. Will you tell your husband that I shall be glad to see him when he comes home this evening?"

"I will, my lady," said Mrs. Gray; "and, my lady, would you please not to mention to Mr. Gray about the charwoman? He's that proud; it would hurt him, I'm sure. If he isn't told he'll never know she's there. A child isn't as easily deceived as Walter."

"I shall certainly not tell him," Lady Anne said graciously. She did not object to the honest pride in Walter Gray. He was probably a superior man for his station, being Mary's father. As for that poor slattern, Lady Anne had lived too long in the world to be amazed by the marriages men made, either in her own exalted circle or in those below it.

Walter Gray came, in a flutter of tender anxiety, at half-past six in the evening, to Lady Anne's garden, where Mary was sitting in her wicker chair under the mulberry tree. Lady Anne had given orders that he was to be shown out to the garden when he called.

"My poor little girl!" he said, with an arm about Mary's shoulder.

Then he took off his hat to Lady Anne. There was respect in his manner, but nothing over-humble, nothing to say that they were not equals in a sense. His eyes, at once bright and dreamy, rested on her with a friendly regard.

"The man has gentle blood in him somewhere," said the old lady to herself. She had a sense of humour which kept her knowledge of her own importance from becoming overweening. "I believe his respect is for my age, not for my rank. I wonder what the world is coming to!"

She went away then and left the father and daughter together. Walter, who had taken a chair by Mary's, looked with a half-conscious pleasure round the velvet sward on which the shadows of the trees lay long. The trees were at their full summer foliage, dark as night, mysterious, magnificent.

"What a very pleasant place." Walter Gray said, with grave enjoyment. "How sweet the evening smells are! How quiet everything is! Who could believe that Wistaria Terrace was over the wall?"

"I have been missing Wistaria Terrace," Mary said. "You don't know how lonesome it feels for the children. I wonder how Mamie is getting on without me. I want to go home. Indeed, I feel quite able to. I don't know how I shall do without going home."

"If you went home," said Walter Gray, unexpectedly practical, "your arm would never set, Mary. You'd be forgetting and doing all manner of things you oughtn't to do. If Lady Anne is kind enough to ask you to visit her, stay a while and rest, dear. Indeed, you do too much for your size."

"You will all miss me so dreadfully."

"Indeed, I don't think we shall miss you — in that way. Oddly enough — I suppose Matilda was on her mettle — the house seemed quieter when I came home. The children were in bed. I smelt something good from the kitchen. Don't imagine that we shall not be able to do without you, child."

Mary, who knew no more of the capable charwoman than Walter Gray did, looked on this speech of her father's as a mere string of tender subterfuges. She said nothing, but her eyes rested on her grey woollen skirt, faded by wear and the weather, and she had an unchildish sense of the incongruity of her presence as a visitor in Lady Anne's house. Walter Gray's glance roamed over his young daughter. He saw nothing of her dreary attire. He saw only the spiritual face, over-pale, the slender, young, unformed body, graceful as a half-opened flower in its ill-fitting covering, the slender feet that had a suggestion of race, the toil-worn hands the fingers of which tapered to fine points.

"You have always done too much, child," he said, with sudden, tender compunction.

When he rose to go Mary clung to him as though their parting was to be for years.

"I will come in again tomorrow," he said. "I shall sleep better tonight for thinking of you in this quiet, restful place. Get some roses in your cheeks, little girl, before you come back to us."

"I wish I were going back now," said Mary piteously. She looked round the old walls with their climbing fruit trees as though they were the walls of a prison. "It is awful not to be able to come and go. And Mamie will never be able to do without me. The children will be ill —"

He left her in tears. As he re-entered the house by its iron steps up to a glass door Lady Anne came out from her morning-room and called him within. He looked about him at the room, walled in with books, with yellowed marble busts of great men on top of the bookcases. His feet sank in soft carpets. The smell of a pot of lilies mingled with the smell of leather bindings. The light in the room, filtered through the leaves of an overhanging creeper, was green and gold. It seemed to him that he must have known such a room in some other world, where he had not had to make watches all day with a glass screwed in his eye, but had abundant leisure for books and beautiful things. Not but that there might be worse things than the watch-making. Over the works of the watches, the fine little wheels and springs, Walter Gray thought hard, thought incessantly. He thought, perhaps, the harder that he had neither the leisure nor opportunity for putting down his thoughts on paper or imparting them to another like-minded with himself. How his fellows would have stared if they could have known the things that went on inside Walter Gray's mind as he leant above his table, peering into the interior of the watch-cases!

"Sit down, Mr. Gray," said Lady Anne graciously; "I want to talk to you about Mary."

She approached the matter delicately, having wit enough to see that Walter Gray was no common person. While she talked she looked with frank admiration at his face: the fine, high, delicate nose; the arched brows, like Mary's own; the over-development of the forehead. The dust of years and worries lay thick upon his face, yet Lady Anne said to herself that it was a beautiful face beneath the dust.

"I want to talk to you about Mary," she went on. "The child interests me strongly. She is a fine vessel, this little daughter of yours. Pray excuse me if I speak plainly. She has been doing far too much for her age and her strength. Haven't you noticed that she is pulled down to earth? Those babies, Mr. Gray — they are remarkably fat and heavy; they are killing Mary."

"Her mother died of consumption," Walter Gray said, his face whitening with terror.

"Ah!" the old lady thought; "she is the child of his heart. Those three twins are merely the children of his home. That poor drudge of a mother of theirs! Mary is the child of her father's heart and mind."

Then aloud: "You had better let me have her, Mr. Gray."

"Let you have her, Lady Anne? What would you do with my Mary?"

He looked scarcely less aghast than he had done a moment before at the suggestion of consumption.

"Not separate her from you, Mr. Gray. This house is my home, and I am not likely to leave it, except for a month or two at a time, at my age. I think the child will be a companion to me. I have no romantic suggestions to make. I am not proposing to adopt Mary. I shall pay her a salary, and give her opportunities for education that you cannot. She interests me, as I have said. Let me have her. When I no longer need her — I am an old woman, Mr. Gray — she will be fit to earn her own living. Everything I have goes back to my nephew Jarvis Lord Iniscrone. But Mary will not suffer. Think! What have you to give her but a life of drudgery under which she will break down — die, perhaps?"

She watched the emotion in his face with her little keen, bright eyes.

"It is not a fine lady's caprice?" he said. "You won't make my Mary accustomed to better things than I could give her and then send her back to be a drudge?"

"The Lord judge between thee and me," she answered solemnly.

"Then I trust you, Lady Anne Hamilton," he said.

The strange thing was that the proud old lady was gratified, almost flattered, by the confidence in Walter Gray's unworldly eyes.

"Thank you, Mr. Gray," she said; then, as he took up his hat to go, she laid a detaining hand on his shabby coat sleeve.

"Why not have dinner with Mary in the garden?" she suggested. "Do, pray. I want you to tell her what we have agreed upon. I can send word to Mrs. Gray."

Walter Gray was pleased enough to go back to his little girl whom he had left in tears for the comfortless house and the burden of the young stepbrothers and stepsisters. It was pleasure, half pain, to see the uplifted face with which Mary regarded him when she saw him return. How was he going to put the barrier between them that this plan to which he had given his consent would surely mean? He had no illusions. Over the wall, Lady Anne had said. But the wall that separated Wistaria Terrace and the Mall was in reality a high and a great wall. He would never have Mary in the old close communion again. All passes. How good the old times were that were only a few hours away, yet seemed worlds! Never again! They would never be all and all to each other in a solitude which took no count of the others. Yet it was for Mary's sake. For Mary's sake the wall was to rise between them. As he began to tell her the strange, wonderful thing, his heart was heavy within him because a chapter of his life was closed. He had come to the end of an epoch. Henceforth things might be conceivably better, but — they would be different.

CHAPTER III

THE NEW ESTATE

Mary took the news of her great promotion in an unthankful spirit.

"Lady Anne is very kind," she said tearfully; "but I don't want to stay with her. I couldn't bear to live anywhere but in Wistaria Terrace. It is absurd that you should say you have given your consent, papa. How could you possibly have consented when the house could not get on without me? You know it could not. Why, even for a day things would be all topsy-turvy without me."

"And so you have not gone to school," the father answered, with an accent of self-reproach. "You have been weighed down with responsibilities and cares that you ought to have been free of for years to come. You have even been stunted in your growth, as Lady Anne said. It is time things were altered. I don't know how I was so blind. We ought to be grateful to the accident that has opened a door to us."

When he had gone, Lady Anne came and comforted Mary. There was a deal of kindness in the old lady's heart.

"You shall help them," she said. "Dear me, how much help you will be able to give them! Imagine beginning with a salary at fifteen! You are to leave things to me, Mary. I have sent help to your step-mother — an excellent woman, Mrs. Devine, whom I have known for many years. She is very capable. I will tell her that she must remain with your stepmother. It is amazing what one really capable woman can do. And afterwards there will be the salary."

The salary, and perhaps a quick, warm feeling for Lady Anne which sprang up suddenly in Mary's heart, settled the question. After all, as Lady Anne said, despite her greatness she was very lonely. She had lost her son and her grandson, and she could not endure her nephew or his family. She had only a few old cronies. As a matter of fact, although she had taken a fancy to Mary Gray and captured the child's susceptible heart, she was not a particularly amiable or lovable old lady to the rest of the world. She was too keen-sighted and sharp-tongued to be popular.

Mary slept that night in such a room as she had never dreamt of. There was a little bed in the corner of it with a flowing veil of white, lace-trimmed muslin like a baby's cot. There was white muslin tied with blue ribbons at the window, and the dressing-table was as gaily and innocently adorned. There was a work-box on a little table, a writing-desk on another; a shelf of books hung on the wall. The room had really been made ready for a dear young cousin of Lady Anne's, who had not lived to enjoy it. If Mary had only known, she owed something of Lady Anne's interest to the fact that her eyes were grey, like Viola's, her cheek transparent like Viola's.

Apart from the discomfort of the broken arm, as she lay in the soft, downy little bed, she was ill at ease, wondering how they were getting on without her at Wistaria Terrace. Her breast had an ache for the baby who was used to lie warm against it. Her good arm felt strange and lonely for the familiar little body. She kept putting it out in a panic during her sleep because she missed the baby.

In the morning Simmons, Lady Anne's maid, came to help her dress. It was very difficult, Mary found, to do things for one's self with a broken arm. Her head ached because of the disturbed sleep and the pain of the broken limb. Simmons had come to her in a somewhat hostile frame of mind. She did not hold with picking up gutter-children from no one knew where and setting people as were respectable to wait upon them. But at heart she was a good-natured woman, and her indignation disappeared before the unchildish pain and weariness of Mary's face.

"There," she said, "I wouldn't be fretting, if I were you. Lor' bless you, there's fine treats in store for you. Her ladyship sent only last night for a roll of grey cashmere. I'm to fit you after your break-fast and make it up as quick as I can. Then you'll be fit to go out with her ladyship in the carriage and get your other things."

It was the last day of the ugly linsey. Simmons got through her task with great quickness. She was a woman of taste, else she had not been Lady Anne's maid. Lady Anne was more particular about her garments than most young women. And, having once made up her mind to like Mary, Simmons took an interest in her task.

"You are so kind, Mrs. Simmons," Mary said gratefully, feeling the gentleness and dexterity with which the woman tried on her new garments without once jarring the broken arm.

"I'm kind enough to those who take me the proper way," said Simmons, greatly pleased with Mary's prefix of Mrs., which was brevet rank, since Simmons had never married. It would have made a great difference to Mary's comfort at this time if she had been suf-ficiently ill-advised to call Simmons without a prefix, as Lady Anne did.

Dr. Carruthers had called to see Mary the morning after the accident. He had interviewed his patient in the morning-room, and was passing out through the hall when Lady Anne's voice over the banisters summoned him to her presence.

"You can give me a little while, Dr. Carruthers?" she said. "I shall not be interfering with your work?"

"I am quite free" — a little colour came into his cheeks. "The friend whose work I was doing at the House of Mercy returned last night. Yesterday was my last day."

"Ah! and yesterday brought you an unexpected patient. How do you find her?"

"She has less physique than she ought to have."

"Yes, she has been underfed and overworked. I am going to alter all that. I have taken her into my house as my little companion."

Dr. Carruthers stared in spite of himself.

"You think it very odd of me? Well, I *am* odd, and I can afford to do what pleases me. Mary Gray is going to live here. You should know her father. A quite remarkable man, I consider him. Now, about yourself. I have heard of you, Dr. Carruthers. I have heard that you are a very clever young man and devoted to your work, that you have all the knowledge of the schools at your fingertips, but very little experience, and no practice to speak of."

"Excuse me, Lady Anne. I was three years house surgeon at the Good Samaritan; and I have done a great deal of work since I have been here. I will confess that my patients have been of a poor class."

"Who have not paid you a penny. I don't know whether you do it for philanthropy or to keep your hand in —"

"A little of both," the young man said with a faint smile.

"But it is a good thing to do." the old lady went on, without noticing his interpellation. "You're spoken well of by the poor, if the rich have not heard anything about you. I know you're living beyond your means in a big house, hoping that a paying practice will come to you. My dear man, it never will, so long as people think you are in need of it. They like Dr. Pownall at their doors with his carriage and pair, even if he can only give them five minutes. Pownall forgot himself with me. I remember his father — a very decent, respectable man who used to grow cabbages. That's nothing against Pownall — creditable to him, I should say. Still, he hadn't time to listen to my symptoms, and he was rude. 'A woman of your age,' he said. I should like to know who told Dr. Pownall my age. A lady has no age. 'It's time you retired,' I said to him. 'I don't think of it,' said he; 'not for ten years yet. My patients won't hear of it.' 'You're greedy,' said I; 'if you weren't your patients might go to Hong Kong.' He thought it was a joke — hadn't time to find out whether I was serious or not. I made him, Dr. Carruthers. It's time for him to retire now. I shall mention to all my friends that you are my body-physician."

She spoke like one of the Royal Family. But Dr. Carruthers had no inclination to laugh. His eyes were dim as he murmured his acknowledgments. It was fame, it was fortune, in those parts to be approved by Lady Anne Hamilton. Hitherto she had been understood to swear by Dr. Pownall.

"It means a deal to us, Lady Anne," he said, stumbling over his words. "We had made up our minds to give up the big house and look for a slum practice. The children — I have two living — are not very strong, any more than Mildred. We put all we could into the venture of taking the house. It was our bid for fortune."

"I wouldn't approve of it in a general way," said Lady Anne. "Still, it has turned out well. Will your wife be at home tomorrow afternoon? I should like to call upon her."

"She will be delighted."

Dr. Carruthers was regaining his self-control. He knew that the presence of Lady Anne's barouche at his door for an hour in the afternoon would be more potent in opening doors to him than if he had made the most brilliant cure on record.

Mary was with Lady Anne next day when she went to call on Mrs. Carruthers. It was characteristic of Lady Anne that she thought to tell Jennings, the coachman, to drive up and down in front of the house and round the sides, for Dr. Carruthers' house was a corner one with a frontage to three sides. It was a hot summer day, and Jennings wondered disrespectfully what bee the old lady had got in her bonnet. Such a jangling of harness, such a flashing of polished surfaces! Every window that commanded the three sides of Dr. Carruthers' house had an eye at the pane. The tidings flew from one to another that Lady Anne Hamilton was visiting Mrs. Carruthers, and was making a very long call.

Mildred was still on her sofa. She would have risen when Lady Anne came in, but the old lady prevented her. Lady Anne could be royally kind when it pleased her.

She drew a chair by the sofa and sat down. Mary, who had come in with her, listened in some wonder to Lady Anne's sympathetic questions about the children. That was something in which Mary was interested, in which Mary had knowledge and experience; but though she listened she would not have spoken a word for worlds.

As she sat there on the edge of one of Mrs. Carruthers' chairs — the drawing-room furniture was of the sparsest; a chair or small table dotted here and there on the wilderness of polished floor — she could see herself in a pier-glass at the other end of the room. It was a quite unfamiliar presentment she saw. This Mary was dressed in soft dove-grey. She had a little white muslin folded fichu about her shoulders. She had a wide black hat, with one long white ostrich feather. Her good hand was gloved in delicate grey kid. There was something quaint about her aspect; for that artist, Simmons, had discovered that Mary, for all her fifteen years, looked her best with her soft fine brown hair piled on top of her head. When she presented Mary so to Lady Anne the old lady was fain to acknowledge that Simmons was right. There was a quaint and delightful stateliness about Mary which made Lady Anne say to herself once more that the child had gentle blood in her.

"Dear me," Mildred Carruthers thought, as her eyes wandered again and again to the elegant little figure, "Kit said nothing of this. I expected to find a rather interesting child of the humbler classes. I remember particularly that he said she looked as though she had had a hard time."

Mary's changed aspect had one unforeseen result. When she presented herself at Wistaria Terrace the baby did not know her. Her stepmother shed a few tears, which were half-gratification. The elder children were already a bit shy of her, the baby's immediate predecessor even murmuring of her as "the yady," and surveying her from afar, finger in mouth. But the baby could in no way be brought to recognise her, and only shouted lustily when she tried to force herself upon his recognition.

"I shall come tomorrow in my old frock," Mary said, bitterly hurt by this lack of perception on the baby's part. "I hate these hideous things; so I do. Tomorrow he will come to his Mary, so he will."

But when the morrow came, and she sought for her old work-a-day garments in that pretty white and blue wardrobe where she had hung them when she had discarded them for the grey frock and hat, they were not to be found. There were numbers of things such as Mary had never dreamed of. Lady Anne had provided her with an outfit, simple according to her thoughts, but splendid in Mary's eyes. A white cashmere dressing-gown, trimmed with lace, hung on the peg where the grey linsey had been.

Mary flew to Simmons to know where her old frock had gone to. The good woman, who by this time had taken Mary under her wing to uphold her against the rest of the household if it were inclined to resent the new inmate, looked at her reprovingly.

"You never wanted that old frock, and you her ladyship's companion? No, Miss Mary — for so I shall call you, as by her ladyship's orders, let some people say what they like — that frock you never will see, for gone it has to a poor child that'll maybe find it a comfort when winter comes. I wonder at you for thinking on it, so I do, seeing as how I've taken so much trouble with your clothes."

Mary turned away with a desolate feeling. The grey linsey might have been like the feathers of the enchanted bird that became a woman for the love of a mortal, the feathers which, if she wore them again, had the power of transporting her back to her kindred and her old estate. The old life was indeed closed to Mary with the disappearance of the grey linsey; and it was long before she lost the feeling that if she could only have kept her old garments she need not have been so separated from the old life.

CHAPTER IV

BOY AND GIRL

It was during those early days that Mary made the acquaintance of Robin Drummond. She had a comfortless feeling afterwards about the meeting; but it was not because of Sir Robin or anything he did: he was always a kind boy in her memory of him. It was because of his mother, Lady Drummond. Mary knew from Lady Anne, who always thought aloud, that Lady Drummond made a good many people feel uncomfortable.

They had driven out all the way from the city to the Court, the big house on its wide plain below the mountains. It was a long drive — quite twenty miles there and back — and Jennings, who liked to have a good deal of his time to himself, had been rather cross about it. Not that he dared show any temper to Lady Anne, who was easy and kindly with her servants, as a rule, but could reduce an insubordinate one to humble submission as well as any old lady ever could. But Mary, who knew the household pretty well by this time, knew that Jennings was out of temper by the set of his shoulders, as she surveyed them from her seat in the barouche. It was a road, too, he never liked to take, because of a certain steam tram which ran along it and made the horses uncomfortable when they met it face to face. And there his mistress was unsympathetic towards him. She had been a brilliant and daring horsewoman in her youth and middle age.

"I never thought I should live to amble along like this," she confided to Mary as they drove between golden harvest fields. "Rheumatic gout is a great humbler of the spirit. Ah! here comes one of those black monsters to make the pair curvet a little. They are too fat, Mary. They have too easy a life. It is only on such an occasion as this that they remember their hot youth."

They reached the Court without mishap, although once or twice the horses behaved as though they meditated a mild runaway.

"You shall take the other road home, Jennings," Lady Anne said graciously, as she alighted in front of the great square, imposing house, amid its flower-beds of all shapes, its ornamental fountains flinging high jets of golden water in the sun.

"It's time we gave up the horses, my lady," Jennings said, with bitterness, "with the likes o' them black beasts on the road."

Later, as she and Mary waited in the great drawing-room for Lady Drummond, she returned to the subject of Jennings and his grievance.

"He is always bad-tempered when we come to the Court," she said. "For all its grandeur it is not a hospitable house. Jennings will have to go without his tea this afternoon."

Mary looked with wonder down the great length of the magnificent room. Her feet sank in the Turkey carpet. The walls, which were papered in deep red, were lined with full-length portraits, some of them equestrian. The place had an air of rich comfort. Was it possible that the mistress of so much magnificence could grudge a visitor's coachman his tea?

"Her ladyship looks after the bawbees," Lady Anne went on, thinking aloud as usual, rather than talking to Mary. "And those who are in her employment must think of them too, or they go. Ah! you are looking at Gerald Drummond's portrait. What do you think of it, child?"

It was one of the equestrian portraits. The subject, a man in the thirties, dressed in a lancer uniform, stood by his horse's head. His helmet was off, lying on the ground at his feet; and it was easy to see why the artist had chosen to paint the sitter with his head uncovered. The upper part of the face — the forehead and eyes — was strikingly handsome. The sweep of golden hair, despite its close military cut, was beautiful also. For the rest, the nose was too large and not particularly well-shaped, the chin was rugged, the mouth stern. Lantern-jawed was the epithet one thought of when looking at the portrait of the man whose deeds were written in his country's history.

It was an epithet Mary Gray would not have thought of. Indeed, she stared at the hero in fascinated awe, but would not have known how to express an opinion regarding his looks. Fortunately, Lady Anne did not wait for an answer to her question — had not, perhaps, ever intended that it should be answered.

"It is very like," she went on. "Half Greek god, half fanatic. He led his charges with Bible words on his lips. He spent the night before a battle in prayer and fasting. He was as stern as John Knox, and as sweet as Francis de Sales. The only time his light deserted him was when he married Matilda Stewart. We were all in love with him. I was, although I ought to have had sense, being ten years his senior and a widow. He picked the worst of the bunch. Luckily, he could get away from Matilda, for he was always fighting somewhere, and perhaps he never found out. He kept his simplicity to the day he died. Some people thought he married Matilda because she was one of the Stewart heiresses, and the Drummonds were as poor as church mice. They didn't know him. It was more likely he'd marry her because she was plain, with a face like a horse, and was head over ears in love with him. I will say that for Matilda. She was desperately in love with her husband, although no one would believe now that she had ever been in love with anybody."

Lady Drummond delayed about coming to her guests. Lady Anne tapped an impatient small foot on the floor.

"She's heckling someone now — take my word for it," she said.

Then her face wrinkled up, shrewdly humorous.

"What are you thinking, child?" she asked. "Thinking of how oddly we in the world talk of the friends we go to visit? I don't trouble the Court much. But I am interested in Gerald's boy. I should like to know how he is going to turn out. Not much of her Ladyship in him, I fancy."

However, there was no question of Mary's judging her benefactress; and Lady Anne smiled as she noticed that the girl had not heard her question, and watched the innocent, tender, worshipping look with which she was gazing at Sir Gerald's portrait. The smile faded off into a sigh. *"Ah, le beau temps passe!"* The expression on Mary's face recalled to Lady Anne the one romantic passion of her life, which had come to her after widowhood had put an end to a marriage in which esteem and liking for an elderly husband had taken the place of love.

"You must excuse me, Anne."

A monotonous, important voice broke into Lady Anne's dream like a harsh discord, shattering it to atoms.

"You must excuse me. I've been interviewing my gardener. In your town life you are spared much. Considering the size of the gardens here and the labour I pay for, the yield is far too little. I expect the gardens to pay for themselves, and send the fruit to market. This year there is a great falling-off."

"It has been a wet summer," said Lady Anne.

"Ah! and who is this young lady?"

Lady Drummond's voice told that she had no need to ask the question. She had heard of Anne Hamilton's extraordinary freak and had suggested that for the protection of the interests of Anne's relatives she had better be put under proper restraint. Still, she asked the question. One would have said from the deadly monotony of Lady Drummond's voice that she could not get any expression into it. Yet she could on occasion; and the chilling disapproval in it now made Mary look up in a frightened surprise.

"This young lady, Miss Gray, is my companion," Lady Anne said, with a stiffening of herself for battle and a light in her eye which showed that she had not mistaken Lady Drummond's challenge, and had no objection to take it up.

"Ah!" Lady Drummond again lifted the lorgnette that hung at her belt and stared at Mary through it. "The young lady is very young for the post, and a companion is a new thing — is it not, Anne? — for you to require."

"You mean that I never could get one to live with me," Lady Anne said good-humoredly. "Well, Mary and I get on very well together — don't we, Mary?"

"Miss Gray is very young."

"If we are going to discuss her, need she stay?" Lady Anne asked. "I am sure she is longing to see the gardens. I couldn't get round myself. The damp has made me stiff."

"Can you find your way, Miss Gray?"

Lady Drummond was plainly anxious to be rid of Mary, and made an effort at politeness which was only awkward and discouraging.

"I think so," said Mary, looking round with an air of flight.

Lady Drummond's disapproval chilled her. She was not accustomed to be disapproved of, and it filled her with a vague terror as though she had done something wrong ignorantly.

She glided out of the room like a shadow. As she went, Lady Drummond's unlowered voice followed her.

"Your choice is a very odd one, Anne Hamilton. That gawky child, all eyes and forehead. I remember I wanted you to have my excellent Miss Bradley."

"I wouldn't have your excellent Bradley for an hour...."

But Mary had fled beyond the hearing of the voices. She had no curiosity to hear any more of Lady Drummond's unflattering remarks concerning her.

Once again she longed for Wistaria Terrace. There was no place for her in *this* world, she said to herself; and sent a tender reproach in her own mind to the father who had given her up for her good. Then she felt contrite about Lady Anne. How good the old lady was to her, and how she stood up for her, would stand up for her, even to the terrible Lady Drummond! Still, it was not her world; it never would be. She thought, with sudden childish tears filling her eyes, that the next time Lady Anne went to see any of her fine friends she would pray to be left at home.

The great suite of rooms opened one into the other. Mary was in the last of them — a library walled in books from floor to ceiling. The heavy velvet curtains that draped the arched entrance by which she had come had fallen behind her. The silence in the room where the feet fell so softly could be felt. There was not a sound but the ticking of a clock on the mantel-shelf.

Suddenly she came to a standstill. She had entered the room, but how was she to leave it? The doors were constructed of a piece with the book-shelves. The backs of them were dummy books. Mary did not know in the least how to discover the doors. In fact, she supposed that there were not any. She would have to retrace the way she came — perhaps even ask the terrible Lady Drummond how to get out.

She looked up at the long windows with the eye of a bird who has strayed in and cannot find the way out. The elusive air of flight that was hers was more pronounced at the moment.

Suddenly there was a sound, and, as Mary thought, the book-shelves opened. She saw light through the opening. A tall boy came in, whistling, and pulled up short as his eyes fell on her. He was about her own age, or a little older.

Mary never forgot in after years the kindness and friendliness of his face as his eyes rested upon her. He came forward slowly, putting out his hand. The colour flooded his face to the roots of his fair hair.

"You came with Lady Anne Hamilton," he said. "I found the carriage outside. I have sent it round to the stables and told the man to put up the horses for a while. He will want some refreshment; and they need a rest."

Mary put a limp hand into the frankly extended one.

"I couldn't find my way out," she said, with a sigh of relief. "I thought there were no doors. I was going to see the gardens while Lady Anne and Lady Drummond talked."

"Let me come with you," the boy said eagerly. "I don't know how anybody stays in the house on such a day. Do you like puppies? I have a beautiful litter of Clumber spaniels. And I should like you to see my pony. I have just been out on him. It's a bit slow here, all alone, after so many fellows at school. I'm at Eton, you know. I am going back next Thursday. Shan't be altogether sorry, either, though I'll miss some things."

They went out together into the golden autumn afternoon. First they went round the gardens, where the boy picked some roses and made them into a little bunch for Mary. He took a peach from a red wall and gave it to her. They sat down together on a seat to eat their fruit. Gardeners and gardeners' assistants passing by touched their hats respectfully. It was, "Yes, Sir Robin," and "No, Sir Robin." The young master had a good many questions to ask of the gardeners. He was evidently well liked, to judge by the smiles with which they greeted him.

"They're no end of good fellows," he confided to Mary. "The mater's rather down on them; thinks they don't do enough. It's a mistake, a woman trying to run a place like this. She can't under-stand as a man does. Now, if you've finished your peach, Miss Gray, we'll go round to the stable yard and see the puppies. After that I'll show you the pony. His name's Ajax, and he's rather rippin'. Do you like Kerry cows? The mater has a herd of them — jolly little beasts, but a bit wicked, some of them. You needn't be afraid of them. They wouldn't touch you while I'm there."

Mary inspected the Clumber puppies, and was promised the pick of the litter if Lady Anne would allow her to accept it.

"She won't refuse," said the boy, confidently. "She thinks no end of me."

"Unless the puppy might worry Fifine."

"The puppy wouldn't take any notice of that thing — the old dog, I mean. Besides, she lives in her basket, doesn't she? You might keep the puppy in the stables and take him for walks whenever you can. He'll have a beautiful coat like his mother, and if he's half as clever as she is...!"

"He's a lovely thing," said Mary, hugging the puppy, who was licking her face energetically and patting her with tremendous paws.

They visited the paddock next; and Sir Robin, springing on Ajax's back, trotted him up and down for Mary's inspection. He had a good seat in the saddle, and he looked his best on horseback. To be sure, Mary had not discovered that Sir Robin was plain, his mother's plainness militating in him against what share of beauty he might have inherited from his father. There was something so exhilarating to Mary in the afternoon's experience, after its beginning so badly, that she forgot what had gone before. She thought Sir Robin a kind and delightful boy. They saw the Kerries, and afterwards there were the rabbits, and the ferrets, and the guinea-pigs to be visited. Inti-macy advanced by leaps and bounds. Before the inspection had con-cluded she was "Mary" to her new-found friend, although she was too reticent by nature to think of addressing him so familiarly.

They had forgotten the time till half-past five struck from a clock in the stable-yard. At this time they were down by a pond in the shrubbery, where there was an islet with a water-hen's nest and a couple of swans sailing on the water. There was a boat, too, and Sir Robin was just getting it out preparatory to rowing Mary round the pond.

"Oh!" she said, with a little start. "What time is that?"

"Half-past five. I'd no idea it was so late."

"Nor I. I must go back at once. Lady Anne said we should be returning about five. I hope she will not be very angry with me."

Mary had begun to tremble. She always trembled in moments of agitation, as a slender young poplar might shiver in the wind.

The boy jumped out of the boat hastily.

"There, don't be frightened," he said. He had caught a glimpse of Mary's face. "Lady Anne won't mind. She's a good sort. You should see the hampers she sends me. The mater doesn't approve of school hampers. You must put the blame on me. It was my fault entirely, for I had a watch."

They hurried along the path leading back to the open space in front of the house. When they emerged into the open a breathless maid came towards them.

"I've been looking everywhere for you and the young lady, Sir Robin," she said. "Lady Anne Hamilton is waiting for Miss Gray."

Poor Mary! When they arrived in the drawing-room it was not with Lady Anne she had to count. Lady Anne sat with an air of humorous patience on her face, but Lady Drummond's brow was thunderous. The haughty indignation in her pale eyes terrified the very soul in Mary. She shrank away from it in terror.

"I had no idea you were with Miss Gray, Robin," she heard the lady say in glacial accents.

"I discovered Miss Gray trying to find her way out of the library. No one could find those doors without knowing something about them. And we went to see the puppies and the pony and the other beasts."

"We'd better be going, Mary," Lady Anne said, standing up. "You and Robin have made my visit quite a visitation."

"The horses had to rest and the coachman to have his tea," said Sir Robin, sturdily.

"You take too much care of your horses, Anne," Lady Drummond said. "They are too fat; they can't be healthy. And your coachman is very fat, too."

"Oh, they take it easy, they take it easy," Lady Anne said, laughing; "they've only my temper to worry them."

They left Lady Drummond looking as black as thunder in the drawing-room. Sir Robin escorted them to their carriage.

"So sorry, Lady Anne," he said, apologetically. "It was my fault. I hope you won't be angry with Miss Gray."

"It is your mother's annoyance has to be considered, my dear boy," answered Lady Anne, while he tucked the rug about her.

"All the same, Miss Gray and I had a rippin' time," he said, flinging back his head with an air of humorous defiance. "And — I say — you're too good to me, you know, you really are." Lady Anne had pressed something into his palm. "The mater doesn't see what boys want with so much pocket-money. Sometimes I don't know what I'd do only for you. There are so many things a fellow has to subscribe to."

The carriage rolled off, leaving him bare-headed on the drive in front of the house.

"That's a good boy," said Lady Anne, emphatically. "He has his father's heart. He's getting the ways of the master about him, too. I can tell by Jennings' back that he's had a good tea. He'll be a good son, but the time will come when he'll choose for himself. Well, Mary, I hope you've enjoyed yourself. Matilda won't want to see me for a month of Sundays again. Nor I her, for the matter of that. Dear me, she can make herself unpleasant."

Mary sat in a conscience-stricken silence during that homeward drive. Yet Lady Anne was not angry with her — that was very obvious. She seemed to be enjoying herself, too, judging by the smile that played about her lips. Now and again she cast a humorous glance on Mary. Once she chuckled aloud.

"Never mind me, my dear," she said, in answer to Mary's glance. "I was only thinking of something Denis Drummond, Gerald Drummond's elder brother, said of her Ladyship. Ah, poor Denis! He'd face a charge of the guns more readily than he would her Ladyship. Odd, isn't it, Mary, how those thoroughly disagreeable women can make themselves feared?"

CHAPTER V

"OLD BLOOD AND THUNDER"

Sir Denis Drummond had been his brother Gerald's senior by some seven or eight years. He, too, was a soldier, and had inherited the baronetcy from his father, upon whom the title had been bestowed by a grateful country for services in the field. A second baronetcy in the family had been specially created for Sir Gerald. It would not have been easy to say which was the finer soldier of the two brothers; for while Sir Gerald had made his name famous by the most dare-devil and brilliant feats, Sir Denis was rather the old type of soldier — cool as well as daring, always reliable and steady. Worshipped by his men, his name was one to be held in constant regard by the British public, which calls its heroes by their Christian names abbreviated, if they do not happen, indeed, to have a nickname for them.

"Old Blood and Thunder" was the name by which Sir Denis was known to his men, and that from a certain violence of speech of which he had never been able, or perhaps had never desired, to divest himself. This violence had somewhat annoyed his brother Gerald, who could get as much exhortation out of a verse of Scripture as ever he needed. Sir Denis, like many old soldiers, was quite a devout man in his way; but he had none of the zealot passion of his younger brother. The hidden fires which had given Sir Gerald a certain haggardness of aspect, as though a sculptor had hewed him roughly in marble, had never burned in Sir Denis's breast. He was a red-faced, white-moustached veteran, as blustering as the west wind, but with a heart as soft as wax in the hands of his daughter Nelly, and, indeed, in the hands of anyone else who knew the way to it.

His servants adored him, as did the dogs and all animals and children. He was beautiful in his manner to women of high and low degree, with perhaps one exception. He was as simple as a child, and loved the popular applause which fell to him whenever he made any kind of public appearance, for he had been so long a Londoner that now the London crowd knew him and had a sense of possession in him. His rosy face would beam all over when the crowd shouted itself hoarse for "Old Blood and Thunder." He did not at all object to the name, which had filtered from regimental into common use. The crowd was always "Boys!" to him. He had a most amiable feeling towards it, were it ever so frowsy and undersized and sallow. But he loved a soldier-man, and could hardly bear to pass one in the street without stopping to speak to him.

One delightful thing about Sir Denis was the esteem in which he held his own calling of arms. It might be questioned whether he held the Church even in higher honour. He was no subscriber to the belief that the army must necessarily be a refuge of rapscallions. "Straighten your shoulders, sir; hold your head high; for, remember that you are now a soldier!" he would say to the newest recruit who had just scraped through with a margin of chest. His thunderous wrath and sorrow when one of his "boys" was guilty of conduct unbecoming a soldier were something which, in time, impressed even the least impressionable. His old regiment, which he delighted to talk about, he had left a model regiment.

"There's a deal of good in the soldier-man," he would say to his daughter Nelly. "The poor fellows, they're good boys, they're very good boys."

Sir Denis had married, as he was approaching middle age, a very beautiful young girl, who had fallen in love at first with the soldier, and afterwards with the man.

His Nell had left him in his daughter Nelly a replica of herself. During the years of service that remained to him the child was always as near to him as might be. Fortunately, by this time the period of his foreign service was all but at an end. Wherever he had his command the child and her nurse were always within riding distance. He did not believe in barracks and towns for the rearing of anything so fresh and tender. His Nelly must have the fields and the woods and the waters. In later years her milkmaid freshness owed, perhaps, something to this upbringing.

Later, she went to school. Sir Gerald's widow, to whom Sir Denis always referred as the Dowager, who had taken an unasked-for interest in the motherless child from her birth, had found the ideal school for Nelly — a school where the daughters of the aristocracy were kept in a conventual seclusion while they learnt as little as might be of the simpler virtues, but a deal of the way to step in and out of a carriage, to comport themselves with dignity, to bear themselves in the presence of their sovereign, and so on.

Sir Denis, who had not been consulted, made a pretence of interviewing the Misses de Crespigny, by whom this aristocratic preserve was safeguarded.

He had listened to Miss Selina de Crespigny's eloquent exposition of the system adopted at De Crespigny House. Then he had torn it all to pieces as one might the delicate fabric of a spider's web, constructed at infinite cost.

"And, tell me now, do you teach them to be good daughters and wives and mothers?" he asked, with his air of convincing simplicity. "Do you teach them their duties to their husbands and children, ma'am, may I ask?"

Miss de Crespigny positively gasped. There was an indelicacy about the General's speech, to her manner of thinking.

"We expect our young ladies' mothers to teach them all that," she said, stiffly.

"And they don't. In nine cases out of ten they don't. They've too much to do otherwise. Whether it is philanthropy or politics, or just amusing themselves, they've all got too much to do," Sir Denis said, with a simple air that made it doubtful if this criticism of Society's ways was adverse or not.

Nelly did not go to De Crespigny House. She went, instead, to a much less pretentious school, kept by a family of four sisters, for whom the dry bones of teaching had been clothed with life. The house was perched on a high, windy cliff. The sisters, Miss Stella and Miss Clara, Miss Lucy and Miss Marianne, did their own teaching, and did it in a perfectly unconventional way to the twenty or so girls who made up their school.

When Nelly came home to her father at seventeen years of age, it would not have been easy to find a fresher, franker specimen of young girlhood. In fact, to her father's eyes she was somewhat alarmingly bright and fair.

"The young fellows will be about her thick as bees," he said to himself in a frightened way. "I won't have any nonsense about Nelly. I want my girl to myself for a little while. Afterwards there is that arrangement of the Dowager's about Nelly and Robin. I don't care for the marriage of first cousins. And I'm not sure that I care for Robin; still, he is poor Gerald's son. There can be nothing against poor Gerald's son."

He was so afraid of possible lovers for Nelly that he actually suggested to her that she should go to a smart finishing school for the couple of years that separated him from the sixty-five limit.

"After that," he said, faintheartedly, for there was a sparkle in Nelly's eye which discouraged him, "we shall settle down in London, and you shall see all you want to see. There are quiet nooks and corners to be had, even in London. I think I know the one I shall choose. Be a good girl, Nelly, and go to Madame Celeste's. A garrison town is no place for you. Unless, indeed, you would like to go to the Dowager, as she wishes."

"I shan't go to the Dowager, and I shan't go to Madame Celeste's," said Nelly, dimpling and sparkling. "I shall stay with my old

Dad and take care of him."

"What, Nell? 'Shan't'! You forget you're talking to your commanding officer. Rank insubordination — that is what I call it!"

"Call it what you like," Miss Nelly replied. "I'm going to stay. A finishing school at seventeen! I never heard the like!"

With that she put her arms round the General's neck, and that was the final argument. Secretly, indeed, he was not altogether sorry to be worsted. He had done his best to ward off the things that might happen. Now he was going to trust in Providence and keep his little girl with him. To be sure, he had known that she would never go to the Dowager's. Nelly had never considered that possibility. After all, it was a relief that they were not going to be parted.

During the two years Nelly, indeed, had many admirers and lovers, but she was not attracted by any of them. She was kind and friendly and engaging; but she was unconscious with her lovers, or so it seemed to the jealous, fatherly eyes, to the verge of coldness.

He often said to himself that he could not understand Nell. None of the gay, handsome, gallant soldier lads seemed to have the least attraction in that way for her. To be sure, she was a child, and there was plenty of time. Why shouldn't her old father keep her for the years to come? Unless — unless, that fellow Robin had been beforehand with the others — Robin, who had refused point-blank to be a soldier, and had even, to the General's bitter offence, actually spoken at the Oxford Union "On the Waste and Wickedness of a Standing Army." The General had nearly had a fit over that. Good Heavens! Gerald's son, Sir Massey Drummond's grandson, to be found on the side of the Philistines like that! What chill was in the boy's blood? What crook in his character? What bee in his bonnet?

The General had sworn then that Robin never should have his Nelly. But the Dowager had been sapping and mining and laying plans to bring about the marriage almost from Nelly's infancy, when she had come in and altered the constituents of Nelly's baby bottles, and had infuriated Nelly's wholesome country nurse to the point of departure. The General had come just in time then to find Mrs. Loveday fastening the cherry-coloured strings of her bonnet with fingers that trembled, and had been put to the very edge of his simple diplomacy to undo the Dowager's work. He knew his own helplessness where women were concerned. Nelly might see something in Robin, confound him, that the General could not.

At this point he would remember that, after all, Robin was poor Gerald's son, if an unworthy one, and be contrite. But then the grievance would revive of a far-back Quaker ancestor of Lady Drummond, whom the General blamed for the peace-loving instincts of poor Gerald's boy; and once again he would be furious.

Meanwhile, Nelly's frank, innocent eyes, blue as gentians, had no consciousness of a lover. Her old father seemed to be enough for her. At one moment they gave him the fullest assurance; the next he was in heats and colds of apprehension about the lover, be it Robin or another, who would take his little girl from him.

CHAPTER VI

THE BLUE RIBBON

The half-dozen years or so following Sir Denis's retirement were years of peace, in which he forgot for long periods, broken only by the Dowager's visits to London, his fear of losing his Nelly.

He had taken a house in Sherwood Square, where there is a space and breeziness that the fashionable districts could not possibly allow.

The square sits on top of one of the highest hills in London, and entrenches itself as a fortress against the poverty and squalor that are creeping up the hill towards it. Around the square there are still gardens and crescents and roads of consideration, but ever dwindling in social status as one goes down the hill, till the consideration vanishes in the degradation of cheap boarding-houses and the homes of Jews of the shopkeeping classes.

Sir Denis had discovered Sherwood Square for himself, and was uncommonly proud of it. He liked to point out to his friends that he rented a palatial mansion for what a *pied-à-terre* in Mayfair would have cost him. The houses had been built by wealthy merchants and professional people in the eighteenth century. They had splendours of double doors and marble pavements, of frescoed walls and ceilings, and carved mantelpieces. They were entered from a quiet street which showed hardly a sign of life. There were lions couchant guarding the entrances. The walls on that side showed mostly blank, uninteresting windows. With an odd pride the great houses showed only their duller aspects to the world.

All the living-rooms except one looked on the other side; and what a difference! There was a great stretch of emerald-green turf such as one would never look to see in London; to be sure, gardeners had been watering and mowing and rolling it for over a century. In the turf were many flower-beds, and here and there were forest trees which had been there when the district was fields. Country birds came and built there year after year. You might hear the thrush begin about January. And in the spring it was a wilderness of sweet hyacinths and daffodils, lilac and may. The rooms were spacious and splendid within the big cream-coloured house; and the General used to say that in the early morning, when the smoke had cleared away, it was possible from the upper windows to see as far as the Surrey hills. However, that was something which nobody but himself had tested.

In the house love and friendliness and good-will reigned supreme. The General had insisted on engaging his own servants, much to the disgust of the Dowager, who had several *protégés* of her own practically engaged. When the General had outwitted Lady Drummond on this occasion by a flank movement, he was very gleeful in his confidential moments alone with Nelly.

"She wanted to put in her spies and satellites, did she, Nelly, my girl? Pretty stories of us they'd have carried to her Ladyship. The only womanly thing your aunt has, my girl, is an invincible curiosity. She'd like to know what we had for lunch and dinner, who came to see us, and what clothes we wore. I'm glad you wouldn't have that mantua-maker of hers. Cannot my girl have her frocks made where she likes? I'll tell you what, Nelly: your aunt is a presumptuous, meddling, overbearing, impertinent woman — that she is."

"Why don't you tell her to leave us alone, papa?"

But the General, whose courage had never been doubted during all the years of his strenuous life, had very little bravery when it came to a question of telling hard truths to a woman, and that woman the Dowager.

"We must remember, after all, Nelly," he would say then, "that she is your Uncle Gerald's widow. Poor Gerald! what a dear fellow he was! No matter what we say between ourselves, we can't quarrel with Gerald's widow."

And Sir Denis, who was becoming garrulous in old age, would slip off into some reminiscence of the younger brother to whom he had been tenderly attached, and for whom he had also a certain hero-worship because he had been so fine and heroic a soldier.

Certainly it said well for the servants whom Sir Denis and Nelly had chosen for themselves that they fell in so completely with the kindness and honesty and good-will of the house. Some credit was doubtless due also to Sir Denis's soldier servant, whom he had installed as butler; for Pat's loyalty and devotion to "Old Blood and Thunder" must have influenced the class of persons who are so susceptible of impressions from those of their own station, while the standards and exhortations of their social superiors are as though they were not. Pat was lynx-eyed for a malingerer in his Honour's service; and, indeed, where the rule was so easy and pleasant there was no excuse for malingering. Pat, too, was ably seconded by Bridget, the cook, who had come in originally as kitchen-maid, and had in time taken the place of the very important and pretentious functionary with whom they had started, and whose cookery did not at all suit Sir Denis's digestion, impaired somewhat by long years in India. The young kitchen-maid had taken the cook's place during the latter's holiday, and had sent up for Sir Denis's dinner a little clear soup, a bit of turbot with a sauce which was in itself genius, a bird roasted to the nicest golden brown, and a pudding which was only ground rice, but had an insubstantial delicacy about it quite unlike what one associates with the homely cereal.

"You've saved my life, my girl," said Sir Denis, meeting Bridget on the stairs the morning after this banquet, and presenting her with a golden sovereign, "and if you like to stay on as cook at forty pounds a year, why so you shall."

"You could shave yourself in her sauce-pans, your Honour," said Pat, when he heard of this amazing promotion. It was Pat's way of saying that Bridget polished her utensils till they reflected like a mirror. "She's a rale good little girsha, that's what she is, the same Bridget; and I'm rale glad, your Honour, that ould consiquince isn't comin' back again."

After that there were few changes. The servants were in clover, and since Pat and Bridget knew it, and impressed it on their subordinates, it came to be a generally recognised fact. To be sure, it made it pleasanter for everyone in the house when, thanks to Bridget's excellent plain cooking. Sir Denis forgot he had such a thing as a liver, and had no more of the gouty attacks which made his temper east-windy instead of west-windy. During those peaceful years he forgot to be choleric. He was overflowing with kindness and helpfulness to those about him, and took a paternal interest in the affairs of his household.

"Sure," Pat would say to Bridget, "'tis for marrying us he'd be, if he knew how it was with us, same as he married off Rose to the postman and gave them a cottage; and that new girl isn't up to Rose's work yet, nor ever will be, unless I'm mistaken."

"'Twould be a sin to take advantage of him," Bridget would answer. "And we're both young enough to wait a bit, Pat. There'll be new ways when Miss Nelly marries Sir Robin. Maybe 'tis going to live with them he'd be."

"He never will, so long as her Ladyship's alive," said Pat, emphatically.

"Then maybe we'd be havin' him for a furnished lodger," said Bridget. "I'd rather it 'ud be something in the country. Why wouldn't you be his coachman as well, Pat? Sure, anything you don't know about horses isn't worth the knowin'."

"True for you. We might have a little lodge," said Pat.

They were really the quietest and most peaceful years — unless the Dowager happened to be in town. Then something went dreadfully wrong with the General's temper, and he would come roaring downstairs and along the corridors like a winter storm. The servants' hall used to take a tender interest in those bad days.

"Somebody ought to spake to her," said Bridget. "Supposin' the gout was to go to his heart! He was bad enough after the last time she was here."

"She'll never lave hoult of him," said Pat, solemnly. "The sort of her Ladyship houlds on the tighter the more you wriggle. He's preparing a quare bed of repentance for himself, so he is, the langwidge he's usin' about her all over the house. By-and-by he'll be rememberin' she's Sir Gerald's widdy, and'll be askin' me ashamed-like, 'I hope I didn't say too much about her Ladyship in my timper, Pat. She's a tryin' woman, a very tryin' woman. I'm afraid I'm apt to forget now an' agin that she's my dear brother's widdy, so I am.'"

Pat's imitation of Sir Denis was really admirable.

"'Tis a pity he doesn't run her out of the house," said Bridget, "instead of lettin' her bother the heart out of him like that."

"He couldn't say a rough word to a woman, not if it was to save his life," said Pat. "Nothin' rougher thin 'No, ma'am,' and 'Yes, ma'am,' I ever heard him say to her. Whirroo, Bridget, you should ha' heard him whin his timper was up givin' it to us long ago in the barrack square. I hope it isn't the suppressed gout she'll be giving him the next time! 'Tisn't half as bad whin it's out."

However, the storms were few and far between. The household lived by rule. Every morning, winter and summer, the horses were at the door by eight o'clock for the morning canter of the General and Miss Nelly in the park. At nine o'clock the household assembled for prayers. After breakfast Sir Denis walked to his club in Pall Mall, wet or dry. He would read the papers and discuss the cheeseparing policy of the Government with some of his old chums, lunch at the club, play a game of dominoes or draughts, and return home in time for dinner. Frequently they entertained a friend or two quietly at dinner. But, company or no company, there were prayers at ten o'clock, after which the General took his candle and went to his bedroom.

There were times, of course, when Nelly went out to balls and entertainments, and then Sir Denis was to be seen on duty, even though there were a good many ladies who would be willing to take the chaperonage of his daughter off his hands. But that was an office he would relinquish to no one. He was the most patient of chaperons, too, and never grumbled if the daylight found him still at the whist-table, although he would rise at the same hour as usual and carry out his appointed round for the day as if he had not lost his sleep over-night. Of course, Nelly might stay a-bed. He wouldn't have Nelly's roses spoilt, and the young needed their proper amount of sleep. As for himself, he couldn't sleep a wink after seven, no matter how late he had been up the night before.

But, on the whole, they lived a quiet life. Nelly was too unselfish, too fond of her father, to cost him many nights without his usual sleep. She had really the quietest tastes. Her few friends, her books, her music, her dogs and birds, sufficed for her happiness. They had a houseful of dogs, by the way, and any description of the way of life in Sherwood Square which made no mention of dogs would be quite insufficient. Duke the Irish terrier and Bonaparte the pug, usually Boney, and Nelson the bull terrier, were as important and characteristic members of the household as anyone else, except, perhaps, Sir Denis and Miss Nelly. Nelly used to explain her stay-at-home ways to her friends by saying that the dogs were offended with her if she went out for a walk without them. The dogs had many tricks. They knew the terms of drill as well as any soldier, and were always ready for parade, or to die for their country, or groan for their country's enemies, at the General's word of command. Nelly had to be much out-of-doors, as the dogs were clamorous for walks, and she kept her roses in London with the old milkmaid sweetness.

There was one happening of the quiet day that stood out for Sir Denis, and, although he did not know it, for his daughter also.

Sir Denis's old regiment happened to be stationed at a barracks in the immediate neighbourhood. To reach their parade-ground it was possible for the troops, by making a little detour, to pass along the quiet street on which the houses in Sherwood Square opened. It became an established thing that they should pass every morning about nine o'clock. How that came Sir Denis did not trouble to ask. He was quite satisfied and delighted that "the boys" should do him honour.

The breakfast-room was one of the few rooms that did not overlook the square but the street. Every morning, just as Sir Denis concluded prayers, there would come the steady trot of cavalry and the jingle of accoutrements. If he had not quite finished, he would say "Amen" in a reverent hurry. "Come now, boys and girls," he would say to the servants, "I want you to see my old regiment."

He would step out on the balcony above the hall-door with a beaming face, and his arm around his Nelly's waist. The servants would press behind him, the dogs push to the front with the curiosity of their kind. Down the street the soldiers would come, all flashing in scarlet and gold, the sleek horses shining in the morning sun with a deeper lustre than their polished accoutrements. There would be a halt for a second in front of the house. The men would salute their old General, the General salute his old regiment. Then the cavalcade would sweep on its way and the street be duller than before.

One morning — it was a bright, breezy morning of March — the wind had caught Nelly's golden hair and blown it in a halo about her face. She was wearing a blue ribbon in it. She was fond of blue, and the simplicity of it became her fresh youth. Just as the soldiers halted the wind caught Nelly's blue bow, and, having played with it a little, sent it drifting down like a little blue flower among the men on horseback.

It was such a slight thing that the General might not have noticed it. Anyhow, he made no comment, but watched the troops out of sight as usual. The odd thing was that Nelly passed over her loss in silence, although she must have missed her blue ribbon, since without it her hair had become loose in the wind.

At breakfast, when the servants had left the room, the General made a remark.

"That young Langrishe sits his horse well," he said. "He's a good soldier, Nelly, my girl. A very good soldier, or I'm much mistaken."

But Nelly was apparently too absorbed in her duty of making the tea to answer the remark. For an instant she was redder than a rose. No one would have suspected Sir Denis of slyness, but the look he shot at the girl was certainly sly. Under the white tablecloth he rubbed his hands softly together.

CHAPTER VII

A CHANCE MEETING

It was worse for the General when Sir Robin Drummond left Oxford and settled in London, with an avowed intention of reading for the Bar, and at the same time making politics his real career.

"A man ought to do something in the world," he said to his irate uncle. "The Bar is always a stepping-stone. I confess I don't look to practice very much; my real bent is for politics. But the law interests me, and it is always a stepping-stone."

"I should have thought that the profession of arms, which your father and your grandfather adorned, as well as a good many of your forbears, might serve you as well," Sir Denis said, hotly.

"You leave out my uncle, sir," the young man replied, with urbane good humour. "Yes, the Drummonds have done very well for the profession of arms. Still, with my beliefs on the subject of war —"

"Pray don't air them, don't air them. You know what I think about them. Your father's son ought to be ashamed of professing such sentiments."

"One must abide by one's sentiments, one's convictions, if one is to be good for anything. Uncle Denis," Sir Robin said, patiently.

"You'll have no chance in politics. No constituency will return you. What we want now is a strong Government that will strengthen us, through our Army and Navy, sir, against our enemies. Such a Government will come in at the next election a-top of the wave. The people, or I am much mistaken, are not going to see the bulwarks of our power tampered with. The country is all for war. Where do you come in?"

Sir Robin smiled ever so slightly. It was that smile of his, with its faintest hint of intellectual superiority, that riled the General to bursting point.

"I don't believe there is a war feeling, Uncle Denis," he said. "The country has had enough of war. However, I should not come in on top of a wave of war feeling in any case. You would be quite right in asking where I should come in. To be sure, I look to come in on top of the anti-war wave. My side is pledged against war. The working man —"

"You don't mean to say that you're going to appeal to *him*!" Sir Denis shouted. "You don't mean to say that you're going to side with the Radicals! I've lived to see many strange things, but — Gerald's son a Radical!"

He brought out the ejaculations with the sound of guns pop-ping. His face was red with indignation, his eyes leaping at his degenerate nephew. The next words did not tend to calm him.

"Do you know, Uncle Denis, I believe that if my father had been a politician he would have been a Radical? His profound feeling for Christianity, his adherence to the creed of its Founder, Whose whole life was a glorification of toil —"

"Spare me, spare me!" cried the General, restraining himself with difficulty. "So a man can't be a Christian and a gentleman! And you think your father would have been a Radical! I can tell you, young gentleman —"

At this moment Nelly came into the room, charming in her short-waisted frock of white satin, with a little cap of pearls on her hair. Both men turned and stared at her, pleasure and affection in their eyes.

"So you've been heckling poor Robin as usual," she said, strok-ing her father's cheek. "Heckling poor Robin and getting your hair on end like a fretful porcupine. I'll never be able to make you into a nice, sweet, quiet old gentleman."

"Turn your attention to him," said the General, indicating his nephew by an unfriendly nod. "What do you think, Nell? He's a Radical. He's going to contest a seat for the Radicals. What do you say now?"

"Pooh!" said Nelly, with her pretty chin in the air. "Pooh! Why shouldn't he? Lots of nice people are Radicals. If he feels that way, of course he ought to do it."

Robin's unpractical eyes thanked her mutely. He was as plain-looking a man as he had been a boy, more hatchet-faced than ever. He was long and lean and angular, and his positions were un-graceful. But his eyes were the eyes of Don Quixote. The eyes had appealed to Nelly as long as she could remember.

"Oh, if you're against me, Nell!" said Sir Denis, lamely. "Ah! there's the bell! And a good thing, too. I couldn't eat my lunch today for old Grogan of the Artillery. He's a man with a grievance. It soured my wine and spoilt my food. Well, well, Robin, if you're under Nelly's protection you may do what you like — join the Peace Society, if you like."

"I mean to, sir," Sir Robin said, placidly. "In fact, I'm speaking on 'The Ideal of a Universal Peace' on Monday evening at the Finsbury Democratic Debating Club."

When Sir Robin came to town there had been an apprehension in his uncle's breast, too well-founded, that the Dowager would follow him. She was devoted to her son, and not at all disposed to take the General's views about his recreancy in politics.

"A good many good people are on the Radical side, after all," she said, "and there is, perhaps, more room, too, for a young man of Robin's ambitions in the Radical party."

"So far as I can see," said the General, acidly, "his ambitions are rather to succeed at the bottom than at the top. The applause of the multitude appeals to him more than the praise of his equals or superiors."

Lady Drummond glanced coldly at his heated face.

"I fancy you've an attack of gout coming on, Denis," she said. "I should send for Sir Harley Dix, if I were you."

She had stopped the General just as he was on his own doorstep, setting his face cheerfully eastwards on his way to Pall Mall. He had come back with her. He knew his duty to his brother's widow better than to do anything else. It was Wednesday, and on Wednesday there was always a particular curry at lunch which he much affected. He was a connoisseur in curries, and the *chef* always made this with an eye to Sir Denis's approval. He would have to shorten his walk and 'bus part of the way, or the curry would be cold. He hated to be put out in his daily routine.

"I never was freer from gout in my life, Matilda," he said, with indignation. "I don't trouble the doctors much. When I want their advice I shall ask for it. I always ask for advice when I want it."

She looked at him with unconcern.

"Do you think Nelly will soon be back?" she asked.

"I don't know. When she takes the dogs for a walk she is often out for a couple of hours. Perhaps it would be too long a time to wait."

In his mind he could see the curry disappearing before the other men who liked it as much as he did. Grogan would always eat curry — that special curry — to the General's indignation. Why, curry was the last thing Grogan ought to eat! Wasn't he as yellow as the curry itself with chronic liver? Grogan was greedy over that curry — a greedy fellow, the General said to himself, remembering the many occasions when it had been impossible for him to break away from Grogan and his grievances. If her Ladyship was going to sit on endlessly! The General's manners were too good to leave her to sit by herself. And she was untying her bonnet strings! He might as well lunch at home. No, he wouldn't do that, not if her Ladyship was going to stay to lunch. He supposed he could have lunch somewhere, if not at his club.

"Pray, don't put yourself out for me, Denis," her Ladyship was saying, with what passed for graciousness in her. "I know your usual habits. At your age a man doesn't like to be put out of his habits. Don't mind me, pray. I can amuse myself very well till Nelly comes in. Plenty of books and papers, I see. You subscribe to Mudie's. I thought no one subscribed to Mudie's now that we have so many Free Libraries. I have never been able to afford myself a library subscription, even although we lived in the country. Now that I am going to settle in town —"

"Settle in town!" The General's eyes were almost starting from his head. "I'd no idea, Matilda, you were going to settle in town. What's going to become of the Court?"

"I have an idea of letting it for a few years. Mr. Higbid, the very rich hide merchant, has taken a fancy to the place. I have yet to hear what Robin will say. Mr. Higbid is prepared to pay a fancy price —"

"He'd have to before I'd let him into my drawing-room," said the General, with disgust. "Imagine letting the Court! And to a man who sells hides!"

"His money is as good as anybody else's. And he is received everywhere. You are really too old-fashioned, Denis. Your ways need altering."

"I am too old to change, ma'am," said the General, getting up and giving himself a shake like a dog. "If you don't really mind being left —" He wanted to get away to think over the fact that the Dowager was going to settle in town. He could hardly keep himself from groaning. His peace was all at an end. If he had not been too old to change, he would have fled from London and left it to the Dowager. But big as it was, it was too little to contain himself and the Dowager with any prospect of peace.

"I'll stay and have lunch with Nelly," the Dowager went on, quite ignorant of his perturbation. "Afterwards, I'm going to take her to see houses with me. *Of course*, I shall settle in your immediate neighbourhood, if I can find anything suitable. I'm going to take Nelly off your hands a bit, take her about and advise her as to her frocks. She was wearing white chiffon the last time we dined here — a most perishable material. I don't think your purse is long enough for white chiffon, Denis. Then the young people ought to see more of each other. We ought to be talking about trousseaux —"

But at this point the General fled. If he had stayed another second he would have said things that his kind and chivalrous heart would have grieved over later. He fled, and left her Ladyship staring after him in amazement.

He clean forgot about the curry in the fretting and fuming of his mind, or it occurred to him only to be consigned to Grogan, as though Grogan were a synonym for something much stronger. His fiery indignation between Sherwood Square and Pall Mall was quite amazing. The Dowager in the next street! Why, he might as well order his coffin. And talking about taking Nelly from him. That muff, Robin, too! When had the fellow shown any impatience? He didn't want the girl to marry an oyster. He remembered the glory and glamour of his own love affair, of that golden year of marriage. His Nelly ought to be loved as her mother had been before her, as her mother's daughter deserved to be. He wasn't going to yield her to a fellow who would only give her half his tepid heart, who would leave her to spend her evenings alone while he spouted in Radical clubs or in that big talking shop, the House of Commons. He wouldn't have it. And still — Robin was poor Gerald's son, and there was nothing against him but his politics. Somewhere, at the back of his mind, the General recognised the fact that he could have forgiven the politics if it had not been for the Dowager.

He had almost reached the doors of his club — Grogan might eat the curry for him, and be hanged to him! — when he saw advancing towards him the spare, elegant figure that sat its horse in front of the regiment below the General's window every morning. The oddest gleam came into his eyes. The young man had recognised him, and was blushing like a girl as he came towards him. He had velvety brown eyes and regular features, was a handsome lad, the General said to himself as young Langrishe lifted his hat from his sleek, well-shaped head. He had the barest acquaintance with Sir Denis, and he would have passed by if the old soldier had not stopped him.

"How do you do, Captain Langrishe?" he said. "I am very much obliged to you for the pleasure you give me every morning. I take it as uncommonly kind of you to bring 'the boys' past my house. I assure you I quite look forward to it — I quite look forward to it."

Langrishe stammered something about the regiment delighting to do honour to its old General, growing redder and redder as he did so. His confusion became him in the General's eyes. He was certainly a pleasant-looking, well-mannered boy, the General decided, and the confusion of the young soldier in the presence of the old soldier an entirely natural and creditable thing.

"I'll tell you what, my lad," said Sir Denis, putting his arm within the other's: "if you've nothing better to do, supposing you come and lunch with me. I'm just going in to the club. And you — on your way to it? I thought so. You'll give me the pleasure of your company?"

The General was half an hour late, yet he found a small table in a window recess unappropriated. It was set for two, and a screen was drawn about it so that the two could be as retired as they wished. More — the General had not been forgotten in the distribution of the curry. Their portions came up piping hot. From where they sat the General could see Sir Rodney Vivash and Grogan button-holing each other. They were the bores of the club, and for once they had foregathered, willingly or unwillingly.

After all, there were compensations — there were compensations; and the General was hungry. His manner towards young Langrishe had an air of fatherly kindness. There was a gratified flush on the young fellow's lean, dark cheek. What was it the General had heard about Langrishe? Oh, yes, that he had had rough luck — that his old uncle, Sir Peter — the General remembered him for a curmudgeon — had married and had a son, after rearing the young fellow as his heir. No wonder the lad looked careworn. The regiment was an expensive one; not too expensive for Sir Peter Langrishe's heir, but much too expensive for a poor man.

However, it was no business of the General's — not just yet.

"You have met my daughter, I think?" he said. They were at the cheese by this time, and the General was apparently divided between the merits of Gruyère and Stilton. He did not glance at Captain Langrishe, but he knew quite as well as if he had that the colour came again to his cheek, that the brown eyes looked unhappily conscious.

"I have met Miss Drummond several times," he answered.

"Ah, you must dine with us one evening."

Young Langrishe looked at him in a startled way.

"Thank you very much, sir," he said, "but, as a matter of fact, I am negotiating a change into an Indian regiment. I don't know how long I shall be here. And I shall be very busy, I'm afraid."

"Ah! Just as you like — just as you like." The General, by the easiest of transitions, passed on to the subject of soldiering in India. He had an unwontedly exhilarated feeling which later had its reaction in a consciousness of guilt.

"What would poor Gerald have said?" he thought, as he walked homewards that evening. "And I've nothing against Robin — I've nothing really against Robin, except his Peace Societies and all the rest of it. And the Dowager — yes, there's always the Dowager. I should like to know what on earth ever induced poor Gerald to marry the Dowager."

CHAPTER VIII

GROVES OF ACADEME

After that keen disappointment about the baby's forgetting her, although she excused it to herself, arguing that at twenty months one cannot be expected to have a long memory, Mary was more reconciled to the changed conditions of her life.

"I hope we are going to be together for a good many years," Lady Anne said, "and presently you must be able to play and sing to me, to read to me and take an interest in the things in which I am interested. You are to go to school, Mary."

So Mary went to school, first to the Queen's Preparatory School, then to the Queen's College. Her years there were very happy ones, especially those years at the College, after she had found her feet and made friends, and gained confidence in herself and the world.

"She sucks up knowledge as a sponge sucks up water," was the report of the Principal, Miss Merton, to the delighted Lady Anne. "I hope Lady Anne, that you will permit her to go in for her B.A. I should not be surprised, indeed, if she captured a fellowship."

"No fellowships," Lady Anne said, firmly. "What would she do with a fellowship? I propose, as soon as she has done with you, to take her abroad. I have a mind to see the world again through young eyes. And it will put the coping-stone on her education. I shouldn't dare leave her too long with you. Learning so often destroys a woman's imagination. They work too hard, I suppose. It doesn't seem to come natural to them yet as it does to men."

"There's no question of Mary's working too hard," the Lady Principal said, bearing these hard sayings of Lady Anne's with composure. "She has fine brains. Whatever she wants in an intellectual way she can come at easily."

Mary, indeed, took her B.A. without over-much burning of the midnight oil. Afterwards she always spoke with the tenderest affection of her old school-days. She recalled with delight the spacious class-rooms, the old garden with its great woodland trees, and the tiny rooms of the girls who were in residence at the College, with their quaint and pretty adornments — the place of so much young *camaraderie* and soaring ambition and happy emulation. "I can hardly remember that anyone was ever unkind," she used to say long afterwards.

As a matter of fact, the band of elder students with whom Mary was connected in her latter days at the College had a generous enthusiasm for her beauty, taking it as in a sense a credit to themselves.

"You will be a living answer to them," said Jessie Baynes, who was small and plain-looking, "when they say that learned women are always ugly."

And the whole of the class applauded her speech.

"I shall love to see you in your cap and gown," Jessie went on, firing at the picture in her own imagination. "Very few of the men will be taller than you, Mary. How they will shout!"

Jessie had no thought at all of her own lack of height and grace, as she had no idea of how pleasant her little brown face was despite its plainness. She was going to earn her living by teaching, and, what was more, going to make living easier and pleasanter for her mother and her young sister. To get her mother out of stuffy town lodgings to a seaside cottage, which was an unattainable heaven to the mother's thoughts, to educate Edie and give her a chance in life — these were the things that filled Jessie's mind to the exclusion of fear whenever she thought of her ordeal at the conferring of the University degrees. To be sure, she trembled a little when she thought of the long, brilliantly lighted Hall, and all the fine ladies, and the scarlet robes of the Senators, and the young barbarians in the gallery, and all the thousands of eyes fixed on the one little dumpling of a woman going up to receive her degree. If she might only win the fellowship! She would not care what ordeal she passed through for that. So she put away the fear from her mind. If she could only win the fellowship! But she was too humble about her own attainments to have more than a little, little hope of that.

How generous they all were, Mary thought, with an impulse of gratitude towards those dear class-fellows that brought the tears to her eyes.

"When we are photographed in our caps and gowns," said another, "you must stand up in the middle of us, Mary, so that they will see how tall you are."

Mary reported their generosity to Lady Anne, with whom, by this time, she was on the loving terms that cast out fear.

"Very creditable to them," the old lady said, twinkling. "Don't let it make you vain, Mary. You're well enough, but you aren't half as pretty as a rose, or half as tall as a tree, and there are thousands of trees and roses in the world."

"I don't think myself pretty," Mary said, in a hurt voice. "There are several of the girls far prettier. As for being tall, it is no pleasure. I would much rather be little."

"Your skirts will always cost you more than other girls'."

"It is only because they are so kind and generous that they think well of me," Mary went on. "And, oh! I do hope that Jessie will win the fellowship. Everyone does, even —"

"Even her opponents," the old lady said, drily. It was always Lady Anne's way to seem cynical over things, even with those she loved best.

"She has worked so hard for it," said Mary, "and Alice Egerton, who is in the running, too, has shaken hands with Jessie, and told her that if she wins it will only prove she is the better man."

"Dear me, we are cultivating the manly virtues, too," said Lady Anne. "Let me see: there are twenty young ladies in your class, and not a spiteful one among them. I have never heard of so low a percentage."

"If women were given something to think of besides petty interests," Mary began hotly. "If they were educated, if they were given ideals —"

"You are only on your trial yet, child," Lady Anne suggested. "We produced very good women before Women's Colleges were heard of. I'm glad they've not spoilt you, anyhow. No stooped shoulders, no narrow chest, no dimmed eyes. I couldn't have forgiven them if they had made you pay a price for your learning."

When Mary received her B.A. degree she was applauded more rapturously from the gallery than even the new Fellow, Miss Jessica Baynes, B.A., who knew little enough about her own reception, since, as she left the daïs, she had glanced up and made out her mother's little nutcracker face, so like her own, in one of the circles of faces overhead.

There was a little group in the balcony watching Mary with fond pride. Lady Anne Hamilton's face shone again as the tall, slender young figure went up amid the furious applause of the undergraduates, through which the general clapping of hands could hardly be heard. Behind Lady Anne were Mary's father and stepmother. Lady Anne had taken care that they should not be forgotten in the distribution of tickets. Walter Gray looked on quietly. He was very proud of his girl; but he had, perhaps, too great a wisdom to set much store by the plaudits of the many. Mrs. Gray, in a bonnet Mary had made for her and a mantle which had been Mary's gift, was in a timid rapture. She was older by some years than she had been when Mary went to Lady Anne first, but she was far more comely. Her family seemed to have reached its limits, for one thing, and she was no more the helpless drudge she had been. Several of the children were at school, and that wonderfully elastic salary of Mary's had done miraculous things in the way of bringing comfort and even refinement to Walter Gray's home.

"Well," said Lady Anne, turning round, and touching Walter Gray's arm, "I have not made too bad a fairy godmother, have I, now?"

"She would never have grown so tall," Walter Gray said, with absent eyes. He had yielded up Mary for her good, but he had never ceased to miss her.

One person who sat among the most distinguished group in the Hall looked at Mary with a lively interest.

"What a charming girl!" she said to her host, a very great person.

"I believe she has been adopted as a sort of companion by old Lady Anne Hamilton, who is a cousin of my wife's," he responded. "The girl has been educated at her expense. Yes, it's a pretty thing. I only hope it won't become a blue-stocking."

"I must positively know her," said the lady. "She interests me."

"You make me jealous," returned the great person, with playful gallantry.

Lady Agatha had been a peeress in her own right since she had attained the tender age of two years. Her father and mother had died too early for her to miss them, and she had shown from her childhood a capacity to think for herself, which nurses and governesses and all such persons looked on as absolutely shocking. She had had a guardian, a soft, woolly, comfortable gentleman whose will she had brushed aside and replaced by her own from the time she was eight years old. Legally, she was not of age till twenty-one; in reality, she was of age at fifteen or thereabouts. She consulted Colonel St. John, her guardian, about her affairs, as an act of grace, because she was so fond of him and wouldn't hurt his feelings for anything; but she made no secret of the fact that at twenty-one she was going to be absolutely her own mistress.

"You are your own mistress now," Colonel St. John said once, a little ruefully. "You never do what I wish — you make me do what *you* wish. Don't go too fast, Agatha, my dear. At twenty-one one is not wiser than old people, though one may feel so."

But he knew that he was talking to empty air. She was so eager to lay hold on life. And she was equipped for it — there was no doubt of that. Mr. Grainger, of Grainger, Ellison and Wells, who had had charge of the business of the estate from time immemorial, whose trade it was to be cautious, was cheerful over the Colonel's misgivings.

"You wouldn't feel anxious if she was a lad," he said. "I'd set her against nine hundred and ninety lads out of a thousand for sound common-sense. She won't do anything foolish. Take my word for it, she won't do anything foolish."

She did not do anything foolish. She took her own way about some things against Colonel St. John, and even against Mr. Grainger, but she turned out to be right in the end. She had a good many people dependent in one way or another upon her for their well-being, and she insisted on coming face to face with these — on dealing with them without an intermediary. And she made no mistakes. She could see through shifty dishonesty as well as if she had had three times her years and a wide knowledge of the seamy side of human nature. She had always been an outdoor girl, and now she displayed a knowledgeable interest in her own Home Farm and in the affairs of her tenants.

She used to say that the days were not long enough for all she had to do. Certainly, she contrived to cram into them three times as much pleasure, business, and philanthropy as her neighbours.

She had an idea of the obligations of her position as lady of the soil which made poor Colonel St. John gasp when she talked about it. There was so much to be done for the people — churches to be built, or chapels, if they preferred them, and school-houses, industries to be fostered — so much encouragement to be given to honest endeavour. Her idea was that the land should afford all the people wished for. She was going to stop the terrible drifting of the people into the towns. Their lives were to be made gayer. There should be entertainments. The farmers' wives and daughters were to make butter and cheese like their forbears, to grow fruit and vegetables, to rear poultry and sell eggs; but they were not, therefore, to lead a life of narrow toil. They were to be rewarded for their skill and industry. The fruit of their labours was to make life sweeter and pleasanter for them. There were to be libraries and reading-rooms, debating clubs, social gatherings.

"Stuff and nonsense!" Colonel St. John said, with his cotton-wool eyebrows puffed out. "She'll dip the estate, and then she'll be coming to ask us to pull her out. Worse, she'll only make them discontented."

"She'll come out all right," Mr. Grainger said, rubbing his hands softly together. "If she blunders, she'll learn wisdom from the experiment. You'll see she'll come out all right, Colonel. The only thing that troubles me is that she may have no time to get married. We don't want her to be a spinster, hey? I confess I should like to see the succession assured."

It was this notable young lady who came in not so long after to Queen's College, where a distinguished woman of letters was giving a series of lectures on "The Poetry of the Sixteenth Century." Her entrance created somewhat of a flutter. She was as tall as Mary Gray, but much more opulently built. She had short, curling, dark hair, irregular features, and violet eyes — not a bit handsome, but big and bonny and lovesome. Her dress fluttered even these students. It was of purple velvet, with a great stole of sables, and her sable muff had a big bunch of real violets, which brought an odour of the quickening and burgeoning earth.

She sat by the Lady Principal, and afterwards had tea with the students. She asked especially for an introduction to Mary Gray, and then she insisted on driving her as far as the Mall in her motor-car, which she drove herself, while the chauffeur sat with folded arms behind. On the way she talked poetry and politics with the same fervour she brought to all her pursuits.

"It has been borne in on me," she said vehemently, "that in working among my own people as I have been doing I have been only tinkering at things, just tinkering. One has to go to the root of the matter, to abolish unjust laws, to replace them by good ones. Supposing I made my estate, as I hope to make it, a Utopia, still there would be hundreds of estates where the people would be in misery. It ought not to be left to our good will to do things. We should be compelled to do them."

Mary watched the flashing eyes with the greatest admiration. She felt that Lady Agatha was a glorious creature, for whom she could do anything. The hero-worship which is latent in the heart of all young people worth their salt sprang into sudden life. Lady Agatha glanced at her, noticed her expression, and smiled a rich, sweet, gratified smile. She had made a disciple. To make a disciple was very pleasant to one of her temperament. Like most women, she was a thorough propagandist.

As she swept up to the gate of Lady Anne's house, the old lady herself was standing just within it. She had come in from driving her little pony phaeton, which she liked to drive herself. She had a little wild, bright-eyed mountain pony, which would eat sugar and apples from her hands, and was as much of a pet as a dog.

"Well, Mary," she said, "introduce me. How do you do, Lady Agatha? I know you by sight already. Won't you come inside and have some tea? I'm very glad my Chloe didn't meet that uncanny monster of yours. I have something to do to get her past the trams, I can tell you, much less the motorcars."

"You shouldn't go out alone," Mary said, with tender concern. "Her little pony is very wild, Lady Agatha, and she won't take the carriage, unless she goes visiting."

"You want to make me out an old woman," Lady Anne said,

"and I shall never be that. Come along in, Lady Agatha. I've been hearing about you. What do you mean by making my tenants discontented? They're very well as they are. We shall have to form a league against you, we indolent ones."

Her Ladyship had a way of winning her welcome wherever she went. Lady Anne had begun, like a good many other people, with a certain distrust of the brilliant young woman who desired to conquer so many kingdoms. In the end she yielded unreservedly.

"A fine, big-hearted, generous creature," she said. "It makes me young to look at her and hear her talk. And so she has taken a huge fancy to my Mary. Very well, then, she can come and go; but she's not to have my Mary for all that, for I want her for myself."

"No one really wants me," said Mary, with suddenly dimmed eyes, "except you and papa. But if they did they couldn't have me. I belong to you and papa."

CHAPTER IX

THE RACE WITH DEATH

It might have been considered great promotion for the daughter of Walter Gray, who attended all day to the ailments of watches with a magnifying glass stuck in his eye, to be the friend of Lady Agatha Chenevix as well as the adopted child almost of Lady Anne Hamilton. Indeed, in the early days, when Lady Agatha's friendship for Mary brought her into the finest society the country provided, Lady Anne sometimes watched Mary narrowly, to see how she was taking it. The result of these observations must have been quite satisfactory to the old lady, judging by the energetic shaking of her head after one or two of these occasions when she was alone and thought over things. Once she spoke her thoughts to Lady Agatha, to whom, indeed, she found herself often talking in a way that surprised herself. There was something about the minx that forced even a suspicious and reticent old lady into trust and confidence, and as her trust and confidence increased so did her affection for the brilliant young peeress.

"People said I was mad," she remarked, "when I took Mary Gray into my house, and into my heart. Matilda Drummond even said — and I have never forgotten it to her — that if she was my nephew, Jarvis, she'd have my condition of mind inquired into. Yet see how it has turned out! Is she spoilt? Is she an upstart? Is she set above her family? She's over there this minute with that poor little drab stepmother of hers. She worships her father. The joys and sorrows of the poor little household are as much to her today as the day she left them."

"I know," said Lady Agatha. "She's pure gold. I saw it in her face the first day I laid eyes on her. The only quarrel I have with her is that so many people push me out with her. I don't mean you, of course, Lady Anne. But yesterday I could not have her because she must go to your doctor's wife, and today she was going for a long walk with that little Miss Baynes. Tomorrow it will be her father. It is his free afternoon."

"I heard an amusing thing about the father the other day," said Lady Anne. "Of course, Mary knows nothing about it. I called at Gordon's — that is where Mr. Gray is employed — about a new catch for my amethyst bracelet. I have known Mr. Gordon for years. He is a thoroughly respectable man. It seems there is a very ill-conditioned person who works in the same room as Mr. Gray — a good workman, but most ill-conditioned. When he is especially bad-tempered he vents his anger on his quiet room-fellow, who never seems to hear him but works away as though he were a thousand miles distant from the grumbling and scolding. Well, it seems that the other day, despairing, perhaps, of rousing Mr. Gray by any other methods, he made a reference to Mary as having got into fine society and looking down on her father. It's a little place, after all, my dear, and you and your motor-car are known as well as the Town Hall. Mr. Gray got up very quietly and threw the man downstairs; then went back to his work without a word. Gordon saw it in quite the right way. He said that the person thoroughly well deserved it, but that the next time he mightn't get off with a few bruises, and that would be awkward for Mr. Gray. So he has given him another room."

"Ah, bravo!" Lady Agatha clapped her hands together. "That's where Mary gets it. I've seen the light of battle in her eye — haven't you?"

"Sometimes — when she has heard of cruelty and injustice."

Now that Mary's schooling was over, she was to see the world under Lady Anne's auspices. They were to go abroad soon after Christmas, to be in Rome for Easter, to dawdle about the Continent where they would and for as long as they would. Everything was planned and mapped out. Mary had her neat travelling-dress of grey cloth, tailor-made, her close-fitting toque, her veil and gloves, all her equipment, lying ready to put on. Her old friend, Simmons, had packed her travelling trunk. It had come to almost the last day.

And, to be sure, Mary must be much with her father and the others during those last hours. She had gone with her father for a long country walk.

"I wish you were coming, too," said Mary, clinging closely to his arm.

"You will be bringing me back fine stories," her father said, patting her hand. "I shall be seeing the world through your eyes, child."

"I shall write to you every day."

"I shan't expect that, Mary. You will be moving from place to place. I know you will write when you can, and I am always sure of your love."

While they talked Lady Anne was receiving Dr. Carruthers professionally. She had had symptoms, weaknesses, pangs, of which she had told nobody.

"I was inclined to go without telling you anything about it, doctor," she said. "I was as keen upon it as the child. I am more disappointed than she will be. I have been wilful all my life, but I am glad I did not take my own way this time. It would have been a nice thing for poor Mary if I had been taken ill in some of those foreign places."

"You will be much better in your own comfortable home."

Dr. Carruthers spoke cheerfully, but he could not keep the anxiety out of his face.

"You must have suffered a deal lately," he said pityingly. He had not forgotten what Lady Anne had done for him and his Mildred. She had been their faithful and kind friend from that propitious day when he had picked Mary Gray from under the feet of the tram-horses. His position was now an assured one, and he and his wife had a tender affection for their benefactress.

"I'm an obstinate old woman," said Lady Anne, with very bright eyes. The doctor's visit had been an ordeal to her. "I have had the pain off and on for the last few months, but I assured myself that it was merely indigestion, which mimics so many things. I am glad my common-sense came to the rescue at last. Do you think I shall go off suddenly, or shall I have to lie, panting, like those poor creatures I've seen at the hospital, labouring for breath? I shouldn't like that."

The doctor shook his head. How was he to know when the worn-out heart would cease to perform its functions, and after what manner?

"We must hope that you will not suffer," he said gently. "I will do my best to save you that."

"And I've plenty of spirit for whatever the good God sends," Lady Anne said, her face lighting up. "I've always had great spirit. They said I pulled through my childish illnesses twice as well because of my spirit. I remember my dear mother telling me that when I had croup at two years old I mimicked the cows and sheep and cats and dogs between the paroxysms. I was just the same later on. I ought to have married a soldier. My poor husband was a man of peace. He couldn't bear a loud voice. Have a glass of wine before you go, doctor. I've just had a bottle of Comet port opened. Try it. There's very little like it left in the world."

After Dr. Carruthers had taken his departure she went to her desk and set about writing a letter. But she paused after she had written a few lines, looked at the clock, and sat for a minute thinking.

"No," she said aloud. "I won't wait till tomorrow. Mary shan't take the chances. Who knows if I shall be here tomorrow? If I drive out to Marleigh I shall just catch Buckton. He will be pottering round that orchid-house of his. He will just be home from the office. He can make me a new will there as well as here. Indeed, I ought not to have postponed it for so long."

She ordered her little pony phaeton. It was nearly five o'clock.

There would be plenty of time to drive to Marleigh Abbey, where her lawyer lived, to interview him, and get back again before it was dark. She would make Mary's interests safe. She had come to care for the child more than she had ever expected to care. She was going to make a provision for her, so that she should be secure against the chances and changes of this life. Nothing very startling, nothing that need make Jarvis grumble to any great extent; just a modest provision which would not keep Mary from making use of the talents with which God had endowed her and the education her fairy godmother had given her.

It was not long before she had left the town behind, and was driving along the winding road that ran by the foot of the mountains. The road was very lonely.

Chloe was rather nervous, not to say hysterical, on this particular afternoon. Her mistress had not considered her as was her wont. She had taken the shortest road, forcing her to meet a black monster of a steam-tram which she had sometimes seen at a distance, a thing which was her special abomination. Chloe had made a bolt for it, and had passed the tram safely and got away on to the back road. She had been accustomed, when she had made her small run-aways before, to be petted and soothed afterwards. Indeed, as soon as her terror had calmed a little, and she was on the road she knew to be harmless, she slackened down, expecting to hear her mistress's voice of tender scolding, to have her mistress alight and stroke her with soft words. Instead of that she was touched up pretty sharply.

"Get me there, my girl," said Lady Anne. "Get me there quickly. You can take your time going home, and we'll go the lower road. I feel as though Death and I were running a race. I could never forgive myself if I died before I'd provided for Mary."

The pony gave her head a shake as though in answer to her mistress's words, pricked up her ears and set off at a sharp canter.

Suddenly something happened. Lady Anne had at first no realisation of what it was. Jennings, the coachman, said afterwards that it must have been the work of one of the mischievous lads whom he had driven with his whip from staring in at his stable door. What happened was that the pony's bridle, which had been snipped with a knife, had come apart, fallen about her neck and then under her feet. She was off like the wind.

As for poor Lady Anne, suddenly rendered helpless, she caught at the side of the little carriage, which was being dragged violently at the pony's heels. She had need of all her spirit. Fortunately, the road was a straight one, but there was not a soul in sight to help her, not a sower in the fields, not a ploughman, not even a boy herding cattle along the road. Her right hand still grasped the useless rein. She stared before her, while the rocking of the little carriage grew more and more violent, and the hedges and trees flew past them. How long would it be before the terrified pony shook herself free of the carriage altogether, or upset it on one of those mud-banks?

The old spirit kept wonderfully calm and collected. There was just one chance — that Chloe might keep the middle of the road, and presently pull up of herself, being exhausted. If only the phaeton would not rock so much. It was swaying from side to side at a terrific rate. The few seconds of the runaway seemed æons of time to Lady Anne. She was holding on now to both sides of the carriage, but her arm was through the reins. Thank Heaven, the road seemed absolutely open and Chloe must exhaust herself soon.

Then — her eyes were distended in her face. They had swung round a little incline, with a miraculous escape of running on a heap of shingle intended for mending the roads. Just ahead of them were the lodge gates and lodge of a big house. The gates were open. Out through them there toddled a small child about three years old. The child set out to cross the road. His attention was arrested by the noise of the runaway. He stood in the middle of the road staring.

Lady Anne uttered a loud, sharp cry. The child moved a few steps, fell, and lay directly in the path of Chloe's feet. A woman ran out of the lodge, screaming "Patsy, Patsy; where are you, Patsy?" Then she began to wring her hands and call on all the saints.

The pony, however, had of herself come to a standstill. The child was under her feet, between her four little hoofs. She was shaking and sweating and looking down. As for the child, after a second or so he broke into a lusty roar. He was only frightened, not hurt, but it took a little time for the mother to find that out by reason of the mud on his face and the noise he was making. When she had reassured herself, she carried him inside and closed the door of the lodge upon him. Then she returned to the pony-carriage.

Chloe was still standing there, in a piteous state of terror. Some-one was coming along the road — a policeman. Someone else was running from the opposite direction.

As for Lady Anne, the little figure had fallen forward. Her fore-head was down on the reins. Her eyes were wide open, and had a mortal terror in their gaze. She would never set things right for Mary in this world. She and Death had run a race together, and she had been beaten.

CHAPTER X

DISPOSSESSED

Lady Anne's nephew and heir, Lord Iniscrone, showed no friendly face to Mary. He came as soon as possible, and took possession of the premises. Lady Iniscrone was with him. She was a lady with a wide, flat, doughy face. Her eyes were little and pale and cold. Mary thought afterwards that if it had not been for Lady Iniscrone, Lord Iniscrone might have been kinder. She remembered that Lady Anne had detested Lady Iniscrone to the extent that she would never have her inside the house. She had an idea, which she could not put away, while she hated it, that Lady Iniscrone remembered that fact. She took possession of everything thoroughly, as though she revenged herself on the dead woman. In her cold speech she disparaged the things Lady Anne had held dear.

Their attitude towards Mary was as though she were a servant no longer necessary. She was not to eat at their table; she was to eat in her own room or in the servants' hall.

"Is it Miss Gray, my lady?" Saunders, the elderly parlourmaid, asked, aghast. "Her Ladyship thought the world of Miss Gray. She might have been her own child. And I will say, though we didn't hold with it at first, yet —"

Lady Iniscrone closed the discussion haughtily.

"Miss Gray will have her meals in the servants' hall, or in her own room if she prefers it, till after the funeral. We shall make other arrangements then, of course."

Saunders flounced out of the room. Although she was elderly and had lived in Lady Anne Hamilton's house since she was fourteen, when she had come as a between-maid, she had not forgotten how to flounce.

"Mark my words," she said in the kitchen, "she'll make a clean sweep of us, same as Miss Mary, as soon as ever the funeral is over. Supposing as how *we* gives the notice!"

And they did, to Lady Iniscrone's discomfiture, for she had intended to stay on at the Mall and to keep the staff as it stood till she had supplied its place. However, she showed her dismay only by her bad temper.

"I suppose you've all pretty well feathered your nests," she said acridly, "and can afford to retire."

Nor was her bitterness lessened by the fact that Lady Anne had left handsome legacies to each of the servants, annuities to the elder ones, sums of money to the younger. But the will, dated some years back, made no mention at all of Mary Gray.

"It seems clear to me," said Mr. Buckton, talking the matter over with Lord Iniscrone, her Ladyship being present, "that Lady Anne intended to make some provision for her *protégée*. In fact, the letter which she had begun writing to me, which was found in her blotter after her death, plainly indicates that. She was, apparently, on her way to my house when the lamentable accident happened. Dr. Carruthers had seen her that afternoon, and had told her that her heart was in a bad way. I believe she grew alarmed about the unprovided state in which she would leave Miss Gray if she had a sudden seizure, and hurried off to me. In the circumstances —"

"Of course, we could not think of doing anything more for Miss Gray," Lady Iniscrone put in, anticipating her lord. "She has already been dealt with very handsomely out of the estate. She has had a most unsuitable education for a person in her rank of life. She has lived like a lady; been clothed like one. When I saw her she was wearing ornaments — a brooch of amethysts, with pearls around it, I remember, which, I am sure, ought to belong to the estate. I can't see that Lord Iniscrone is called upon to do anything more for the young person. What with those absurd legacies to the servants and the way Lady Anne lived — a big house and a staff of servants and carriages and horses for one old lady! — the estate has been impoverished."

"Lady Anne had a great sense of her own dignity," the lawyer put in. "And this house had been her home for more than fifty years."

"Everything needs replacing," Lady Iniscrone grumbled, with a disparaging look around. "Those curtains and carpets —"

"Your Lordship will, I am sure, feel that, in making some little provision for Miss Gray, you will be doing what Lady Anne wished and intended to do," Mr. Buckton said earnestly, turning from the lady to her husband.

Lord Iniscrone's eyes fluttered nervously. He was not a bad little man at heart, but he was entirely ruled by his wife.

"I don't think the estate will bear it, Mr. Buckton," he said in a peevish voice. "It is heavily burdened as it is. If a five-pound note would be of any use —"

"I can't see that we are called upon to do anything, Jarvis," his wife put in again. "In fact, Mr. Buckton, you may take it that we do not intend to do anything more for Miss Gray."

"Very well, Lady Iniscrone."

Mr. Buckton turned away and busied himself with his papers. He could not trust himself at the moment to speak lest he should forget his professional discretion.

But Mary had not waited for the result of his intercession on her behalf, of which, indeed, she knew nothing. Mary, who was sensitive to every breath of praise and blame, had fled out of the dear house, the atmosphere of which had become suddenly unfriendly. A good many friends would have been glad to have had her. Lady Agatha Chenevix was away, else she would have been by her friend's side to take her part with passionate generosity and indignation. She was away, but Jessie Baynes's little house on the edge of the sea, a bare little homely place, full of sunlight and the sea-wind, had its doors open to her. One could not imagine a better place for a sad and sorrowful heart than Jessie's little spare room, with its balcony opening like the deck of a ship on to the blue floor of the sea. Mildred Carruthers had come at once, in the first hour of the girl's grief, to carry her off to the big house, which was now amply justified by the size of the doctor's practice.

Only, where would Mary go to but home? In all those years in the great house on the Mall she had never come to find Wistaria Terrace too little and lowly for her. Indeed, there was a wonderful wholesomeness and sweetness to her mind about the little house. The transfiguring mists of her love lay rosily over even the drudgery of her childish days. To be sure, there had been hard work and short commons. She had been insufficiently clad in winter, too heavily clad in summer. Her people had gone without fires and many other things which some would have considered essential. But there had always been love. Looking back on those days, Mary saw with the eyes of the spirit which miss out immaterial material things.

She fled back home. She took nothing with her but what she stood up in. Only her friend, Simmons, while Lady Iniscrone was absent from the house, packed up all Mary's belongings, and conveyed them, with the assistance of the coachman, across the lane to Wistaria Terrace. The servants had made up their minds that Mary was not coming back.

Lady Iniscrone had hoped, in conversation with Lord Iniscrone, that Mary would not give them any trouble. Never was anyone less inclined to give trouble than Mary. Not for worlds would she have gone back to the house where the new cold rule was, to meet Lady Iniscrone's unfriendly eyes. Only while the body of her benefactress was yet above ground she had stolen across at quiet hours, in the absence of the enemy, to look for the last time on the quiet face. She had carried away little Fifine. Fifine was seventeen years old now, and shook incessantly and moaned in a lost way in her darkness. But she knew Mary's voice. Mary was the one that could comfort her. At Wistaria Terrace they went to the unheard-of extravagance of having a fire in Mary's room, day after day, so that Fifine might lie before it in a basket, and feel the warmth in her little bones, and hear Mary's voice.

The day of the funeral came. Mary stood by the graveside quietly, with a veil down over her face. Walter Gray was by her side. She had come in the doctor's carriage, and she had no leisure or thought for the insolence with which Lady Iniscrone stared at her, as though her presence there required explanation.

She was going to work, to begin at once. Her dear, kind old friend, who had meant to do so well by her, had at least equipped her for earning her own bread. The Lady Principal of Queen's College had found her work — temporary work, to be sure, but something to go on with till she could look about her. The Lady Principal and Dr. Carruthers were against her making any definite plans till Lady Agatha Chenevix should return — she was in America, arranging for a display of her industries at a forthcoming exhibition. They had an idea that Lady Agatha would expect to be consulted in any plan that affected her friend's future.

Returning home after the funeral Mary found that all her attention would be required for a short time for Fifine. The little dog had had a fit or something of the kind, and had rallied wonderfully, considering her great age. She had missed her one friend during that hour of absence. Dr. Carruthers came in and looked at the dog, stooping to examine it with as much tender care as though it had been human and a paying patient. "Keep her warm," he said. "There isn't much else possible. There is nothing the matter, only old age. She seems to know you, Mary. She is positively wagging her tail."

"She is miserable without me," Mary said, wondering what she was to do about Fifine when she took up that temporary work which the Lady Principal of Queen's College had found for her. Meanwhile she devoted herself to the little creature. But about three days after Lady Anne's funeral Fifine solved all difficulties concerning her by dying quietly in the night.

Mary slipped in stealthily to the garden of the old house when the new owners were not likely to be about, and placed the little rigid body in the grave Jennings had dug for it, lined with a few flowers that had come up in the beds, snowdrops and wallflowers and little pale mauve double primroses. She wept a few bitter tears above the grave. The death of the little dog was like her last link with her dear old friend. The day had the bright, clear, strong sunshine of March. There were yet drifts of snow in the valleys among the hills, but spring was coming, and the bare boughs would soon be thick with the buds of leafage. She took one look at the sunny, green place and the old house which had harboured her so kindly. Then she went away with a drooping head.

That very afternoon Lady Agatha came. She rushed in on Mary like the March wind, big and beautiful, in her long cloak of orange-tawny velvet, breathing fire and fury over the unkindness to Mary. She had interviewed Lady Iniscrone, and had gathered from her what had been happening.

"In one way I am selfishly glad, Mary, because you will belong so much more to me. I am going to take possession of you. For the first time for many years Chenevix House is to be opened this season. I am going to be among the political hostesses. I shall do all sorts of things. I have found a dear old lady to live with us, my father's twenty-second cousin, Mrs. Morres. She will make it possible for me to do the things I want without running tilt against all the windmills of prejudice. I shall respect your mourning. You will have your own room to which you can retire. Chenevix House looks over a quiet, green square. You shall see the spring come even there. Afterwards, when the season is at an end, we shall bury ourselves in the green country."

She paused for breath, and Mary smiled at her. She was so big and bonny and generous it was impossible not to smile at her.

"Where do I come in?" she asked. "I want to earn my bread."

"And so you shall. You shall earn it hard. You are to be my secretary, Mary. I am going to be a leading Radical lady. They want hostesses. There are things a woman can do for a cause much better than a man. I consider my wealth, at least, my comparative wealth, my rank and youth and energy and brains, and my splendid health, as so many weapons given to me by God so that I may help the right."

"You forget your charm," Mary reminded her. "It is the most potent of all."

Lady Agatha suddenly blushed. It was the first time Mary had seen her blush.

"Charm — oh, come, Mary! Why not beauty if you are inclined to flatter?"

"Yes, indeed; why not beauty?" Mary repeated, looking at her with loving eyes of admiration.

"A big, black, bounding beggar!" Lady Agatha quoted against herself merrily.

But Mary was not inclined to make any further excursions from home. The soul in her was chilled by her recent experiences. In her hurt and unhappy state the little house at Wistaria Terrace seemed most desirable. It gave her satisfaction to note the discomforting things about her — the bare floor, the windows that shook and rattled, the ill-fitting doors, the ugliness of the painted dressing-table from which the paint had long departed, the chipped jug and basin that did not match each other. She liked it all, even the carelessness about meals, for there was love with it. Her younger sisters growing up had a kind of worship for Mary. They served her out of pure love. She was not allowed to do anything for herself. Yes, for the present, at least, home was best. She could go out and earn money and bring it home to them. She would stay henceforth in the world into which she had been born. She would make no more excursions.

However, these thoughts of hers were rendered vain by the fact that Walter Gray positively took Lady Agatha's part against her. There was no room for Mary in the cramped life of Wistaria Terrace. She had brains and beauty and sympathy. The opportunity to make use of these gifts was given her. She must not reject it.

The thing was put on a business basis. Mary was to be Lady Agatha's secretary, with a handsome salary. "I shall work you till you cry out," her Ladyship promised, and it seemed like enough to be true. She was talking already of writing a novel when they should retire to the country. Her energy overflowed. She was perpetually seeking new outlets for it. Her secretary was not likely to enjoy a sinecure.

"No one but you could have sent me from you again," Mary said to her father, in tender reproach.

"It is for your good, Moll. You have outgrown Wistaria Terrace. We could not long have contented you."

But Mary shook her head. She thought she would have been very well content at home. She could have got plenty of teaching to do. She thought of the little house as of a resting place from which she was to be debarred. But she would not dispute her father's will for her. He rallied her, saying that if they kept her her head and shoulders would presently be pushing themselves above the slates.

"It was big enough for you," she said indignantly, "and your mind rises to greater heights than mine ever will. You cramped yourself into it, if it were a question of cramping. Why should not I?"

"Sometimes it was not big enough, Moll," he answered. "Sometimes it was sore cramping, and at other times it was big enough to contain the heaven and all the stars. Perhaps the ambition I flung away for myself I keep for you. I would not have you at microscopic work all your days."

So it was settled. For a little while longer Mary stayed on at home. Then, when the leaves were just opening out in pale green silk, and all the world was fragrant and full of the joy of birds, she went, unwillingly, and turning back many times to make her sorrowful farewells.

"I don't want you to stay till you begin to feel cramped," Walter Gray had said. "I had rather you went away with your illusions."

She did carry away her illusions. It was a happy and blessed thing for her that she could make illusions about common things all the days she was to live. Yet somewhere, in her hidden heart, she knew her father was right.

CHAPTER XI

THE LION

Mary was established, high up in Chenevix House. She was amazed at the spaciousness of the rooms, the feeling in them as though the streets were far away. The square was a wonder of waving and tossing green, across which Mary looked from her window and saw other stately old houses like the one she was in. At first she was never tired of admiring the miracle of spring in London. She realised that no country greenness is equal to the glory of the new leaf against the dingy house-fronts, the green freshness about the black stems and boughs and branches.

Lady Agatha was in a perpetual whirl of affairs and gaiety. All her days, and her nights into the small hours, seemed to be filled. At this time Mary had a great deal of her time to herself. In the morning she wrote her Ladyship's letters, and selected from the newspapers such things as her Ladyship ought to read. By-and-by she would be much busier. She was taking lessons in short-hand and type-writing in the afternoons. Her Ladyship would come in only in time to dress for dinner. She had been driving in the park, she had been calling, she had been at a concert, or a matinée, or an "At Home." She had been attending this or that meeting. She was never in bed before the summer dawn, yet she would be at the breakfast-table as fresh as a milkmaid, smiling at Mary and telling her this and that bit of news or event of the time since they had met.

Mrs. Morres, who had to accompany her to many places, slept every hour of the day she could. She confessed to Mary in her dry way, that did not ask for pity, that she found her Ladyship's energy superhuman. Sometimes there was an interesting debate in the House of Commons, and Lady Agatha must drop in after dinner to sit for an hour behind the gilded grille. Afterwards she would go on to a political reception. Later to a ball, where she would dance as though there had been nothing in all the long day to tire her.

Once or twice she had a quiet dinner-party, to which Mary came down in her frock of filmy black, which made a delightful setting for her fair paleness. At these dinners she encountered famous men and women, and looked at them from afar off with wistful interest. In the drawing-room afterwards she saw Lady Agatha the centre of a brilliant group. Someone said of her that she was likely to be the spoilt child of politics, since she could be audacious with even the greatest, and move them to speak when no one else could. The great men shook their heads at her and smiled. They warned her that she went too fast for them, that impulsiveness, charming as it was in a woman, was not to be permitted in politics. "If you would but learn diplomacy, my dear lady!" Sir Michael Auberon sighed. But diplomacy seemed likely to be the last thing Lady Agatha Chenevix would learn.

Mary used to sit under Mrs. Morres's wing, and listen, through her witty and wise talk, to the utterances of the great. She felt very shy of these companies of distinguished men and women. Lady Agatha made one or two attempts to draw her closer. Then, perceiving that she was happier in her corner, she let her be.

In her corner Mary listened. She listened with all her ears. Her cheeks would flush and her eyes shine as she listened. There was a younger school of politicians which was well represented at Lady Agatha's parties. Their theories had the generosity of youth. Sir Michael Auberon would listen to them, nodding his head, his fine, beautiful old face lit up with as great a generosity as warmed theirs. He was very fond of his "boys." If he must show them what was impracticable in their views he did it gently. He rallied them with tenderness. He had none of the mockery which is so searing and blighting a thing to hot youth.

One night Mary, looking down the dinner-table, saw a face she remembered. The owner of the face — a tall, loosely-built, plain-looking young man — glanced her way at the moment, and stared — stared and looked away again with a baffled air. Mary knew him at once for the boy she had met seven or eight years before at the Court. He had aged considerably. Men like him have a way of falling into their manhood all at once. His hair was even a little thin on top — with that and his lean, hatchet face he might have been thirty-five.

Afterwards in the drawing-room he was one of those who stood nearest to Sir Michael. Some of the others laughed at him, calling him Don Quixote, and she heard Sir Michael say that the young man's theories were those of the Gironde. "The Revolution devours her own children," he said, with his fine old ironic smile. "And a good many of us have to eat our own professions before we're forty. The great thing would be if we could keep our youthful generosity with the wisdom of our prime."

Looking towards Mary, he caught the flame of enthusiasm in her eyes, and again he smiled. But this time it was a smile without irony, rather an understanding and, one might have said, a grateful smile. All the world knew that Sir Michael's private sorrows were heavy ones, and that he leant the more on the alleviations and consolations his public life brought him.

Afterwards he asked to be introduced to Mary and talked with her for a little while, making her the envy of the room.

"She has a clear mind as well as a sound heart," he said. "She is on fire with the passion for humanity. Take her about with you" — this to Lady Agatha. "Let her see how the people live — what serfs we have under our free banner. There is fine material in her. She should do good work."

Meanwhile Mrs. Morres sat by Mary, doing crochet, with a quiet smile. Her tongue dripped cold water on all the enthusiasms.

"Believe me, my dear, they will do nothing," she said placidly in Mary's ear. That placidity of hers gave her the air of being as relentless as a Fate. "Parties are Tweedledum and Tweedledee. Let Sir Michael get into office and he'll do nothing. Those fine young gentlemen over there will be the office-holders of twenty years to come, the fat sinecurists and pluralists. The people were better off when, like the lower animals, they had no souls. They were protected by their betters. Now they are at war with them and they are more soulless than before. Dear me, how much fine talk I have heard that never came to anything!"

She would go on till the company had departed, and Lady Agatha would come to her side, laughing, and ask her what horrible feudal theories she had been propounding. The two differed on every point but one, and that was in the mere matter of loving each other. Lady Agatha delighted in her cousin's conservatism; and always said she would not have it otherwise if she could. It was a *sauce piquante* to the dish of their daily lives.

"You shan't lead Mary astray," she would say with pretended indignation. "If she knew the things Sir Michael has been saying about her!"

"My dear Agatha, don't *you* go leading her astray. Politics are no *métier* for a woman, or they should be subservient to something else. Go marry, Agatha, and bring children into the world, and when you have reared them you can set up a political salon and theorise about the regeneration of humanity. Let Miss Gray do likewise. You play with these things when you are young — later on you will find them dry bones."

"Dear me!" Lady Agatha said, with admiration. "What a pity she isn't with us, Mary! What a pity she is only a destructive critic! Don't listen to her, child!"

That first evening of their meeting Sir Robin Drummond had come to Mary's side and turned the page of her music while she sang. She had a fresh and sweet voice, although of no great range or compass, and she could sing, without music, song after song of the old English masters, of Arne and Purcell and Bishop, and their delightful school.

"She brings strawberries and cream to town," said someone who was not particularly imaginative.

Mary was conscious of the young man's scrutiny as he turned her pages, and it embarrassed her, but she made no sign.

Afterwards she met Sir Robin many times. He was at this time the adopted candidate for an East-End constituency, and was becoming well known as an advanced politician. He went further than his party, indeed, and somewhat offended even his particular *clientèle* by the breadth of his views. He and Lady Agatha were at this time engaged in the work of organising labour, especially amongst the girls and women of the worst-paid and most dangerous trades. It brought them often together amid forlorn habitations and hopeless humanity. One of the difficulties was the question of whether the alien women should be brought in. "They will join the Union and they will go on underselling all the same," said someone. But Sir Robin was of those who held that the alien should have equal rights with her English sister, and that it was possible to teach her to stand on her feet like one of the free-born. He was not chary of his denunciations of certain methods among the Trade Unions and the Trade Unionists, and therefore a crowd sometimes howled him down. But there was always a minority at least to stand by him, and the minority included the industrious and sober, the honest and thinking, among those he desired to help.

By-and-by he fell into a quiet friendliness with Mary Gray. He used to take charge of the ladies when they went into the East End. Lady Agatha used to say that he was a drag on the wheel, because he would not let her do imprudent things, because he would veto it when a question of their going into dangerous streets or houses or rooms, because he insisted on their leaving by a side door a meeting which was becoming turbulent, because he was always forbidding some extravagance or other of her Ladyship's.

"There is one thing about that young man," said Mrs. Morres, who was chary of praise of her Ladyship's party: "he has excellent common-sense, and I thank Heaven for it."

"Ah, yes; he has excellent common-sense," Lady Agatha echoed, with a ruefulness which made Mary laugh suddenly.

"You ought to marry him, my dear," Mrs. Morres went on, looping another stitch of the endless crochet.

"Marry Bob Drummond!" Lady Agatha repeated. "Marry Bob Drummond! Why, it is the last thing in the world I should dream of doing."

One evening, just at the end of the season, someone brought the latest lion to a small reception at Lady Agatha Chenevix's. He was a very modest and retiring lion, a quiet, very bronzed young man, who wore his arm in a sling. He had had his shoulder torn in an encounter with an African leopard. He had fought almost hand to hand with the beast over the body of a Kaffir servant, and had rescued the man at the cost of his own life, it seemed at first, later on of his right arm. It was doubtful whether the strength and vitality of it would ever be restored.

He was not merely a brave man, however, this Mr. Jardine. He had gone to the Gold Coast, and from there into Central Africa, inspired, in the first place, by the desire of knowledge and love of adventure. But, amid the thrilling adventures and hairbreadth escapes, there had grown up in his heart the liveliest interest in and sympathy with the people he found himself amongst. He discovered that they had an ancient civilisation of their own. To be sure, what remained of it hung in shreds and patches on some of them; but there were others, civilised after a fashion, which was not the Western one. He discovered traditions, folk-lore, ancient poetry, laws, a wealth of customs. Understanding the people, he came to love them. They interested him profoundly. He was going back to them as soon as he could.

He stayed after the other guests, and was yet talking eagerly to his hostess when the dressing-bell rang.

"We dine alone," Lady Agatha said to the old friend who had brought Mr. Jardine. "And I go nowhere afterwards: I am fagged out. How glad I am that next week sees us at Hazels! If you and Mr. Jardine could dine, Colonel Brind?"

The old friend answered her wistful look.

"Our lodgings are not far off; we have only to jump into a hansom; we should be back before the dinner-bell rings. Only — this fellow has a host of engagements."

"Ah!"

Lady Agatha had hardly sighed when Jardine woke up as if from a dream.

"Have I engagements?" he asked. "I do not remember any. Anyhow, I am a convalescent, and the privileges of convalescence are mine. I vote for that hansom, Brind."

After dinner they sat around the fire and talked. Although it was June, it had been a sunless day of arid east wind, and Lady Agatha, who always snatched at the least excuse for a fire because it was so beautiful, had ordered one to be lit. The three long windows were open beyond the red leather screen that made a cosy corner of the fireplace, and the scent of flowers came in from the balcony.

Paul Jardine talked as much as they desired him to talk. He started on his hobby about those West African peoples, and rode it with spirit and energy. His friend laughed at him.

"Why, Jardine," he said, "I can never again call you the lion that will not roar."

"Am I horribly loquacious?" The hero smiled, but was not more silent. He had great things to tell, and he told them well and modestly. Lady Agatha sat with her cheek shaded by a peacock-feather fan. There was a deep glow in her eyes. Glancing across at her from the opposite corner, Mary thought it must be the reflection of the firelight.

She came to Mary's room after the guests had departed, when Mary was preparing for bed, and sat down in the chair by the open window.

"What do you think of him, Mary?" she asked.

"Of whom?" Mary said sleepily. They had met a good many people during the day, so the question was a pardonable one.

"Of whom! Why, of Mr. Jardine! Who else could it be?"

She lifted her arms about her head, and the loose white sleeves of her gown fell away from their roundness and softness.

"What a man!" she said, with a long sigh. "What a man! That is life, if you like. How tame the others seem beside him!"

"He roared very gently," said Mary, "but it was very exciting."

"Yes, wasn't it? That sail in the canoe down the river, with the jungle on each side of them alive with wild beasts and venomous reptiles, to say nothing of cannibals, and deadly sicknesses worse than any of those. He said so little about the danger. One got an impression of the extraordinary languorous beauty of the tropical vegetation; one smelt it, that African night, with its enormous moon beyond the mists. There was death on every side of him, in every breath he drew. He found what he went for, the antidote to the bite of the death's-head spider. Henceforth life in those latitudes will be robbed of one of its terrors. What a man!"

"It is a pity that we could not have heard him at the Royal Society," Mary said, with a little yawn — they had been keeping late hours. "If it had been a day or two earlier!"

"But I am going," said Lady Agatha. "Why, Mary, it is only to alter our arrangements by a day. Hazels — the dear place — will keep for a day longer."

CHAPTER XII

HER LADYSHIP

At Hazels Mary found her duties more onerous than they had been in town. It was delightful to see Lady Agatha among her own people. She had made life easier for them. Mary marvelled at the prettiness of the red-brick farmhouses, with roses and honeysuckle to their eaves. She could never get over the feeling that it was only a picture. They would walk or drive to them, and the farmer's wife would come out and beg her Ladyship to come in for a glass of cowslip wine; and she and Mary would go in to a rather dark parlour — to be sure, the windows were smothered in jessamine and roses and honeysuckle — and sit down in chairs covered in flowery chintz, and sip the fragrant wine and eat the home-made cake, while the topics of interest between landlord and tenant were discussed. Then the farmer would come in himself, hat in hand, and his eyes would light up at the sight of the visitor, and there would be more pleasant homely talk of cattle and crops, and the harvest and the plans for the autumn sowing, and the state of fairs and markets.

There was Nuthatch Village, which seemed to have stepped out of Morland's pictures. It was all so pretty and peaceful, with its red gabled cottages sending up their blue spirals of smoke into the overhanging boughs of great trees. Mary cried out in delight at the quaint dormers, with their diamond panes, at the wooden fronts, at the gardens chockfull of the gayest and most old-fashioned flowers.

"As for prettiness," said Lady Agatha, "it isn't a patch on Highercombe, a mile away, and, what is more, I've done more than anyone else to spoil its prettiness. I've filled in the pond and driven the swan and the water-hen to other haunts. I've given them a new water-supply and done away with the most picturesque pump, which was sunk in 1770 by Dame Elizabeth Chenevix. I've put new grates and new floors into the houses, and I've seen to it that all windows open and shut. The pity of it is that I can't compel them to make use of their privilege of opening. Also, I've introduced cowls on the chimneys. My friend, Lionel Armytage, the painter, lifted his hands in horror at my doings. I'd have liked to get at the chimneys, but I'd have had to pull down every cottage in the place to rectify them. Oh, I've spoilt Nuthatch, there's not a doubt of it. You must see Highercombe."

"The children seem healthy," Mary said thoughtfully, "and the old people walk straighter than one sees them often."

"Ah, yes, that is it." Lady Agatha's face flushed and lit up. "I've made it healthy for them. Highercombe is a painted lie — a pest-house, a charnel-house, full of unwholesome miasmas from its pretty green, its pond covered with water-lilies. Death lurks in that pond. There is bad drainage and bad water; the damp oozes through the old brick floors of the houses. The whole place is as deadly in its way as those West African jungles of which Mr. Jardine told us."

They were to see Mr. Jardine later. At present he was on a round of visiting at the houses of the great. The names of the people who had elected to do honour to Paul Jardine would have been a list of pretty well the most illustrious persons in the kingdom. When Lady Agatha had suggested to him that he might give a week to Hazels before the summer was done, he had been eager about it, had even suggested dropping some of his other engagements. But that she would not hear of. She seemed to take an odd pride and pleasure in the way he had conquered the world best worth conquering.

"What!" she had said. "Drop Sir Richard Greville and Lord Overbury! Not for worlds! You may find it dull. Sir Richard lives the life of a hermit, and you won't get anything fit to eat at Lord Overbury's. He never knows what he's eating, and his cook has long given up trying to do credit to herself. I believe that only for his dining-out he'd be starved. Even as it is, he's been known to take mustard with his soup and red-currant jelly with his cheese. Still — he's Lord Overbury!"

They led a very quiet life at Hazels, seeing hardly anyone. Lady Agatha had declared that she was going to make up for her rackety life in town, as well as to prepare for the winter. She had looked as fresh as a rose through all the racketing, and when she talked about the need for rest she had smiled.

As a matter of fact, her energy was too overflowing to permit of her resting as other folk rested. A change of occupation was about as much as one could hope for. And now she was restless as she had not been before, for, energetic as she had always been, she had never driven others. Indeed, many people had found absolute restfulness in her Ladyship's big, wholesome presence.

"The life in town has only stimulated me, Mary," she confessed; "just stimulated me and excited my brain. I must work it off some-how. Let us begin at the novel tomorrow."

They began at the novel. Lady Agatha dictated it, and Mary took it down in short-hand. They worked out of doors. Mary had her seat under the boughs of a splendid chestnut tree on a little green lawn. The lawn was at the side of the house, not over-looked, enclosed on three sides by a splendid yew hedge. The dogs would lie at Mary's feet. There were Roy the St. Bernard, and Brian the bull-dog, a toy Pomeranian, and a little Chow. The dogs always stayed at Hazels. "If I took them up to town," Lady Agatha said, "they would see more of me, to be sure, but then they would always be losing me, for, of course, I couldn't take them out in town. And they always know I'll come back — they're so wise. The parting is dreadful, but they know I'll come back."

Mary sometimes wondered how her Ladyship had found time to think out her novel. For it seemed all ready and prepared in her mind. She would sweep up and down the grass while she dictated. Mary used to say that it meant a ten-mile walk of a morning. The train of her white morning-dress lopped the daisies in their places; the incessant passage of her feet made a track in the grass. Sometimes she would pass out of her secretary's hearing and have to be recalled by Mary's laughing voice of remonstrance.

"Am I afflicting you, Mary?" she asked on one of these occasions. "Am I overwhelming you? It's a horrible flood, isn't it?"

"You are very fluent," Mary answered, looking down at the queer little dots and spirals on her paper. "I daresay we'll have to prune it before it's printed. But it is a good fluency, a rich fluency. To me it is irresistible — like a spring freshet, like the sap rushing madly through all the veins of spring."

"Ah, you feel it? — you feel it like that, Mary? I feel it so myself; I riot in it."

"It will have no sense of effort — it is vital. I hope we shall be able to keep it up."

"Why not, O Cassandra?"

She stood with one hand on the back of Mary's chair, and looked up into the tree.

"The book should have been written in spring," she went on. "I feel the spring in my blood. Why should I, Mary, now when it is full summer, and the trees are dark?"

"I don't know, unless that you were so busy in spring that you had not time to enjoy it. Come, let us get on; perhaps presently you will flag. We must get the book done before anyone comes to interrupt us."

"Never was there such a willing co-worker. You mustn't overdo it, Mary. How many words did I dictate to you yesterday?"

"Six thousand."

"And you gave them to me typewritten this morning."

"I wanted to see how they looked in type. It is all right, Agatha. Even you cannot go on for long, dictating six thousand words a day. We must take the tide at the flow."

"Afterwards I shall do a play — after I have given you a rest."

"More kingdoms to conquer," Mary laughed. "There is only one person like you — the Kaiser."

"I have an immense admiration for him."

Mrs. Morres meanwhile sat and smiled to herself. She had given up the crochet for point-lace, which, as it had more intricate stitches, necessitated the more care. Sometimes she knitted and read with a book in her lap. But when she was not reading, she smiled quietly to herself. It was a curious smile, half-satisfied as one whose prognostications have come true, half-dissatisfied as though there was no great cause for congratulation.

Once Mary was curious enough to ask her why she smiled. Lady Agatha at the piano was playing Wagner like a professional musician. Mrs. Morres's smile grew more inscrutable.

"It amuses me," she said, talking loudly, so that her words might reach Mary through the storm of the music, "to find that Agatha is just a woman, after all. It amuses me — and yet — it had been happier for you and me if she had contented herself with the unrealities of life a little longer."

Mary did not understand at the moment. She began to understand a little later when Mr. Jardine came. The novel, after all, had not been finished. For the last week or so before the visitor arrived her Ladyship had apparently lost interest in it.

"My brain has dried up, Mary," she said. "I should only spoil it if I went on. Put it away in a drawer, and when I feel like it we can go on again. You want a rest. I've over-tired you."

"I felt I couldn't rest till it was done," Mary said, with a little sigh. "I wanted to know what became of them all. And it is such an interesting point. Tell me, does Clotilde marry Mark, after all?"

"How should I know? I have nothing to do with what she does. Clotilde knows her own mind. I do not. Wait till we get back to it."

"Ah! you should finish it — you should finish it. You'll never get that young green world in it again. It was an inspiration. We should have held on to it like Jacob to the angel's robe."

But for the time Lady Agatha's literary energy was exhausted.

"I daresay there's a deal of fustian in it. There's sure to be," she said. "I don't think anything could be really good that was produced with so little pain. I daresay I'll be for tearing it up, so you'd better lock it away. Do you feel equal to walking ten miles? If not, get your bicycle and I'll walk beside you. I've been cramped up too long."

This time it was a mood of physical restlessness. She walked and rode and went out golfing, and played tennis, and rowed on the river, and did a thousand things, while Mrs. Morres made her delicate wheels and trefoils, and smiled a more Sibylline smile than ever.

At last he came. When the sound of his footstep and of his voice reached them where they stood in the drawing-room awaiting him, her Ladyship turned to Mary, and her face was full of an immense relief.

"I didn't really believe he'd come," she said. "I've been feeling quite sure that something would occur to prevent his coming."

"The weeks have been endless," Paul Jardine said, coming in and taking her Ladyship's two hands. "How could you put me off till September? I've had a heavy time. I don't like being made much of by other folk, so I am going out again after Christmas."

Then, to be sure, Mary knew. The pair leaped to each other as though they had been two halves of one whole separated long ago, and now drawn together in a magnetic rush. Mary had always known that when Lady Agatha attracted she attracted irresistibly; there was no half-way, no haltings, no looking back possible.

"We are out of it, Mary, we two," Mrs. Morres said, and the smile had become a trifle weak and wavering. "What do you suppose is going to become of us? Hazels is a pleasant place, and there has always been something of assurance and comfort about Agatha. I had a hard life, my dear, before I came here. Yet what would she do with us? She can't very well take us out to Africa. I, at least, should not know what to do in those places."

It was a wooing that was not long a-doing. Her Ladyship and Mr. Jardine came in one evening in time for afternoon tea. The days were closing in by this time, and a fire was welcome. There had been rain, and the fire sparkled on her Ladyship's black curls and her eye-lashes as she stood by the fire, taking off the long cloak in which she wrapped herself when she went out walking in bad weather. Her eyes were at once bright and shy.

"Congratulate me," she said. "He has consented to take me with him. He held out for a long time, but I was determined to go. As though I should take the chances!"

"It is I who am to be congratulated," said Paul Jardine, and the happiness in his voice thrilled his listeners. "Of course, I wouldn't have listened to her if she wasn't so splendidly strong. It will be an odd place for a honeymoon. Do you think I ought not to have con-sented to take her, Mrs. Morres?"

"For how long?"

Mrs. Morres's voice shook. All the Sibylline quality was gone from it now.

"For a year. I must fulfil my engagements. Afterwards I must do my best for them over here. I never thought that I could do as I would as a married man. Do you think I ought not to have consented?"

"She would have gone without your consent."

Lady Agatha came over and put a hand on her shoulder, a kind, caressing hand.

"You are quite right," she said. "Oh, he has wriggled, but it had to be. It had to be, from the first minute we met."

"I knew it."

"You did, you wise woman. And you will keep house for me when I am gone? You will take care of the dogs for me? You will oscillate between Hazels and town? You will keep the places ready against our return? You are never to leave us."

Mrs. Morres's eyes overflowed.

"My dear," she said, "it would have broken my heart to have left you. And Mary — what is to become of Mary?"

"I have a plan for Mary, unless she will stay here with you."

"I must earn my bread," said Mary.

"For all the bread you eat, I eat four times as much as you. Still, you have talents to be used for the many, as Sir Michael Auberon said. I have no right to keep you from them. You will talk to Robin Drummond about that. He is starting a bureau for purposes of organisation amongst the women. He has had his eye on you. I told him he could not have you. Now, it will fill a gap, perhaps. I shall need you again."

"The funny thing," said Mrs. Morres, and the amusement had come back in her voice — "is that Colonel St. Leger won't like your marriage at all. He has always wanted you to be married. But now — this African marriage — he will talk about it as though you were marrying a man of colour, Agatha, my dear. How his eyebrows will go out!"

"To think," said Mary, with a little sigh, "that the novel is unfinished, after all."

"A novel is so much more interesting," said Lady Agatha, "when you live it, Mary. Besides, it has troubled me that if I published the novel I must come into competition with the legitimate workers. They should form a Trades' Union against us, women of leisure and money, to keep us from poaching on their preserves. They really should. My dears, I have a presentiment that the novel never will be finished."

CHAPTER XIII

THE HEART OF A FATHER

Oddly enough, seeing the General's feeling towards his sister-in-law, seeing, too, that he and Nelly had hardly ever had a thought or taste that was not in common, a certain affection grew up on Nelly's part for Lady Drummond. An acute observer would have said that the affection had something conscience-stricken about it. There were times when Nelly's eyes asked pardon of the Dowager for some offence committed against her, and this usually happened when the Dowager was making much of her, as of a daughter-in-law who would be dearly welcome when the time came. Something of the love Lady Drummond had borne for her husband had passed on to his niece. She was immensely proud, in her secret heart, of the deeds of the Drummonds. Despite her hectoring ways, she looked up to and admired the General, although he had been too simple to discern the fact and profit by it. Robin's divergence from his father's ways was, secretly, an acute disappointment to her. When she caressed Nelly with a warmth which none of her friends would have credited her with possessing, there was compunction with the tenderness. The child ought to have had the delight of marrying a soldier, a hero whom she could adore, as she herself had adored her Gerald. When she pressed the golden head to her angular bosom she was asking the girl's pardon for her son's shortcomings.

"I shall have heroic grandchildren," she said to herself. "Although Robin is a throwback to the Quaker, the grandsons of Gerald and Denis Drummond must be fighting men."

She pondered long over those grandchildren, and derived a grim pleasure from the thought of them. She even spoke of them to the General, when Nelly was out of hearing.

"It was a disappointment to both of us that Robin is a man of peace," she said, acknowledging the fact for the first time. "Not but that he is a good boy — a very good boy. The fighting strain will recur in the next generation. We shall have soldiers among our grandchildren."

"Grandchildren!" growled the General, turning very crimson in the face. "I call it indelicate to discuss such subjects. As for Nelly's marrying, why, she's only a child. I should feel very little obliged to the man who would want to take her from me at her age."

"Nelly is nineteen," the Dowager reminded him, "and the marriage can't be delayed much longer. It ought to be a source of satisfaction to us that the young people are so pleased with the arrangement. I know that Robin has never thought of anyone but his cousin, and I am sure it is just the same with the dear child."

The General grew red again — not this time with anger, but rather as though the Dowager's words had stirred some sense of guilt in his breast. He muttered something grumpily, and, discovering that his favourite pipe must have been left in his own den, he escaped from Lady Drummond for a while.

As a matter of fact, his mind had been plotting mischief. He did not care so much that it was against the Dowager, if it had not been that the memory of his dead brother came in to complicate things. And, after all, his plotting seemed to have come to naught. He had gone so far as to invite young Langrishe to dinner for a specific occasion, without result. The young man had written to say that he had effected his exchange into the — th Madras Light Infantry, and would be so very much occupied up to the time of his departure that he feared dining out was out of the question.

The General had known he was going away. He had known it before he received that letter, before he had seen it in the Gazette. He had known from the day the regiment had gone by without Captain Langrishe in his wonted place. He had felt with his arm about his girl's shoulders the sudden shock that had passed through her. So she had not known either. He had not prepared her. There was not an understanding between them. He saluted as light-heartedly as ever to all appearance, but he did not look at Nelly. Nor did he make any remark on the change in the regiment.

After that day the passing of his "boys" ceased to be the old joy to him. Something was gone out of the ceremonial. It took all his *esprit de corps* to pretend to himself as well as to others that he felt no difference. He felt the limpness and dejection in Nelly. He saw that her roses had faded, that she walked without the old joyous spring. He heard her no longer talking to the dogs, trilling to the canary. It was January now, and raw, cold weather. It seemed as though the sunshine had vanished from the house for good. The General had been wont to say that the cheerfulness of his house was within it, not without it. He had come home from London fog and rain with a happy sense of its bright fires and spaciousness, its carpets and furniture, not so new that a muddy foot or a stray shower of tobacco-ash was a thing to be feared — old friends every one of them. The love and loyalty within his doors were something that came out to welcome the General's home-coming like a sudden firelight streaming out into the black night.

Now his little girl was unhappy, and the shadow of her unhappiness was over his nights and days. It was when he felt this that he had written to Captain Langrishe, saying nothing to her about it, stealing out, in fact, at night to post the letter secretly, he whose correspondence, such as it was — he was no great penman — had always lain in the letter-basket on the hall table for the servants to scrutinise the addresses if they would before it was posted.

When the answer came he congratulated himself on his forethought. Luckily, that morning he was first at the breakfast-table. Of late Nelly, who had been wont to rise as cheerfully as a waking bird, was tardy occasionally. The General suspected broken sleep, and had bidden the servants tenderly not to call her, although the breakfast-table was not the same thing with no bright face and golden head opposite to him.

When he had read the letter he thrust it into an inner pocket. The servant, who was attending, went away at the moment, and the General got up quickly, and with a stealthy glance at the door, buried the letter in the heart of the fire, raked the coals over it, and was in his place before the servant returned.

"Confound the fellow!" he said under his breath.

Plainly, there was nothing more to be done. The child had to go through it. People had to endure such things. Yet he was miserable, watching furtively her dimmed roses and the circles about her eyes. His little Nell, who had lived in the sunshine all her days!

It was, perhaps, not to be wondered at that, in the perturbation of his mind, the pendulum should have swung towards Robin. "Confound the fellow!" — (meaning Captain Langrishe) — "What did he mean by making Nelly unhappy?" A still, small voice whispered to the General that the young man was acting on some foolish, overstrained, honourable scruple just as he would have done himself in his youth — nay, today, for the matter of that. But he would not listen to the voice. He fretted and fumed, puffed himself up into a great rage as men of his temperament will. Confound the fellow! He had gone half-way to meet him, for Nelly's sake, and the fellow had refused to budge. Confound him and be hanged to him! The General would have used much worse language if the simple piety which hid behind his blusterousness had not come in to restrain him.

He blamed himself — to be sure, he blamed himself. What a selfish old curmudgeon he had been, always thinking of himself and his own likes and dislikes! Where could his Nelly find greater security for happiness than in the keeping of Gerald's son? Everybody thought well of Robin. There had never been anything against him. Why, not a week ago, one of the finest soldiers in the army, a field-marshal, a household word in the homes of England, had buttonholed the General to congratulate him on a speech of Robin's.

"That young man will be a credit to you, Drummond," he had said. "Mark my words, that young man will be a credit to you."

And the General had been oddly impressed by the opinion, coming from his old comrade in arms, and one of the finest soldiers that ever stepped. And, to be sure, he had been trying to set Nelly against Robin all the days of her life.

When he had come to this point in his meditations he groaned aloud. A thought had come to him of how little Nelly would be really his, married to Robin Drummond. He would have no need for the house then. He would have to dismiss the servants, the old servants of whom he was fond, who adored him, and go into lodgings. He might keep Pat, perhaps. Even the dogs would go with Nelly. He would never have his girl any more. The Dowager would be always there. The Dowager would know better than anyone how to set up an invisible barrier between Nelly and her father. Why, since she had been their neighbour things had not been the same. She had carried Nelly hither and thither, to concerts and At Homes and picture-galleries and what-not. She talked of presenting her at Court, with an air of significance which the General loathed. The question in her eye and smile — the General called it a smirk — the very transparent question was as to whether it was not better to wait and present Nelly on her marriage.

When the Dowager was sly she made the General furious. Was his little girl to be married out of hand to Robin Drummond without being given the chance to see the world and other men? He asked the question hotly, pacing up and down the faded Persian rug in his den. Then a chill came on his heat. He had not been able to keep Nelly from choosing, and she had chosen unwisely. He had had a dream of himself and young Langrishe and Nelly and the babies in the big happy house. They would belong to him — no one would push him away from his girl. They would be together till they closed his eyes. The thought of it now was like a green oasis in the desert; but it was a mirage, only a mirage!

And Nelly must not suffer. Langrishe had rejected her — rejected that sweet thing, confound him! And there was her cousin Robin, patient and faithful, waiting to make her happy. He forgot that once upon a time he had been furious with Robin for his patience. Robin was a kind fellow, a good fellow. He seemed to be always at the beck and call of his mother and Nelly, always ready to escort them. Why, only yesterday Nelly had said that there was no one so comfortable as Robin to go about with, and then, in a fit of compunction, had flown to her father and hugged him hard.

"Never mind, Nell, never mind," the General had said. "I never took you about much, did I? We were great home-keepers, you and I. Never seemed to want to gad about, did we? I ought to have taken you about more. It was a dull life for a young girl — a dull life. I ought to be obliged to your aunt for showing me the error of my ways, for making life pleasanter for you."

He gulped over the end of the speech.

"It was a lovely life," cried Nelly wildly, and then burst into tears.

The General was terribly distressed. He had had no experience of Nelly in tears. She had never wept or fainted or done any of the interesting things young ladies were supposed to do in his time. She had been always the light of the house, always happy and healthy and gay.

While he looked at the bell uncertainly, being half of a mind to summon assistance, Nelly relieved him from his doubt by running away out of the room, and when they met again he did not remind her of the scene. That discretion of his went to her heart. It was so strange and pitiful for him to be discreet, so unlike him.

After that he began to praise Robin Drummond, not too suddenly nor too effusively at first, but by degrees, so as not to awaken Nelly's suspicions. He amazed Robin Drummond by his cordiality in those days, and the young fellow commented on it whimsically to Nelly herself.

"He has been telling me all my life that I am a poor creature," he said, "and here he is, to all intents and purposes, eating his own words. Just fancy his wading through that speech of mine on the estimates and pretending to be interested in it, even praising it, Nell. Seeing that the speech was all against our maintaining our big standing army, on a motion to cut down the expenditure, it is bewildering. Is it a mild joke, Nell dear?"

"You may call it a joke if you like," she said, her eyes filling with tears. "I call it heart-breaking, heart-breaking. If he would only abuse you as he used to do!"

"Dear Nell, what's up?" asked Robin, in great penitence. "I had no idea I was saying anything to hurt you. The dear old man! Why, I never resented his abuse. I'd rather he'd abuse me, like a dog, as they say — though I don't see why anyone should want to abuse a dog — if it made you happier."

Certainly, all Nelly's world was very good to her in those days. As for Robin Drummond, he thought of women with a chivalrous tenderness somewhat strange considering that the Dowager was his mother. To him they were something delicate, mysterious, inexplicable. If he had had a sister he would have adored her. Not having one, he lavished on Nelly the feeling he would have given a sister; and hitherto he had been content with the ardour of his feelings. What could a man wish for sweeter and prettier beside his hearth than little Nelly? He had fallen in love with that plan of his mother's for him and Nell with lazy contentment. He liked Nelly's society, and it did not occur to him that he would be just as well pleased with her daily companionship if he could have it without the tie between them becoming more than cousinly.

CHAPTER XIV

LOVERS' PARTING

It might have been better for Nelly if her father had told her of those tentative advances to Captain Langrishe, for then her pride might have come to her aid. As it was, she had nothing to go upon but those looks of his, and his manner to her when they had met at the houses of friends. For they had met, and that was something the General did not know. More, Nelly had engineered, with the cleverness of a girl in love, an acquaintance with Captain Langrishe's sister, a Mrs. Rooke, who lived in one of the Bayswater squares. Mrs. Rooke was a vivacious little dark woman, with a cheek like a peach's rosy side. She was perfectly happy in her own married life, and she had the happily-married woman's desire to bring lovers together. She had taken a prodigious fancy to Nelly. While Captain Langrishe yet remained in England that house in the Bayswater square had an overwhelming attraction for Nelly.

She had gone there first under the Dowager's wing. Cyprian Rooke, K.C., belonged to an unexceptionable family, and even the proud Dowager could find no fault with Nelly's friendship for his wife.

In those days poor Nelly used to feel a perfect monster of deceit. For, first of all, she was deceiving her dear old father. The name of Rooke signified nothing one way or the other to him. Then there was the Dowager, who had proved the most patient and considerate of chaperons, sitting wide-eyed and cheerful till her charge had danced through the programme if it so pleased her; going hither and thither to crowded At Homes, attending first nights at the play — doing, in fact, everything to give Nelly a good time. To be sure, the Dowager attached no importance to the name of Langrishe any more than the General did to that of Rooke.

Mrs. Rooke gave a good many dances after Christmas, and Nelly was at them all. Sometimes Robin was there, sometimes that was not possible. And Robin was out of his element at such gatherings, since he did not dance and could find no conversation to his mind while he leant against the wall of the ball-room or hung about the doors. Life was so full of work for him that it seemed unreasonable to keep him where there was nothing he could do.

Captain Langrishe turned up at the dances as unfailingly as Nelly herself. He came in spite of many resolutions to the contrary, as the moth comes to singe its wings in the flame of the candle. He did not make Nelly conspicuous for the Dowager or anyone else to see. Sometimes he asked her for several dances. Again, he would be merely polite in asking her for one; and would yield her up coldly to her next partner and never come to her side again for the rest of the evening. Unlike Sir Robin, he danced conspicuously well. Nelly had thrilled to a speech of Robin's: "One cannot despise the art of dancing for a man when a fellow like that thinks it worth his while to excel in it."

One night, when the guests had departed, Mrs. Rooke had something to tell her husband.

"That little wretch, Nelly Drummond!" she said. "I thought she was as innocent and candid as a child. Would you believe it that all the time she has been engaged to that gawky cousin of hers?"

"My dear Belinda, all what time?"

"Well, for a lawyer, Cyprian —"

"I know I'm obtuse, but the law doesn't favour deductions. All what time?"

"Why, all the time poor Godfrey's been falling head over ears in love with her."

Mr. Rooke whistled. He was fond of his wife's brother.

"Are you sure, Bel? I noticed particularly that he was dancing with the wallflowers tonight. He's a good fellow, so that didn't surprise me. Now you mention it, I caught sight of the little girl dancing with Jack Menzies. She didn't look particularly happy."

"She hasn't been looking particularly happy. I have been imagining that Godfrey's poverty stood between them. He is so impracticable. And I have been making opportunities for them to meet. After all, she is Sir Denis Drummond's only child, and is sure to be sufficiently well off. And here, after all my trouble, I find she is engaged to her cousin. I wonder what she can see in that ugly stick to prefer him to Godfrey!"

"She may not prefer him, my dear. It may be a marriage of convenience. And Drummond is not a stick. That is your feminine prejudice. He is a very clever fellow, although he has got the Socialistic bee in his bonnet. However, he's young, and has time to mend his ways."

"I don't want to discuss him. How coldblooded you are, Cyprian! I can only think of my poor Godfrey going off to the ends of the earth, and his being deceived and hurt by that heartless girl."

"You will let him know?"

"I certainly shall. He ought to know. It may be the quickest way to make him forget her."

"Since he seems to have made up his mind to go away without

speaking to her, I can't see that any great harm has been done," Mr. Rooke said, with his masculine common-sense.

"I shall never forgive her," Mrs. Rooke retorted, with true feminine inconsequence.

She took an early opportunity of telling her brother what the Dowager had told her. The occasion was in her own drawing-room at the afternoon-tea hour, and, since the room was only lit by firelight and a tall standard lamp, his face, where he stood by the mantel-shelf, was in shadow. There had been something portentous in the manner of the telling.

For a few seconds he kept silence. Then he spoke very quietly.

"I hope Miss Drummond may be happy," he said. He did not trouble to put on a pretence of indifference with Bel, just as he did not wish to talk about it. He went on to speak of ordinary topics. That evening he stayed to dinner. He had only a week more in England. Under the electric light at the dinner-table his haggardness was revealed.

"For once," said Cyprian Rooke afterwards, "your discovery wasn't a mare's nest, my dear Bel. Godfrey looks hard hit."

The week turned round quietly. Nelly had not heard definitely the date of Captain Langrishe's departure. For six days she kept away from the Rookes' house. On that last evening he had been icily cold. The poor girl was in torture. All the week she was calling pride to her aid. The sixth day it refused to bolster her up any longer. The sixth day she met at lunch a friend of hers and Belinda Rooke's. She asked a question about the Rookes with averted eyes.

"Poor girl," said the friend; "she is in grief over Godfrey Langrishe. He sails tomorrow."

The rest of that luncheon-party was a phantasmagoria of faces and voices to poor Nelly. He was going, and she would never see him again, although he had shown her by a thousand infallible signs that he loved her. Despite his occasional coldness, she was sure he loved her. Her pride was down with a vengeance. She felt nothing at the moment but a desire to see him before he should go — just to see him, to see the lighting up of his gloomy eyes, as they had lit up on seeing her suddenly before he could get his face under control. After that one meeting, the deluge! But she must see him — she must see him for the last time.

The kindly hostess insisted on her going home in a cab. When she had been driven some distance, Nelly pushed up the little trapdoor of the hansom and gave another address than Sherwood Square.

Having done it, she felt happier. However it ended, she was

making a last attempt to see him. She could not have endured a passive acquiescence in her destiny, whatever was to be the end of it.

The luncheon-party had been prolonged, and the gas-lamps in the streets were lit. It was the close of the short winter's day. Night came prematurely between the high Bayswater houses. It was almost dark when she stood at last on Mrs. Rooke's doorstep, asking herself what she should do if Mrs. Rooke was away from home.

Mrs. Rooke was out, as it happened, but the maid-servant, who knew Nelly, and, like all servants, had been captivated by her pleasant, friendly ways, invited her in to await the lady's return. Mrs. Rooke was expected back to tea. With a smile on her lips she held the drawing-room door open for Nelly to enter.

Nelly passed through. There was a big French screen by the door. She had passed beyond it and out into the warm firelit room before she realised that there was another occupant. Someone stood up from the couch by the fireplace as she came towards it. Fate had been on her side for once. The person was Captain Langrishe.

"My sister will not be very long, Miss Drummond," he began, in a tone he tried in vain to make indifferent. "I hope you won't mind waiting in my company."

Mind waiting, indeed! To Nelly, as to himself, the seconds were precious ones. Mrs. Rooke was shopping on that particular afternoon. It was a kind fate that made it so difficult for her to find just the things she wanted, that sent half-a-dozen acquaintances and friends in her way.

He took Nelly's hand in his. It was quite cold and clammy, although it had come out of a satin-lined muff. The hand trembled.

"I heard you were going tomorrow," she said. "I'm so glad I am in time to wish you *bon voyage.*"

"Won't you sit down?"

He set a chair for her in front of the fire. The flames lit up her golden hair, and revealed her charming face in its becoming setting of the sables she wore. He sat in his obscure corner, watching her with moody eyes. He said to himself that he would never see her again, yet he laboured to make ordinary everyday talk. He asked after the General, and regretted that the hurry of these latter days had prevented his calling at Sherwood Square.

"We miss you at the head of the squadron," said Nelly, innocently. "It isn't the same thing now that there is a stranger."

"Ah!" A flame leaped into his eyes. He leant forward a little. "That reminds me I ought not to go without making a confession." He was taking a pocket-book from his breastpocket. He opened it, and held it under Nelly's eyes. There was a piece of blue ribbon there. She recognised it with a great leap of her heart. It was her own ribbon which she had lost that spring day as she stood on the balcony looking down at the soldiers.

"You recognise it? It was yours. The wind blew it down close to my hand. I caught it. I have kept it ever since. May I keep it still? It can do no harm to anybody, my having it — may I keep it?"

She answered something under her breath, which he construed to be "Yes." She had been feeling the cruelty of it all, that their last hour together should be taken up by talking of commonplaces. At the sudden change in his tone — although it was unhappy, there was passion in it, and the chill seemed to pass away from her heart — the tears filled her eyes, overflowed them, ran warmly down her cheeks.

At the sight of those tears the young man forgot everything, except that she was lovely and he loved her and she was crying for him. He leaped to her side and dropped on his knees. He put both his arms about her and pressed her closely to him.

"Are you crying because I am going, my darling?" he said. "Good heavens! don't cry — I'm not worth it. And yet I shall remember, when the world is between us, that you cried because I was going, you angel of mercy."

An older woman than Nelly might have had the presence of mind to ask him why he was going. But she was silent. She felt it over-whelmingly sweet to be held so, to feel his hand smoothing her hair. The bunch of lilies of the valley she had been wearing was crushed between his breast and her breast. The sweetness of them rose up as something exquisite and forlorn. His hand moved tremblingly over her hair to her cheek.

"Give me a kiss, Nelly," he said, "and I will go. Just one kiss. I shall never have another in all my days. Good-bye, my heart's delight."

For a second their lips clung together. Then his arms relaxed. He put her down gently into a chair. She lay back with closed eyes. She heard the door shut behind her. Then she sprang to her feet, realising that he was gone and it was too late to recall him.

Why should he go? she asked herself, as, with trembling hands, she arranged the disorder of her hair. Then the merely conventional came in, as it will even at such tense moments. She asked herself how she would look to his sister, if she appeared at this moment; to the maid, who might be expected at any moment bringing in the lamp. The room was dark but for the firelight. How would she look, with her tear-stained visage and the disorder of her appearance? She could not sit and make small talk. That was a heroism beyond her. And she was afraid to speak to anyone lest she should break down. She adopted a cowardly course. Afterwards she must explain it to

Mrs. Rooke somehow. She put the consideration of how out of sight: it could wait till the turmoil of her thoughts was over.

She stole from the room, let herself out quietly, and was grateful for the dark and the cool, frosty air. About five minutes after she had gone Mrs. Rooke came in laden with small parcels.

"The Captain and Miss Drummond are in the drawing-room, ma'am," said the maid.

"Then you can bring tea."

Mrs. Rooke opened the drawing-room door leisurely, turning the handle once or twice before she did so. She was excited at the thought of the things that might be happening the other side of the door. Supposing that Nelly had discovered that life with a poor foot-captain was a more desirable thing than life with a well-endowed baronet, a coming man in the political world to boot! Supposing — there was no end to the suppositions that passed through Mrs. Rooke's busy brain in a few seconds of time. Then — she entered the room and found emptiness.

"You are sure that neither the Captain nor Miss Drummond left a message?" she said to the maid who brought the tea.

"Quite sure, ma'am. I had no idea they were gone."

"Do you suppose they went away together, Jane?"

Mrs. Rooke was ready to accept a crumb of possible comfort from her handmaid.

"I do remember now, ma'am, that when I was pulling down the blind upstairs I heard the hall-door shut twice. I never thought of looking in the drawing-room, ma'am. I made sure that the noise of the blinds had deceived me into taking next-door for ours."

"Ah, thank you, Jane, that will do."

The omens were not at all propitious. Mrs. Rooke was fain to acknowledge as much to herself dejectedly. Nor did Cyprian think them propitious when taken into counsel. When she went downstairs, she found that her brother had come in. He was to spend the last evening at his sister's house.

Captain Langrishe's face, however, did not invite questions. He made no allusion at all to the happenings of the afternoon, and his sister felt that she could not ask him. She had a heavy heart for him as she bade him good-night, although she called something after him with a cheerful pretence about their rendezvous next morning.

"It *is* nine-thirty at Fenchurch Street, isn't it?" she asked.

"Do you think you will ever manage it, Bel?" Captain Langrishe smiled at her haggardly.

"Oh, yes, easily — by staying up all night," she answered.

But her heart was as heavy as lead for him.

CHAPTER XV

THE GENERAL HAS AN IDEA

When Sir Denis came home from his club that evening he learned that Miss Nelly had gone to bed with a headache.

Pat, who told him, looked away as he gave the information, as though he did not believe in his own words. Miss Nelly with a headache! Why, God bless her, she had never had such a thing, not from the day she was born! To be sure, the whole affectionate household knew that there was some cloud over Miss Nelly. They didn't talk much about it. Pat and Bridget knew better than to have the servants' hall gossiping over the master and Miss Nelly. A new under-housemaid, who was greatly addicted to the reading of penny novelettes, suggested that Miss Nelly was being forced into marrying her cousin by the machinations of his mother, who was not *persona grata* with the servants' hall. But Pat had nipped the young person's imaginings in the bud.

"She may be contrairy enough to give the General the gout in his big toe and the twisht in his timper, as often she's done. But she can't make our Miss Nelly marry where she don't like. If you'd put your romantic notions into your scrubbin' now, Miss Higgs; but I suppose it's your name is the matter with you, and you can't help it."

The under-housemaid, whose name happened to be Gladys Higgs, was reduced to tears by this remark, and the tears brought the kind-hearted Pat to repentance for his hastiness.

"Whatever the dickens came over me," he imparted to Bridget when they were having a snack of bread and cheese between meals in the room allotted to the cook, who was now also housekeeper, "to go sharpenin' my tongue on that foolish little girl? It isn't for you an' me to be makin' fun of their quare names. 'Tis no credit to us if we have elegant names in the counthry we come from."

"Aye, indeed. Where would you find pleasanter thin MacGeoghegan or McGroarty or Magillacuddy? There was a polisman in our town by the name of McGuffin. I always thought it real pleasant."

"Sure what would be on the little girl? — 'tis Miss Nelly, I mean," said Pat, in a manner that showed his real anxiety. "She scared me, so she did, with her nonsense, that Gladys. For it stands to reason that Miss Nelly wouldn't mind marryin' Sir Robin — isn't he the fittest match for her? — if it wasn't that there might be someone else. And who could it be, I ask you, unbeknownst to us that has watched over her from a babby?"

"You're a foolish man to be takin' that much notice of that Gladys girl and her talk. Why shouldn't Miss Nelly have a headache? Why, I remember the Miss O'Flahertys, Lord Dunshanbo's daughters, when I was a little girl; and 'twas faintin' on the floor they were every other minute and everyone havin' to run and cut their stay-laces. They were fifty, too, if they were a day, so they ought to have had more sense. Why wouldn't Miss Nelly have Quality ways?"

"Young ladies aren't like that nowadays," Pat said dolefully. "'Tis the bicycle and the golf. They've no stay-laces to cut, so they don't go faintin' away. And Miss Nelly, poor lamb, she'd never be thinkin' of doing such a thing."

He went off sorrowfully, shaking his head. The mysteriousness of the change in Miss Nelly perturbed him the more. He looked away from the General when he gave the information about the headache.

"Miss Nelly said, sir," he volunteered, "that she was to be called, unless she was asleep, when you came home to dinner. Shall I send up Fanny to call her?"

"Not for worlds," said the General. "I'll go myself. She mustn't be disturbed, poor child, if she has a headache."

He went upstairs softly, pursing out his lips as he went along in troubled thought. He opened the door of his daughter's room, and spoke her name in a whisper. There was not a sound.

"Fast asleep," he said, with a sigh, as he went to his dressing-room to dress for dinner. That was something he would not have omitted for any possible calamity that could befall him.

He ate his dinner in lonely state. Bridget had done her best by way of expressing her sympathy, but he ate without his usual enjoyment.

"Sure," said Pat afterwards, "he didn't know but what it was sawdust he was atin' instead of that beautiful volly-vong of yours. He could barely touch the mutton, and a beautiful little joint it was. Sure, there's a sad change come over the house, anyway."

The General gave orders that Miss Nelly was not to be disturbed again that night. After dinner he retired to his den and made a pretence of reading the papers, but his heart wasn't in it. He missed even a speech of Robin's which would have enraged him in happier times. He sat turning over the sheets and sighing to himself now and again; only when Pat came in with a pretence of replenishing the fire — it was Pat's way of showing his silent sympathy — was the General absorbed in his newspaper. Not that it imposed on Pat, who mentioned afterwards to Bridget that he didn't believe the master knew a word of what he was looking at.

About half-past nine the General relinquished that pretence of reading. He felt the house to be nearly as sad as though someone were lying dead in it, and he could support it no longer. He must find out what was the matter with the child, or at least show her how her old father's heart bled for her. He got up quietly from his big easy-chair, from which he had been used to survey his Nelly's face at the other side of the fireplace for many a happy year. To be sure, it had not been the same since the Dowager had come, and Nelly had gone gadding of evenings. Still, she had always come in to kiss him before she went off, looking radiant and sweet, with the hood of her evening cloak over her bright head and framing the dearest face in the world. She had always clung to him with her soft arms about his neck, and he had not minded her absence since she was enjoying herself as she ought at her age.

He climbed up the stairs of the high house. Nelly had chosen a bedroom right at the top, whence she could look away over the London roofs to the mists that hid the country.

The blinds were up and the cold winter moon lay on the girl's bed. The General came in tip-toe, trying to avoid creaking on the bare boards, which Nelly preferred to carpets. But his precaution was unnecessary. She was lying wide-awake. The darkness of her eyes in her face, unnaturally white from the moonlight, frightened him. He had a memory of Nelly's mother as he had seen her newly-dead, and the memory scared him.

"Is that you, papa?" Nelly asked, half-lifting herself on her pillow. "Come and sit down. I was thinking of dressing myself and coming down to you."

"You mustn't do that if your headache is not better."

"It was nothing at all of a headache," she said with a weary little sigh, "but I must have fallen asleep. If I had not I should have come down to dinner. I only awoke just before the church clock struck nine. Were you very lonely?"

"I am always lonely without you, Nell. You have had nothing to eat, have you? No. Well, perhaps you'd better come down and have a little meal in the study by the fire. Unless you'd prefer a fire up here. The room strikes cold. To be sure, the windows are open. There is snow coming, I think."

"I like the cold. I'm not hungry, but I shall get up presently. I haven't really gone to bed."

She put out a chilly little hand over her father's, and he took it into his. When had they wanted anyone but each other? What new love could ever be as true and tender as his?

"Oh!" cried Nelly, burying her face in her pillow. "I'm a wicked girl to be discontented. I ought to have everything in the world, having you."

"And when did my Nelly become discontented?" he asked, with a passionate tenderness. "What has clouded over my girl, the light of the house? What is it, Nell?"

He had been both father and mother to her. For a second or two she kept her face buried, as if she would still hold her secret from him. His hand brushed the pale ripples of her hair, as another hand had brushed them a short time back. He expected her to answer him, and he was waiting.

"It is Captain Langrishe," she whispered at last. "His boat goes from Tilbury tomorrow morning."

"From Tilbury." The General remembered that Grogan of the Artillery, the club bore, had a daughter and son-in-law sailing from Tilbury next morning, and had suggested his accompanying him to the docks. "Why he should have asked me," the General had said irritably, "when I can barely endure him for half-an-hour, is more than I can imagine!"

"What is wrong between you and Langrishe, Nell?" he asked softly. "I thought he was a good fellow. I know he's a good soldier; and a good soldier must be a good fellow. Has anyone been making mischief?"

He sent a sudden wrathful thought towards the Dowager. Who else was so likely to make mischief? The thought that someone had been making mischief was almost hopeful, since mischief done could be undone if one only set about it rightly.

"No one," Nelly answered mournfully.

The General suddenly stiffened. His one explanation of Langrishe's pride standing in the way was forgotten; it was not reason enough. Was it possible that Langrishe had been playing fast-and-loose with his girl? Was it possible — this was more incredible still — that he did not return her innocent passion? For a few seconds he did not speak. His indignation was ebbing into a dull acquiescence. If Langrishe did not care — why, no one on earth could make him care. No one could blame him even.

"You must give up thinking of him, Nell," he said at last. He could not bring himself to ask her if Langrishe cared. "You must forget him, little girl, and try to be satisfied with your old father till someone more worthy comes along."

"But he is worthy." Nelly spoke with a sudden flash of spirit. "And he cares so much. I always felt he cared. But I never knew how much till we met at his sister's this afternoon and he bade me good-bye."

"Then why is he going?" the General asked, with pardonable amazement.

"Oh, I don't know," Nelly answered irritably. She had never been irritable in all her sunny life. "But although he is gone I am happier than I have been for a long time since I know he cares so much."

"I'll tell you what," — the General got up quite briskly — "dress yourself, Nell, and come down to the study, and we'll talk things over. You may be sure, little girl, that your old father will leave no stone unturned to secure your happiness. I'll ring for your dinner to be brought up on a tray and we'll have a happy evening together. And you'd better have a fire here, Nell. It's a very pretty room, my dear, with all your pretty fal-lals, but it strikes me as being very chilly."

He went downstairs and rang the bell for Miss Nelly's dinner. The fire had been stoked in his absence, and was now burning gloriously.

He drew Nelly's chair closer to it and a screen around the chair. He put a cushion for her back, and a hassock for her feet. The little acts were each an eloquent expression of his love for her. He was suddenly, irrationally hopeful. He reproached himself because he had done so little. He had thought he was doing a great deal when he, an old man and so high in his profession, had made advances to the young fellow for his girl's sake. To be sure, he had been certain that Langrishe was in love with Nell, else the thing had not been possible. Now that his love was beyond doubt the old idea recurred to him. It must be some chivalrous, overstrained scruple about his poverty which came between poor Nell and her happiness. Standing by the fire, waiting for Nelly, he rubbed his hands together with a return of cheerfulness.

In a few minutes she came gliding in shyly. That confidence had only been possible in the dark. The General felt her embarrassment and busied himself in stirring the fire. Pat came up with the tray — such a dainty tray, loaded with good things. The General called for a glass of wine for Miss Nelly. He waited on her with a tender assiduity and she forced herself to eat, saying to herself with passionate gratitude that she would be a brute if she did not swallow to please him.

The wine brought a colour to her cheeks. She watched her father with shy eyes. What could he do to bring her and her lover together, seeing that it was Captain Langrishe's last night in England and that he would not return for five years? Five years spread out an eternity to Nelly's youthful gaze. She might be dead before five years were over. This afternoon she had felt no great desire to live, but that despair, of course, was wrong. She had not remembered at the moment how dear she and her father were to each other. As long as they were together there must be compensations for anything in life.

She had expected her father to speak, but he did not. While he had been standing by the fire awaiting her coming he had had qualms. Supposing she had made a mistake about the young fellow's feeling for her. Such things happened with girls sometimes. Supposing — no, it was better to keep silence for the present. If things turned out well, it would be time enough to tell Nelly. If things turned out well! What, after all, were five years? To the General, for whom the wheel of the days and the years had been turning giddily fast and ever faster these many years back, five years counted for little. He had a hale, hearty old life. Surely the Lord in His goodness would permit him to look on Nelly's happiness and his grandchildren! It was another thing to think of Nelly's children when the match was not of the Dowager's making.

He inspired Nelly with something of his own hopefulness. She saw that he had some design which she was not to share. Well, she could trust his love to move mountains for her happiness. The evening was far better than she could have hoped for, and she went to bed comforted.

"Early breakfast, Nell," he said as they parted. "I've ordered it for eight o'clock. But I shan't expect to see you unless you feel like it. These cold mornings it's allowable to be a little lazy."

This from the General, who rose at half-past six all the year round and had his cold bath even when he had to break the ice on it. Nelly's laziness, too, was a matter of recent date. She had always loved the winter and had seemed to glow the fresher the colder the weather.

The General thought of himself as an arch-diplomatist, but he was transparent enough to his daughter.

"He doesn't want me at breakfast," she said to herself. "He doesn't want me to ask questions. So I shall save him embarrassment by not appearing."

The next morning there was no General to see the squadron of the old regiment gallop past. No family prayers either. What were things coming to? the servants asked each other. And second breakfast at nine for Miss Nelly!

"Take my word for it," said Bridget to Pat, "the next thing'll be Miss Nelly havin' her breakfast in bed like Lord Dunshanbo's daughters. Five of them there was, Pat, all old maids. And they used to sit round in their beds, every one with a satin quilt, and their hair in curl-papers, and a newspaper spread out to save the quilt."

"'Tis too early and too cowld," said Pat, interrupting this reminiscence, "for the master to be goin' out. And he doesn't like bein' put out of his habits, not by the half of a second. I used to think before I was a soldier that punctuality was the most onnecessary thing on earth, but I've come to like it somehow."

"The same here," said Bridget, "though it wasn't in my blood. I wondher what they'd think of us at home?"

CHAPTER XVI

THE LEADING AND THE LIGHT

The General was at Fenchurch Street by half-past nine. He rather expected to see old Grogan on the platform, and was not sure whether he was relieved or disappointed by his absence. On the one hand, he could hardly have borne Grogan's twaddle on the journey to Tilbury, his mind being engrossed as it was. On the other, he looked to him to cover his presence at the boat.

Now that he was started on the adventure he was nervously anxious lest he should compromise his girl by betraying to Langrishe the errand he was come on, unless, indeed, Langrishe gave him the lead. He was as sensitive as Nelly herself could have been about offering her where she was not desired or was likely to be rejected. But he assured himself that everything would be right. In the sudden surprise of seeing him, Langrishe would say or do something that would give him a lead. He would be able to bring back a message of hope to Nelly. Five years — after all, what were five years? Especially to a girl as young as Nelly. They could wait very well till Langrishe came home again.

At the booking-office he was told that the special train for the *Sutlej* had just gone. Another train for Tilbury was leaving in five minutes.

"You will get in soon after the special," the booking-clerk assured him. "Plenty of time to see your friends before she sails. Why, she's not due to sail till twelve o'clock. There'll be a deal of luggage to be got on board."

The General unfolded his *Standard* in the railway carriage, and turned to the principal page of news. A big headline, followed by a number of smaller ones, caught his eye: "Outrage at Shawur. An English Officer and Five Sepoys Caught in a Trap. Death of Major Sayers. Regiment Sent in Pursuit. Statement in the House."

The General bent his brows over the report. He had known poor Sayers — a most distinguished soldier, but brave to rashness. And the Wazees tribe, treacherous rascals! The General had some experience of them too. Ah, so Mordaunt was sent in pursuit. The tribe had retired after the murder to its fastnesses in the hills. He remembered those fortified towers in the hill valleys. He had had to smoke them out once like rats in a hole. Ah, poor Sayers! The brutes! And Sayers had a young wife!

He lifted his head from the paper, and stared out of the carriage windows, where tiny cottages, with neat white stones for their garden borders, showed that the train was passing through a residential district much affected by retired sailor-men. The mast of a ship seemed to be a favourite ornament, and a little flag was hoisted on many lawns. Flakes of dry snow came in the wind, but, cold as it was, a good many of the old sailors were out pottering about their tiny gardens. Here a glimpse of the river, or a church spire with many graves nestled under it, came to break the monotony of the little houses.

The General looked without seeing. He was thinking of Sayers' young wife — to be sure, she was not so young now: she must be well over thirty — an innocent-faced creature, sitting at the piano in a white gown, singing, while he and poor Sayers paced the garden-walk in the twilight. Poor woman! how was she to bear it? Those knives, too! The General ground his teeth in fury.

Then suddenly another aspect of the matter flashed upon him, so suddenly that he almost leaped in his seat. Why, the — th Madras Light Infantry — he remembered now — it was Langrishe's regiment. How extraordinary that he should not have remembered before! It was the regiment sent in pursuit. Langrishe would fall in for some fighting — he would find it ready-made to his hand. Those little frontier wars were endless things once they started. And what toll they took of precious human lives! In the last one more young fellows of the General's acquaintance had been killed than he liked to remember. Such deaths, too! Even the bravest soldier might well shrink from the fiendish things the Wazees were capable of.

Suddenly the train pulled up abruptly, so abruptly that for a few seconds it quivered as a horse will after being hard-driven. The General went to the window and looked out. The houses had been left behind and around them was a country of grey mud-flats with the river dragging its sluggish length through it like a great serpent. There was a windmill on the horizon, breaking the uniform grey of land and river and sky. The sky was heavy with coming snow.

The guard of the train was standing on the line, beating his two arms against his breast to warm them, and answering stolidly the impatient questions of the passengers.

"Obstruction on the line in front, sir." he said, addressing nobody in particular. "Waggon broke away from the siding and got on to our track. There's a breakdown gang doing its level best to get us clear. How long? Can't say, I'm sure, sir. Matter of half an hour, maybe."

The matter of half an hour became a matter of three-quarters, of an hour, of an hour and a quarter. The train grumbled from end to end. Here and there a particularly indignant passenger got out with the expressed intention of walking to his destination. The officials bore it all patiently. It was no fault of theirs. The breakdown gang, was doing its best. It was a very lucky thing the runaway had been discovered just before the train came round the corner. The train for the *Sutlej* must have had a narrow shave of meeting it.

The General sat in his compartment, which he had to himself, with his watch in his hand. He was thinking of Sayers and Sayers' young wife. Mordaunt was not married, but he had an old mother at home in England. It was bad enough for the men, the brave fellows. But that women should have to suffer such things through their love was intolerable.

The cold intensified. Philosophical passengers either wrapped themselves in their rugs or got out and walked up and down, stamping their feet, their hands in their coat-pockets. The General sat, quiet as a Fate, staring at his watch. His thoughts were tending towards a certain conclusion.

At first he had been merely impatient for the train to get on. As time passed he became more impatient as it was borne in on him that he might possibly be too late for the *Sutlej*. He might lose the chance of looking in Langrishe's eyes and getting the lead he desired so that he might say the words which would bring happiness to his Nelly. Still the time went on. His moustache became little icicles. If anyone had been looking at him they might have thought that he suggested being frozen himself, so stiff and grey was he. They were within a few miles of Tilbury. It was now half-past eleven. The *Sutlej* was to sail at twelve. Was there any chance of his being there in time? The guard had said half an hour! If he had not, the General might have walked with those other impatient passengers.

But if the General was a religious man — nay, rather because he was a religious man — he looked for signs and portents from God for the direction of his everyday life. He believed that God, amid all His whirling world of stars and all His ages, had leisure to attend to every unit of a life upon earth. He believed in special Providences. Everything that was dear to him or near to his heart he commended to God in his prayers. He had prayed for direction and guidance in this matter of his girl and young Langrishe. He had thought to do his best. Well, was not the breakdown of the train a sign that his best was not God's best?

At ten minutes to twelve the track was free, and the train resumed its journey. It was now one chance in a thousand that the General would not be too late. If that chance came, if he saw Langrishe he would take it as a sign that God approved his first intention. If the *Sutlej* had sailed — well, that, too, was the leading and the light.

As they ran into Tilbury Station a train was standing at the departure platform. The General beckoned to a porter.

"Do you know if the *Sutlej* has sailed?"

"Yes, sir — sailed at ten minutes to twelve. Might catch her at Southampton, sir, perhaps. There's a good many people as well as you disappointed in this 'ere train. There's another train back in three minutes."

"When is the next train?"

"Three hours' time."

The General went to the door of the carriage and looked out; then retired hastily. He had caught sight of Grogan and Mrs. Grogan and a number of boys and girls of all ages. Not for worlds would he have let Grogan see him. The amazement at seeing him, the questions about his presence there, Grogan's laugh, Grogan's slap on the back, would be more than the General could bear at this moment.

"I shall wait for the next train," he said to the astonished porter. The porter had not thought of Tilbury as a place where the casual visitor desired to wait for three hours.

The General remained in the train till the other had steamed out of the station. When all danger was over he alighted and walked to the hotel of many partings. He ordered his lunch, a chop and a vegetable, biscuits and cheese. While his chop was cooking he would stretch his legs, cramped by that long time in the train.

He walked along the docks, dodging lorries and waggons, getting out at the side of a basin, with a clear walk along its edge. It was empty — the *Sutlej* had left it only three-quarters of an hour ago. He paced up and down by the grey water, lost in thought.

The *Sutlej* had sailed, ten minutes before the time anticipated. God had given him the sign. He had turned him from his presumptuous attempt to be Providence to his Nelly. The General never had been, never could be, passive. He was made for the activities of life. Yet his religious ideal was passivity — to be in the hands of God expecting, accepting, His Will for all things. It was an ideal he had never attained to, and it was, perhaps, therefore the dearer.

He was oblivious of the cold, of the creeping water, of the thickening flakes in the air which nearly blotted out the silent ship the other side of the basin. He saw nothing but the pointing Finger, the Finger that pointed away from the course he had marked out for himself. He felt uplifted, glad, as one who has escaped a great peril. Was his Nelly to suffer the torture of an engagement to a man who would presently be every hour in danger of a horrible death? Was she, poor child, to suffer like Mrs. Sayers? like poor old Mrs. Mordaunt? No. She must be saved from the possibility of that.

He would say nothing. He would have to endure the looks she would send him from under her white eyelids, the looks of wistful entreaty. After all, he had not *said* he was going to do anything. He had implied it, to be sure, but he had not committed himself to anything very definite. Perhaps Nelly would not discover, for a time at least, the dangerous service Langrishe had gone on. She was no more fond of the newspapers than any other young girl. For the moment he was grateful to the Dowager that she claimed so much of Nelly's time.

He began to look forward with a fearful anticipation to Nelly's marriage to her cousin. Something must be settled at once, before she could begin to grieve over Langrishe. He would be alone, of course, but Nelly would be in harbour. He did so much justice to Robin that he believed her happiness would be safe with him. He felt as if he must go home and put matters in train at once. He was impatient till Nelly was safe. It did not occur to him that he was, perhaps, once more wresting the conduct of his daughter's happiness from the Hand in Whose guidance he humbly trusted.

He awoke with a start to the fact that he had been more than half an hour pacing along by the water's edge. He hurried back to the hotel. Fortunately, his chop was not put on the grill till he returned, and it was served to him piping hot, with tomatoes and a bottle of Burton. Rather to his amazement, he enjoyed it thoroughly, but when he had finished it he had still more than an hour to wait.

He drove across country to another station, and arrived home early in the afternoon. During the return journey his mind was quite calm and unperturbed. He had had the guidance he needed, and now he had only to let things be — as though it were in his character to let things be!

He dreaded meeting Nelly's eyes and welcomed the Dowager's presence with effusion. He suggested to the lady that she should dine, and afterwards they would visit a theatre — *A Soldier's Love* at the Adelphi was well worth seeing, he believed. Lady Drummond accepted, flattered by this unwonted friendliness. He would hardly let her out of his sight all that afternoon. She was his safeguard against Nelly's wondering, reproachful eyes.

He had to endure those eyes all the next day. Then — the eyes retired in on themselves, became introspective. It was hardly easier for the General, that look of a suffering woman in his Nelly's eyes.

To be sure, poor Nelly had known of that journey to Tilbury just as well as if she had accompanied him. The only thing she did not know was that he had failed to see Captain Langrishe. And his silence — the looks of tender pity he sent her when he thought he was unobserved, what could they mean but that his mediation had been in vain? For some strange, cruel reason, although he loved her and he must know he was breaking her heart, her lover would have none of her. Even the knowledge that he loved her ceased to be an anodyne in those days.

Everyone was so good to her. She seemed to have found a way to the Dowager's arid heart, as her own son had not. The Dowager seemed dimly aware that Nelly was suffering in some way, and was tender to her. She came to the General with a proposal. Why should they not all go abroad together and escape the east winds of spring? The General leaped at it. Once get Nelly abroad and she would know nothing of what was happening on the Indian frontier. He, and Nelly and the Dowager. He had not imagined the Dowager in such a party — yet, he shrank from the prolonged *tête-à-tête* with Nell which the trip would have been without the Dowager's presence. Robin would join them at Easter. They could all travel home together.

There was a time of bustle when Nelly and the Dowager were getting their travelling outfits. A spark of excitement, of anticipation, lit up Nelly's sad eyes. The General could have hugged the Dowager.

"Your dear father," the Dowager said to Nelly one day, "how calm he grows as he turns round to old age! I see in him more and more the brother my dear Gerald looked up to and reverenced."

The peacefulness, the good understanding, had their effect, too, on Nelly. It was good that those she loved should dwell together in amity. She was in that state that she could not have endured sharpness or rancour.

Only Pat shook his head disapprovingly.

"If he goes on like this," he said, "he'll be goin' to Heaven before his time. I'd a deal sooner hear him grumblin' about her Ladyship as he used to do. It 'ud be more natural-like, so it would. Why would we be callin' him 'Old Blood and Thunder' if 'twas to be like an image he was? Och, the ould times were ever the best!"

"He'll come to himself yet," said Bridget more hopefully.

CHAPTER XVII

A NIGHT OF SPRING

The room was a long bare one, with three deep windows. They were all open so that the fog and the noises of the street came in freely. It had for furniture a long office table, an American desk, several cupboards — the door of one of these last stood open, revealing lettered pigeon-holes inside. Everywhere there were files, letter-baskets, all manner of receptacles for papers. There were a number of hard, painted chairs. An American clock ticked on the mantel-shelf, a fire burned in the grate behind a high wire screen. The unshaded gas-lights gave the room a dreary aspect it need not have had otherwise.

The only occupant of the room was Mary Gray, who sat at a small table working a typewriter. She had pulled a gas-jet down low over her head, and the light of it was on her hair, bringing out bronze lights in it, on her neck, showing its whiteness and roundness. The machine clicked away busily. Sheet after sheet was pulled from it and dropped into a basket. The basket was half-filled with the pile of papers that had fallen into it.

Suddenly there came a little tap at the door. Mary raised her head and looked towards it expectantly as she said, "Come in."

Someone came in, someone whom she had expected to see, although she had said to herself that she supposed the caretaker of the building had grown tired of waiting, and was coming to remind her that the church clock had just struck seven.

"Ah, Sir Robin," she said, turning about to shake hands with him. "Who would have thought of seeing you? I am just going home."

"As I came past this way I looked up and saw your light through the fog. I thought you would be going home, and that you would let me escort you to your own door. There is a bit of a fog really."

"I am glad you did not come out of your way. Thank you. I shall be ready in a few minutes. You don't mind waiting?"

"Not at all. May I smoke?"

"Do. It will be pleasanter than the smell of the fog."

"Ah! I hadn't noticed the smell. I have a delusion, or do I really smell — violets?"

"There are some violets by your elbow. I was wearing them, but they drooped, so I put them into water to revive them."

She turned back again to her work, and the clicking of the

machine began anew. He leant to inhale the smell of the violets. Then, with a glance at her bent head, he drew one from the bunch, and, taking a pocket-book out of his coat-pocket, he opened it, and laid the violet between two of its pages.

While he waited he looked about him. The ugliness of the room did not affect him. The flaring gas, the business-like furniture, the unhomely aspect of the place, did not depress him. On the contrary, in his eyes it was pleasant. He always came to it with a sensation of happiness, which was not lessened because he felt half-guilty about it. To him the room was the room which for certain hours of every day contained Mary Gray. What did it matter if the case was unlovely since it held her?

Presently the clicking of the machine ceased, and she looked up at him with a smile.

"You are very good to wait for me," she said.

"Am I?" he answered, smiling back at her. "There is not very much to do today. The House is not sitting, and my constituency has been less exacting than usual."

She put the cover on her machine, locked up her desk, and then retired into a corner, where she changed her shoes, putting her slippers away tidily in a cupboard. She put on her hat, setting it straight before a little glass that hung in one corner. She got into her little blue jacket, with its neat collar and cuffs of astrachan. Then she came to him, drawing on her gloves.

"I am quite ready now," she said.

They lowered the gas, and went down the stone steps side by side. At the foot of the stairs Mary stopped to call into the depths of the back premises that she was going home, and a woman's voice bade her good-night.

It was cold in the street, and there was a light brown fog through which the street lamps shone yellowly.

The omnibuses crept by quietly, in a long string, making a muffled sound in the fog. As they went towards the nearest station a wind suddenly blew in their faces.

"It is the west wind," she said. "And it breathes of the spring."

"There will be no fog tonight," he answered. "See, it is lifting. The west wind will blow it away."

"It comes from fields and woods and mountains and the sea," she said dreamily.

The fog was indeed disappearing. The gas-jets shone more clearly; the 'buses broke into a decorous trot. The long line of lights came out suddenly, crossing each other like a string of many-coloured gems.

Outside the Tube station they paused as though the same thought had struck both of them.

"It is like the washing of the week before last," Mary said, as the indescribable odour floated out to them.

"Why not take a 'bus?" said he. "The air grows more delicious."

"Why not, indeed?" she answered. "Except that I shall be so late getting home. And it will keep you late for your dinner."

"So it will," he said. "To say nothing of your dinner. I know you had only sandwiches and tea for lunch. You have told me that when you go home you make yourself a chafing-dish supper. You must need a meal at this moment. Supposing — Miss Gray, will you do me the honour of dining with me?"

"Will you let me pay for my dinner? I am a working-woman, and expect to be treated like a man."

"If you insist. But I hope you will not insist."

She looked at him for a moment hesitatingly. There was no prudery about Mary Gray. She had become a woman of the world, and she had had no reason to distrust the *camaraderie* of men or to think it less than honest.

"Very well, then," she said, "if you will let me pay for your lunch another time."

"Why, so you shall," he answered. For a usually grave young man he laughed with an uncommon joyousness. "You shall give me one day a French lunch with a bottle of wine thrown in at one-and-six-pence. Mind, I must have the wine."

"You shall have the wine. But it isn't good form to talk about the price of a lunch you are invited to."

Laughing light-heartedly, they plunged into a labyrinth of dark streets. The west wind had brought a gentle rain with it now. It was benignant upon their faces, with a suggestion of grasses and spring flowers pushing their heads above the earth. They passed by the Soho restaurants, crowded to the doors. They found one at last in a more pretentious street.

Over the dinner they laughed and talked. There was something intoxicating to Robin Drummond's somewhat phlegmatic nature in their being together after this friendly fashion.

"You have a crease in your forehead, just above your nose," he said, while they waited for their salmon, the waiter having removed the plates from which they had eaten their *bisque*. "Have the Working Women been more unsatisfactory than usual today?"

"I was not thinking of the Working Women," she answered. "It is family cares that are on my mind. Supposing you had seven young brothers and sisters whom you wanted to help to place out in the world —"

"Heaven forbid! It's no wonder you look worried. What do you want to do for them, Miss Gray?"

"There's Jim. He's seventeen years old. I think he'd make a very good bank-clerk, but at present he wants to go to sea. There isn't the remotest chance of his being able to go to sea. The question is whether he can get a nomination to a bank. It will be quite a step in the social scale if we can manage it for Jim."

She looked at Drummond with her frank, direct gaze, and he blushed awkwardly.

"I don't know anything at all about your people, or anything of that sort, Miss Gray, but if I could help —"

"I don't think you could help." Mary's big mysterious eyes under their dark lashes, under their beautiful brows, looked at him reflectively. "You see, you don't know anything about us. I am the eldest of a large family. The others are my stepbrothers and sisters. I love them dearly, and I love my stepmother, too. But not like my father — oh, not at all like my father. I would never have left him only he sent me away. Lady Agatha was very good to me. She paid me a disproportionate salary. And besides — after I had been away from them for a time they could really do very well without me. Cis and Minnie grew up so fast. To be sure, none of them make up to father for me. But he was really anxious that I should go. He thought I would be cramped at home, after —" She paused, and then went on: "He would never think of himself when it was a question of me."

What she was saying did not greatly enlighten him. But, without a doubt, something would come out of the desultory talk by-and-by.

As he watched her in the light of the electric candle-lamps on the table, which, sending their shaded light upwards reflected from the white cloth, made her face luminous in the shadow of her cloudy hair, he was struck again by a baffling resemblance to someone he had known. Now and again during the months since they had known each other her face had seemed familiar; then the likeness had disappeared; he had forgotten to be curious about it. At this moment the suggestion was very strong.

They had the top of the 'bus to themselves as they went on westward. At this hour the traffic was eastward, and the mist of rain saved them from fellow-travellers. They were as much alone as though they were in a desert, up there in the darkness at the back of the bus, with the long line of blurred jewels that were the street lamps stretching away before them.

They passed close to the trees overhanging a square, and the branches brushed them.

"The sap is stirring in the trees tonight," she said. "Can't you smell the sap and the earth?"

"I associate you with the country and green things," he answered irrelevantly. "Can you tell me, Miss Gray, how it is that I who have always seen you in London yet always think of you in fields and woods?"

She laughed with a fresh sound of mirth.

"We met long ago, Sir Robin," she said. "I have always been wondering how long it would be before you found out."

"Where?"

"Think!"

A sudden light broke over him.

"You were the little girl who came with old Lady Anne Hamilton to the Court. It is nine years ago. I never knew your name. Lady Anne died one Long Vacation when I was abroad. I did not hear of it for a long time afterwards. I asked my mother once if she knew what had become of you, but she did not. Why, to be sure, you are that little girl."

"Lady Anne was very good to me. She gave me an education. Only for her the thing I am would not be possible. And I mean to be more than that. Do you know that I am writing a book?"

"A novel? Poems?"

"That is what my father's daughter ought to be doing. No — it is a book on the Economic Conditions of Women's Work."

"It is sure to be good, *citoyenne*."

"I am a revolutionary," she said seriously. "I have learnt so much since I have been at this work. I have things to tell. Oh, you will see."

"I remember Lady Anne as the staunchest of Conservatives."

"Yes, yet she was tolerant of other opinions in her friends. She was very good to me, dear old Lady Anne."

"To think I should not have remembered!"

"I knew you all the time. To be sure, there was your name. I don't think you ever knew my name. You called me Mary all the afternoon. Do you remember the puppy you sent me — the Clumber spaniel? He died in distemper. He had a happy little life. I wept bitter tears over him."

"Why didn't you tell me before?"

"I thought I'd leave you to find out."

"I am a stupid fellow." He leant towards her, and inhaled the scent of her violets.

"I don't think I should have guessed it now," he said, "only for the spring. To think you are Mary!" He lingered over the name.

"I am sorry about the Clumber. You shall have another when

you ask for it."

It was a long drive westward. They got down at Kensington Church, and went up the hill. Close by the Carmelites they turned into a little alley. The lit doorway of a high building of flats faced them.

"Now, you must come no farther," she said, turning to him and holding out her hand.

"Let me see you to your door," he pleaded.

"If you will, but it is a climb for nothing."

"What a barrack you live in!" he said, as they went up the stone steps.

"It was built for working men originally, but perhaps there is none hereabouts. It is now chiefly occupied by working women. They are extremely pleasant and friendly. To be sure, they are West-End working women. Now, Sir Robin, I must bid you good-bye."

They were at the very top of the house. The staircase window was wide open, and the sweet smell of wet earth came in. She had put the latch-key in the door and opened it — she had turned on the electric light. Now, as she held out her hand to him in farewell, he caught sight of the pleasant little room beyond. He had the strongest wish to cross the threshold on which she was standing; but, of course, it was impossible.

"When my cousin comes back from abroad," he said, "I want you to know each other, Miss Gray. Perhaps you will ask us to tea here."

"I shall be delighted," she said frankly.

"You like your quarters?"

He was oddly reluctant to go.

"Very much indeed."

"You are near Heaven."

"I hear the singing at the Carmelites. I can see the tops of the trees in Kensington Gardens. To be sure, I ought to live nearer my work. But these things counterbalance the distance. By the way, do you know that Mrs. Morres is in town?"

"I had not heard."

"She has come up for a week's shopping."

"Ah! I must call on her. I like her douches of cold water on all our schemes."

"So do I."

He looked at her with a dawning intention in his eyes. Before he could speak the words that were on his lips the opposite door opened, and a young woman, wearing an artist's blouse, with close-cropped dark hair and a frank boyish face, came out.

"I beg your pardon, Miss Gray, do you happen to have any methylated spirit?"

"Good-night, Miss Gray."

He lifted his hat and went down the stairs. On the next landing he paused and listened with a smile to the conversation overhead. It appeared that Mary had only enough methylated spirit for a single occasion.

"Then you must come to breakfast with me in the morning," said the other girl. "Can you oblige me with a few slices of bacon?"

It was the true communistic life.

He was smiling to himself still as he walked up the hill homewards. "Winter is over and past, and the spring is come," he murmured to himself. And to think that a few hours ago the fog was creeping over the City!

CHAPTER XVIII

HALCYON WEATHER

Mrs. Morres was looking benignantly, for her, at Sir Robin Drummond.

"Well, I must say I'm pleased to see you," she said. "It's very handsome of you, too, to give up the affairs of the nation for an old woman like me. How do you suppose things are getting on without you?"

"The House is not sitting this afternoon. You know it rises for the Easter vacation tomorrow."

"On Thursday I go down to Hazels. I wanted that bad person, Mary Gray, to come with me. She says she has to work at her book. Did you ever hear such stuff and nonsense? As though the world can't get on without one young woman's book. I told her she could do it at Hazels. She says she couldn't — that she'll have to be out all day long. London will not tempt her out, she says. Is she to go bending her back and dimming her eyes while the lambs are at play in the fields and the primroses thick in the woods?"

"She's an obstinate person, Mrs. Morres. When she has made up her mind to do a thing —"

"Ah! you know her pretty well."

"We first met about nine years ago."

"Dear me! I had no idea that you were such old friends. I thought you met first in this house."

"Lady Anne Hamilton, the old lady who adopted Miss Gray, was my mother's friend."

He said nothing about the fact that twelve hours ago he had not known Mary Gray for the child he had played with for one afternoon, nor of the long gap between that occasion and their next meeting. Not from any disingenuousness; but he had a feeling that he liked to keep that meeting of long ago to himself.

"Dear me, to be sure you would be interested in Mary. You would know a good deal about her. Nine years — it is a long time."

If he had been the most consummate plotter he could not better have paved the way for the suggestion he was about to make.

"Put off your return to Hazels till Saturday morning. I want to take you and Miss Gray into the country for a day on Thursday."

"Indeed, young man! And wait for the Saturday crowd of holiday-makers! A nice figure I should be struggling among them."

"I will be at Victoria to see you off."

"Oh, you needn't do that." Mrs. Morres turned about with the inconsequence of her sex. "I've brought one of the maids up with me. She will take care of me better than most men. She is alarming, this good Susan, to the people who don't know her. But I thought you were going abroad?"

"So I am. Saturday morning will do me very well."

"How did you know I was in town? No one is supposed to. All the blinds are down in front and will be till her Ladyship returns."

"Miss Gray told me. I saw her yesterday."

She looked at him sharply. His honest, plain face reassured her. A friendship of nine years, too. What trouble could there possibly arise after a friendship of nine years? Mary must know that he was all but engaged to his cousin.

"Does she approve of the country trip?"

"I have not asked her. I left that to you to do. She has been shut up in London all the winter. She needs a breath of country air."

"So she does. She shows the London winter, though you may not see it. Very well, you shall take us both into the country on Thursday. Mary will not dream of refusing me."

"That is it. She means to spend those six days between Thursday and Wednesday toiling at her book. I have heard her say that she will spend Thursday at the British Museum."

"Stuff and nonsense, she shan't! The world will do just as well without the book. She must come to Hazels on Saturday. You will help me to persuade her?"

"I will do my best. How did you leave Hazels?"

"Lovely. For the rest, a wilderness of despairing dogs. They will forgive me if I bring back Mary. By the way, what have you got for me to do on Friday? If you will keep me in town when all the shops are shut! Not that it matters. I've finished all my shopping. But am I to spend my Good Friday here, in this room? London streets are no place for a poor woman on Good Friday."

"Will you go to church? There is a service at a church near here, with Bach's Passion music."

"I should like to, of all things. Afterwards, perhaps, Mary would give us tea at her eyrie. You and she must dine with me. She is coming this evening to dinner. Come back to dinner at half-past seven and help me to persuade her. I can only give you a chop. Some mysterious person in the lower region cooks for me. She is the plainest of the plain."

"It will be a banquet, with you."

Sir Robin was not a young man who paid compliments easily. When he did pay one it had always an air of sincerity. Mrs. Morres looked pleased. She was very fond of Robin Drummond.

When he and Mary met at the door a few hours later he made a jest about their dining together again so soon, and they laughed about it — to be sure, that dinner at the restaurant was a secret, something that did not belong to the conventional life. There was the air of a little understanding between them when they presented themselves to Mrs. Morres in the book-room which she used for all purposes of a sitting-room during her flying visit to town. It was a pleasant room, with book-cases all round it filled with green glass in a lattice of brass-work. The books were hidden by the glass, but it reflected every movement of a bird or a twig or a cloud outside like green waters. The ceiling was domed like a sky and painted in sunny Italian scenery. It was not dull in the book-room on the dullest day.

"Did you come together?" Mrs. Morres asked curiously.

"I swear we did not," Sir Robin replied, with mock intensity. "I came from the east, Miss Gray from the west. We met on your door-step."

"You looked as if you were enjoying a joke when you came in."

"There was time for one between the ringing of the bell and the opening of the door."

"Ah, you see, the people downstairs are very old."

Mary allowed herself to be persuaded to the country expedition next day. The spring had been calling to her, calling to her to come out of London to the fields. More, she consented to go to Hazels on the Saturday. The spring had disturbed her with a delicious disturbance. It was no use trying to be dry-as-dust since the spring had got into her blood. The book must wait till she came back.

On Thursday the exodus from town had not yet begun. They left soon after breakfast. As Mary hurried from her Kensington flat to Paddington Station she met the church-goers with their prayer-books in their hands. It was Holy Thursday, to be sure — a day for solemn thought and thanksgiving. She hoped hers would not be less acceptable because it was made in the quietness of the fields.

It was an exquisite day of April — true Holy Week weather, with white clouds, like lambs straying in the blue pastures of the sky, shepherded by the south-west wind. The almond trees were in bloom. They had begun to drop their blossoms on the pavements, making a dust of roses in London streets. As they went down from Paddington the river-side orchards and gardens were starred with the blossom of pear and plum. Everywhere the birds were singing jocundly. The promise of spring a few days earlier had been nobly fulfilled.

The sun shone powerfully as they left the country station and went down a road set with bare hedges on either side. A week ago there had been frost. Now there was a grateful odour from the millions and millions of little spear-heads of grass that were pushing above the ground. On the banks by the side of the road there were primroses and violets, while there was yet a drift of last week's snow in the sheltered copses.

They found an inn by the side of the road. To the back of it lay a belt of woods. In front was a great stretch of cornfield and pasturage. In the distance a church-spire and yet other woods.

There was no village in sight. The village was, as a matter of fact, lying about its green and velvety common just a little way down the road. The place was full of the singing of the birds, and of another sound as sweet, the rushing of waters. A little river ran down from the higher country and passed through the inn-garden, turning a water-wheel as it went. The picture on the old sign was of a water-wheel. The inn was called the Water-Wheel.

"What a name to think upon!" said Mary, with a sigh, "in a torrid London August! it sounds full of refreshment."

"Its patrons would no doubt prefer the Beer-Keg," said Mrs. Morres, and was reproached for being cynical on such a day.

While they waited for a meal they explored the delightful inn-garden. It was not Sir Robin's first visit, and he was able to point out to them the lions of the place. There was the landlord's aviary of canary-birds, so hardy that they lived in the open air all the year round. There were the ferrets in a cage. Not far off, in a proximity which must have profoundly interested the ferrets, there was an enclosure of white rabbits. There was a wild duck which had been picked up injured in the leg one cold winter, and had become tame and followed them about now from place to place. There were a peacock and a peahen, a sty full of tiny, squeaking black piglets, hives of bees, all manner of pleasant country things. A lordly St. Bernard, with deep eyes of affection, followed Sir Robin as a well-remembered friend.

"Out in the woods," Sir Robin said, "there is a pond which later will be covered with water-lilies. The nightingales will have begun now. The wood is a grove of them. The landlord owned up handsomely when I came here first that 'they dratted things kept one awake at night.' I was only sorry they did not keep me. But after the first I slept too soundly."

"What did you find to do?" Mrs. Morres asked.

"Fish. There are plenty of trout in the upper reaches of the river."

They found their lunch of cold roast beef and salad, rhubarb tart and cream, delicious. The landlord had some good old claret in his cellar and produced it as though Sir Robin were an honoured guest. They sat to the meal by an open window. There were wallflowers under the window. In a bowl on the table were hyacinths and sweet-smelling narcissi.

After the meal Mrs. Morres was tired. "Let me rest," she said, "till tea-time. What did you say was the train? Five-thirty? Will you order tea for half-past four? It is half-past two now. Go and explore the woods. I believe I shall go asleep if I'm allowed. The buzzing of the bees out there is a drowsy sound."

Mary voted for walking up-stream, and confessed to a passion for tracking rivers to their sources. They stepped out briskly. She was wearing a long cloak of grey-blue cloth, which became her. Presently she took it off and carried it on her arm. Her frock beneath repeated the colour of the cloak. It had a soft fichu about the neck of yellowed muslin, with a pattern of little roses. He looked at her with admiration. He knew as little about clothes as most men, and, like most men, he loved blue. She did well to wear blue on such a day. The grey of her eyes took on the blue of her garments, a blue slightly silvered, like the blue of the April sky.

As the ground ascended, the stream brawled and leaped over little boulders green with the water-stain and lichens. There were quiet pools beside the boulders. As they stood by one they saw the fin of a trout in the obscurity.

They met no one. Presently they were higher than the woods and out on a green hillside. When they first appeared the place was alive with rabbits, who hurried to their burrows with a flash of white scuts.

"If we sit down on the hillside we can see the valley," Sir Robin said. "We can look down into the valley at our leisure. It is filled with a golden haze. This good sun is drawing out the winter damps. You shall have my coat to sit on. Wasn't I far-seeing to bring it?"

He spread the coat, which he had been carrying on his arm, for Mary, and she sat down on the very edge of the incline. The St. Bernard laid his silver and russet head on her skirt. They had lost sight of the river now. It had retired into the woods. When they sat down Sir Robin consulted his watch, and found that they might stay for nearly an hour. There was a bruised sweetness in the atmosphere about them, which they discovered presently to be wild thyme. They were sitting on a bed of it. He thought of it afterwards as one of the sweetnesses that must be always associated with Mary Gray, like the smell of violets. The full golden sun poured on them, warming them to the heart. The bees buzzed about the wild thyme and the golden heads of gorse. Little blue moths fluttered on the hillside. The rabbits, lower down the hill, came out of their burrows again and gambolled in the sunshine.

"How sweet it all is!" Mary said impulsively. "I shall always remember this day."

"And I."

He plucked idly at the wild thyme and the little golden vetches among the coarse grass of the hillside. A fold of the blue dress lay beside him. He touched it inadvertently, and the colour came to his cheek: unobserved, because he had his hat pulled down over his eyes, and Mary was sketching for him in detail the plan of her book. It interested him because it was hers. Her voice sounded like poetry. He had not wanted poetry. Blue-books and statistics had satisfied him very well, hitherto. But, to be sure, he had read poetry in his Oxford days. Lines and tags of it came into his mind dreamily as he listened to her voice. He did not touch that fold of her gown again. If he was sure — but he was not quite sure. And there was Nelly. He supposed Nelly cared for him if she was willing to marry him. If Nelly cared — why, then, he had no right to think of other possibilities.

Something had gone out of the glory and enchantment of the day as they went back down the hillside. Those lambs of clouds had suddenly banked themselves up into grey fleeces which covered the sun. The wind blew a little cold.

"It is the capriciousness of April," said Mary, unconscious of any change in the mental atmosphere.

He stopped on the downhill path, took her cloak from her arm, and with kind carefulness laid it about her shoulders. As he arranged it he touched one of the soft curls that lay on her white neck, and again a thrill passed through him. He began to wish that he had not planned this country expedition, after all. He ought really to have started this morning for the Continent. Going on Saturday, he would have very little time to stay.

On the homeward way Mrs. Morres reproached him with his dulness. What had come to him?

He hesitated, glancing at Mary in her corner. Mary had enjoyed her day thoroughly, and was wearing an air of great content. She was carrying a bunch of the wild thyme. She had taken off her hat and her cloudy hair seemed blown about her head like an aureole. She had a delicate, wild, elusive air. He withdrew his glance abruptly.

"It is a guilty conscience," he said. "I ought not to come back and dine with you tonight. I ought to put you into a cab and myself into another, go home for my bag and take the night-express to Paris. The House only rises for ten days and I have to be in my place on the opening night."

Mary looked up at him with a friendly air of being disappointed. She was engaged in putting the wild thyme into a bunch, stalk by stalk. Mrs. Morres began to protest —

"Well, of all the deceitful persons! After luring me to spend a Good Friday in town. To be sure, I shall have Mary. Will you come to the Good Friday service at St. Hugh's with me, Mary?"

"I should love to come."

"Very well, then. Have your bag packed and come back with me to sleep. We shall get off the earlier on Saturday morning. So we shan't miss you at all, Sir Robin."

He looked at her with great contrition.

"My mother —" he began.

"To be sure, your mother has first claim. To say nothing of another."

He coloured. Mary was looking at him with kind interest. Mrs. Morres sent him a quick glance — then looked away again.

"To be sure, you must go, Sir Robin," she said, in a serious voice. "I was only jesting. Ah! here we are! So it is good-bye."

"Au revoir," he corrected.

"Well, au revoir. I hope you'll have a very happy time at Lugano. But you are sure to."

A moment later they had gone off in their cab, and he was feeling the blank of their absence.

CHAPTER XIX

WILD THYME AND VIOLETS

While Sir Robin and Mary Gray sat on that English hillside, Nelly and her father walked on a hilly road above Lugano. The April afternoon was Paradise. Below, the lake lay blue as a sapphire mirroring a sapphire sky. The space between them and the lake's edge was tinged with a bloom of bluish-rose, for all the almond groves were out in blossom. Below them were drifts of sweet-scented narcissi. All around them lay the mountains, Monte Rosa silver against the sapphire sky. Below the fantastic houses clustered to the lake's edge in their little groves and coppices of green.

They were talking of Robin's coming. The hour of his arrival was somewhat uncertain. They might find him at the hotel when they returned, going home in the evening quietness, when Monte Rosa would be flushed to rose-pink and the blue sky would die off in splendours of rose and orange.

Nelly was certainly looking better. Not a hint had come to her of the frontier war in which, by this time, her lover must be engaged. The General starved for his newspapers in these days, if he did not get the chance of a surreptitious peep at one at the English library, or when some friendly fellow-guest in the hotel would hand him a belated print two days old. Nelly had a wild rose bloom in her cheek and a light in her eye at this moment. Who could look upon such a scene and not praise the Designer? Not Nelly, certainly. As they paused for the hundredth time to look she breathed sighs of content and pressed her father's arm close to hers in a caress. Even though one's lover had been cruel and had gone away without speaking, it was good to be alive.

The appealing influence of the season was about them, too. They had just peeped into a little wayside chapel, where there was a small altar ablaze with lights set amid masses of flowers. The place was heavy with sweetness. Here and there knelt worshippers with bent heads. The General had bowed with a reverent knee, and Nelly had knelt with him before they had gone out into the blaze of the day again.

"There are only two armies, after all, Nell," the General had said, explaining himself. "The army of the Lord and the army of the Prince of Darkness. Let us rejoice that we have so many fellow-soldiers in the Lord's army, though we fight in different regiments."

"Tomorrow," said Nelly dreamily, "the lights will be all out and the little chapel draped in black. There will be the service of the Three Hours' Agony. Do you think we might come?"

"I'm afraid the Dowager would be shocked," her father replied hastily. "She would look upon it as deserting the flag. Many excellent women are very narrow-minded."

They went along in silence. At intervals they sat down to enjoy at leisure the beautiful world about them. They did not say much. There was little need for talk between two who understood each other so thoroughly. While they dawdled, half-way round the lake from their hotel, the sun dropped behind the hills and left them in shadow. It was time for them to go home.

As they went along leisurely, Nelly's face, uplifted towards the sky, seemed to have caught an illumination from it. It was the eve of the Great Sacrifice. Already the shadow and the light of it lay over the world. Nelly was thrilled and touched. That visit to the wayside chapel had set chords vibrating in her heart. Sacrifice for love's sake appealed to her as it does to all generous, impressionable young souls. Though her own personal happiness had vanished, gone down under the world with the *Sutlej*, there was yet the happiness possible of making those she loved happy. She had understood her father's wistful looks and tentative speeches. She knew that he desired her happiness to be in her cousin's keeping. The old days were over, the sweet days before that other had come, when she and her father had sufficed for each other. They could never come again, and he wanted her to marry Robin. Robin's mother, who was good to her, had suggested that she was trying Robin's patience too far. Why, if she could make them all happy — she was not in a state of mind to appreciate what marriage with one man while she loved another was going to cost her — if she could make them all happy, ought she not to do so?

"Father!" she whispered. "Father!"

"What is it, Nell?"

She rubbed her cheek slowly against his arm, not speaking for a second or two.

"Father, I am ready to marry Robin whenever you will."

The General's heart bounded up with an immense relief.

"Whenever I will?" he said, with an air of rallying her. "Is it not rather whenever you will? Poor Robin has been waiting long enough."

"You are quite sure he wants me: I mean soon?"

"He'd be a dull fellow if he didn't."

The General had suddenly a memory of the time when he had called Robin a dull fellow in his secret heart because he had been content to wait, endlessly to all appearances. He put the memory away hastily as an uncomfortable one.

"To be sure, he wants you soon, Nelly, my dear," he said. "As soon as your old father can give you up to him. You have always been Robin's little sweetheart from the time you were a child. He has never thought of any girl but you."

He made the speech with a gulp, as though it were distasteful to him.

"I never thought there was any girl," Nelly said simply. "Robin is not at all a young man for girls. Only he cares so much for politics. He has not seemed in any hurry."

"God bless my soul, to be sure, he is in a hurry. He must be in a hurry. When you get back to your looking-glass, little Nell, ask yourself whether it is likely that he should not be in a hurry!"

He was talking as much to reassure himself as Nelly. To be sure, Robin must be as eager a lover as it was in his capacity to be. There was nothing volcanic about Robin. He was steady, sensible, reliable! Yes, better let the affair be settled at once. June would be a good month for the wedding. He could go afterwards and take the cure at Vichy for his gout. Pat could go with him. Perhaps Nelly would take over Bridget and some of the other servants. Why shouldn't Robin and Nelly have the house just as it stood? He would make them a deed of gift of it. He could have a bachelor's flat somewhere near the Parks and the Clubs, with Pat to look after him. It would be easier for him if the old house sanctified by many memories were not to be broken up.

Nelly's exaltation carried her on to Saturday afternoon. Sir Robin had arrived on the morning of that day while the General and Nelly were out climbing the lower range of a hill. The Dowager was no climber. More than that, she had acquired tact and good feeling it seemed in her latter days, for she left father and daughter very much together. The General's heart had begun to soften towards her. He had begun to ask himself how it was that he could have so persistently misjudged her all those years. If Gerald had liked her well enough to marry her, surely he could have done her more justice than so to dislike her.

The Dowager had her son to herself for some hours of the Saturday forenoon. He had suggested following Nelly and her father up the mountain track, but she had detained him with a demonstrativeness unusual in her, which struck him like a jarring note. What had come over his mother? She had always been a woman of a cold and even harsh manner, at least to him. To be sure, he had noticed with amazement that she had been different to Nelly. She ought to have had a daughter instead of a son. He had no idea that if he had been a dashing soldier he might have been a far less dutiful son, a far less satisfactory member of society than he was and yet have awakened a feeling in his mother's breast which she had never given to him. Now he was embarrassed somewhat by her playful insistence on her mother's right to her boy for a time. Playfulness sat as ill on her as could well be imagined, and he was captious over her raillery on his hurry to be at his cousin's side, calling it atrocious taste in his irritable mind, he who had never been irritable, to whom it would have seemed the worst of taste to question good taste in his mother.

More than one person was irritable with the Dowager that day. The General was furiously irritable over the transparent manoeuvre by which she packed off the young people together.

"Enough to spoil the whole thing," he thought, pursing his lips and pushing out his eyebrows as he did when he was annoyed. "Indelicate! Stupid! I'd rather have her when she was disagreeable. My poor Nell! She did not look very happy as she went. I had a great mind to go with her and spoil things, after all."

The cousins found their way to Nelly's favourite haunt, the little coppice of low almond trees with the troops of narcissi and violets and primroses colouring all the brown earth. They went into the little chapel together. It smelt of incense after the ceremonies of the morning. The mournful black had been removed. There were flowers on a side-table, and the sacristan was setting the candlesticks on the fair white cloth which he had just laid along the altar. The scents in the woods at home had been thin and faint by these. Standing with his hat in his hand at the threshold of the little chapel, Robin Drummond had a memory of the scent of wild thyme.

He was not one to hesitate when he had made up his mind. His mother had told him that Nelly was waiting, ready for the word which might have been hers any time those two or three years back. Her father thought the time had come to arrange a date for their marriage. His mother, too, was anxious to see him settled. Neither she nor the General was young any longer. They had a right to look upon their children's happiness for the years that were left to them of life.

The young people were high on a mountain path, where few were to be met with except an occasional Englishman climbing like themselves, or the goatherds with their little flocks. He had helped her up a steep bit of climbing. The exertion had brought an unwonted colour to her face. Her hand lay in his, soft and warm. His closed on it and held it. It was the hand of one who had never done anything toilsome in her life, the hand of a petted darling. He remembered another hand, thin, brown, capable. None of Mary's later years of ease had given her the hand of a woman of leisure. It was the hand of a comrade, a helpmate. Nelly's hand fluttered in his and was suddenly cold.

"Well, Nell," he said, "do you know what I came here in the mind to ask you?"

"Yes." He saw the quick rise and fall of her bosom; he noticed the almost terrified look of her eyes. Was that how women showed their happy agitation when their lovers claimed them? Poor little Nell! How easily frightened she was! She had turned quite pale. He would have to be very good to her in the days to come.

"Haven't you kept me waiting long enough, little girl?" he went on with a tenderness which might easily have passed for a lover's. "I've been very patient, haven't I? But now my patience has come to an end. When are you going to fix a date for our marriage?"

"We have been very happy," began Nelly with trembling lips.

"Not so happy as we are going to be. God knows, Nell, I will do my best to make you happy, and may God bless my best!"

As he said it the scent of some little plant, bruised beneath his feet, rose to his nostrils, sharply aromatic. It was the wild thyme, the fragrance of which had hung about him those few days back, no matter how he tried to banish it.

"I will be very good to you, Nelly, if you can trust me with yourself."

It was not the least bit in the world like the love-making of Nelly's dreams. To be sure, he was good and kind, the dear, kind old Robin he had always been. She was grateful that he was not more lover-like according to her ideals. If he had taken her in his arms and kissed her passionately like that other — she smelt lilies of the valley where Robin Drummond smelt the wild thyme — she could not have endured it. As it was, she answered him sweetly.

"I know you will be good to me, Robin. When were you ever anything but good?"

Then he kissed her, a light kiss that brushed her lips. He felt his own shortcomings as a lover when he saw the blood rush tumultuously to her face, cover even her neck. Why, she must care for him with some passion to blush like that for his kiss. He had no idea that it was the memory of another kiss which had caused that wild flush of colour.

"Well, Nell, when is it to be?" he asked, trying to galvanise himself out of his coldness, trying to make the pity and tenderness which she awoke in him take the place of passion.

"When you will, Robin."

"You will never repent it, God helping me," he said again.

They came back, as they were expected to, with things settled between them. Robin had consulted a calendar in his pocket-book and named a date — Thursday, 23rd of July. He would be free then. The House would have risen and he would be able to devote himself to his honeymooning with a clear mind. He had not asked for an earlier date, but it did not occur to Nelly to wonder at that. She was relieved to find it so far off. Already she thought of the time between as a respite, the "Long day, my Lord!" of those condemned to death.

The Dowager saw nothing wrong with the date. They could wander about the Continent leisurely, coming home early in June to prepare Nelly's wedding-clothes. The General, after his first irritation had passed, had brought himself to tell her of his plan about the house. She approved graciously as she thought. It was very generous of the General. To be sure, Robin must have a town house now he was married. Sherwood Square was a little out of the way and quite unfashionable. Still, it was a fine house in an excellent situation to balance those drawbacks. And of course it must be new-papered and painted and modern conveniences placed in it. That could be done while the young couple were away honeymooning. Robin must be on the telephone, of course. That was indispensable. And the furniture must be fresh-covered, so much of it as they decided to keep. A deal of it was old-fashioned and had better go to a sale-room. New carpets too. Already the Dowager was making calculations of what it was going to cost the General. She was capable of a certain grim enjoyment in the spending of other people's money.

"Do you propose to live with them, ma'am?" the General asked at last, in a constrained voice.

She looked at him in amazement.

"Why, to be sure. Poor child, she will need someone beside her. Those servants of yours, Denis, they've had their own way too much. I've no doubt there's a terrible leakage in the establishment."

"If you propose to live with them, ma'am," the General went on, bursting with fury, "I don't give up my house at all. Robin can find his own town-house. The servants have done very well for me and Nelly. So have the chairs and tables and carpets. I'd nearly as soon send my own flesh and blood to an auction-room."

The Dowager was alarmed. She tried to propitiate the General after her usual manner towards him. It was as though she tried to distract a froward child.

"Dear me," she said, "dear me! I didn't mean to offend you, Denis. The house is shabby. Those dogs have always sat in the chairs and on the carpets. I only thought that we might put our heads together for the good of the young people."

"I'm a Dutchman if we will, ma'am!" shouted the General. "As for the dogs, did you intend to exclude them, too, from the fine new house? You'd never teach them not to sit in chairs at this time of their lives."

This outbreak was followed by the usual fit of repentance, in which the General reproached himself for his hastiness. To be sure, he had been annoyed that the wedding should have been put off for so long. In his haste he had said derogatory things about Robin in his heart, which was unreasonable. The fellow was a Member of Parliament and had to stick to his post, to stick to his post like a soldier. Yet, there would be all those weeks of June and July when bad news might come any day about Langrishe: and Nell would be in London and would hear of it.

So, although the thing had come about which he desired, the General was not happy.

CHAPTER XX

JEALOUSY, CRUEL AS THE GRAVE

It was the latter end of April when Sir Robin Drummond presented himself again in the big bare room where Mary Gray transacted the business of her Bureau. The windows were wide open now, and the dull roar of the distant street traffic came in. It had been a showery day, and he had noticed as he came up the stairs the many marks of muddy feet which showed that business at the Bureau was brisk. The women were coming at last to be organised, to learn a spirit of *camaraderie*, to see that their good was the common good, to have hope for a future which would not be always starvation and deprivation, sufferings in cold and heats, intolerable miseries crowding upon each other.

He came up the stairs, looking sadder and sterner than was his wont. He remembered how all last winter he had run up those stairs like a school-boy, being so glad at last to get to the hour he had desired all day. As he passed up the staircase now he looked at the walls, distempered a dirty pink. Outside Mary's door they were adorned by the effusions of amateur artists, the children of the working women, messenger boys, casual urchins, with the desire of their kind for scribbling. It was all quite unlovely, yet it had made him happy to come there. It was a happiness that he had had no right to and now it must be relinquished. This was the last time he should come after this intimate fashion.

He turned the handle of the door and went in, rather dreading to find Mary engaged with other visitors; but she was alone. She turned round from her desk as he came in, and, jumping up at sight of him, she came to meet him with an outstretched hand.

"Congratulate me," she said. "The book is finished and accepted. Strangmans have taken it. They took only a week to decide. I am wild with pride and joy. Maurice Ilbert is one of their readers. He got it to read and recommended it enthusiastically. They are to publish it in June. Wasn't it generous of him, because there is so little of it he can agree with?"

"Oh, Ilbert's conscience is pretty elastic, I should say, and he can agree with many things," Sir Robin answered. He felt vaguely annoyed that Ilbert should have had anything to do with Mary or her book. Ilbert was one of the younger school of Tories, a free-lance he called himself, handsome, conceited, immensely clever, a golden youth with an air of Oxford and the Schools added to him. He was one of the youngest members of Parliament, and was gifted with a dazzling and impertinent wit. Sir Robin had occasionally smarted under Ilbert's sallies. He was a target for them, with his serious and simple views, his lean air of Don Quixote.

Mary looked at him reproachfully, as though the speech grieved her.

"He is very generous," she repeated. "He has come to see me. I found him most sympathetic. It is not a question of parties. He thinks awfully well of the book. He says it will stir the public conscience. To be sure, it is written out of experience, just the plain story of things as they are. I have learned so much since I began this work."

He had got over his first ill-temper, and now he spoke gently.

"I am sure it is a good book," he said. "I have always felt that you would make a good book of it because you know. Ilbert is a very capable critic."

He did Ilbert justice with some difficulty. He had a sharp thought of Ilbert coming in and out as he had been used to, when he should come no more. For the first time in his life, which had had no room for self-consciousness, he compared himself with another man, handsome, debonair, and remembered the lean visage over which mornings he passed the razor, dark, lantern-jawed, almost grotesque. It was the only aspect of himself he knew, the one which was presented to him when he shaved.

"Now you are like yourself," Mary said sweetly. "It was not like you to throw cold water on my pleasure."

He turned away his head from her reconciled eyes. She was making what he had come to say doubly hard for him.

"I want to tell you something," he said. "I should like you to hear it from me first, because you have been so good a friend to me. I have spoken to you of my cousin, Nelly. I wanted you to be her friend. Well — I am to marry my cousin in July."

There was silence for a moment after he had said it, a silence broken only by the ticking of the noisy clock on the mantelpiece, by the sounds of the street outside.

"There has been an implicit engagement between my cousin and myself," he went on as though he set his teeth to it. "I couldn't tell you when it began. It was made for us. I was always ready to be bound by it. She is as sweet a thing as ever lived; but sometimes I have thought that perhaps, perhaps, the cousinly closeness would make the other tie a difficult thing for Nelly to accept. I was wrong. She has no desire to break through that implicit bond."

He was making an explanation, and Mary Gray was not the girl to misunderstand him.

"I am very glad," she said cheerfully, "very glad. I hope you will be very happy. I am sure that you will be."

He looked at her with relief, which was not altogether agreeable. He had not done her any wrong after all. She was not angry with him. But, to be sure, why should she be? It was unlikely that she would have taken more than a friendly interest in him. He mocked at himself, and thought of his harsh uncomeliness. If he had been Ilbert now his conduct of all this winter past would have been unpardonable. But Ilbert and he were made in a different mould. Oddly, the thought did not comfort him — was a bitter one, rather.

"Won't you sit down and tell me about it?" Mary said, her eyes looking at him frankly and kindly. "I am not at all busy. The business of the Bureau is pretty well over for the day, and I can finish my proofs at home. Do, Sir Robin."

She pushed a chair towards him, and he sat down in it. He felt that he ought to go. It was a concession to his own weakness that he stayed. And he had no inclination at all to talk about his engagement. He tried to say something, tried to imagine what a man happily engaged to be married would find to say to a sympathetic woman-friend about it. He could think of nothing, only that so far as he could see there was no consciousness in the serious bright eyes that watched him. To be sure he ought to be glad. He would be the most miserable hound on earth if he wished her to be unhappy because he was marrying his cousin. Yet he was not glad of that ready sympathy.

"Well," she said at last, "you have nothing to tell me."

"What can I say" — he laughed awkwardly — "that I have not already said? We have been brought up like brother and sister, but our elders always expected us to marry when we should be old enough. We have been taking it easy, Nell and I; thought there was plenty of time, you know."

"And at last you have decided that the plenty of time is up?" she said, filling the gap in his speech. Her eyes were wondering now. It was a strange thing to her that lovers should take it easy.

"Yes, that was it."

"Of course, I understand now why you felt you had to go that Thursday in Holy Week. It was very good of you to give us so much of your time."

"You didn't tell me how you got on, what you did," he said eagerly. He was glad to escape from the discussion of his too intimate affairs. "What did you do on Good Friday, after all?"

"Mrs. Morres spent the day with me. It was a lovely day. We went to the service at St. Hugh's. The music was wonderful. Afterwards we sat by the open window and talked. My window-box was full of daffodils. They are just over now. Mrs. Morres said it was like the country. Afterwards I locked up the flat, put the key in my pocket, discovered a hansom — it wasn't easy, but 'Tilda, who comes in to tidy up for me every day, managed it. Her young man is a hansom-driver. I stayed the night at the Square, and we went down to Hazels next morning."

"Was it good?"

"Exquisite. I finished the book there. We had miraculous weather. I was able to work out of doors in the very same green garden where her Ladyship and I worked at the novel last year. The dogs used to sit all around me: and I believe the birds remembered me. I am sure I recognised one robin. I came back like a lion refreshed, with the full copy of the book done up in my portmanteau. Since then I have been enjoying the sweets of a mind at ease."

"You look it."

She did, indeed, look like a flower refreshed. She was wearing a soft grey gown with a little good, yellowed lace about the shoulders. The lace had been a gift from Lady Anne. It gave the final touch of distinction to Mary's air. She had the warm, pale complexion that goes well, with grey, and her hair seemed to have more than usual of gold in it. Standing against the light it was blown out like a little aureole full of stars. He had thought that he could like her in nothing so well as her dark blue frock, but now he thought that grey should be her only wear.

"What time do you leave?" he asked, glancing at the clock.

"Not for a long time yet. It is only half-past five. People come in and out here up to quite late. I foresee that my hours will be later and later."

"You mustn't let them take too much of your time. You must have time for exercise, for meals, for rest, for your friends —"

"I am so profoundly interested in the work that I don't grumble. As for my friends, they can see me here. For exercise I walk most of the way between Kensington and this, either coming or going. Society is not likely to claim me — at least, not in her Ladyship's absence. My few friends can find me here."

It was on his lips to ask her to let him walk part of the way home with her. He might have this last pleasure since he was coming here no more, at least not in the old way. But, as though her words had been a challenge, there was a clatter of wheels and horses in the narrow street below.

"A carriage," Mary said. "It will be one of the fine ladies who are interested in philanthropy and politics."

There was a rustle of silks and murmur of voices coming up the stairs. Sir Robin sat holding his hat in one hand, vaguely annoyed. Why should one of those meddlesome fine ladies choose for the hour of her empty, unimportant visit his last hour with Mary Gray?

He sat irritated, shy, awkward, his feelings faithfully reflected in his face. The door opened. A lady came in whom he had occasionally met in drawing-rooms, a slight, tall woman, with a brilliant brunette face. A delicate perfume came with her entrance. She was finely dressed, as fine as a humming-bird, and it became her. She looked incredibly young to be the mother of the slim youth who followed her. The youth was Maurice Ilbert. His mother, Mrs. Ilbert, was well known as one of the most brilliant and exclusive hostesses in fine London circles. Now she was holding Mary's two hands in her own grey-gloved ones.

"I insisted that my son should bring me to see you, Miss Gray," she was saying with *empressement.* "I hope you will excuse my descending on you like this. But I positively had to. This wonderful book of yours — my boy has been talking of it every hour we have been alone. It is such a pleasure to meet you. Ah — Sir Robin Drummond, how do you do? Are you also privileged to know about the wonderful book?"

To Robin Drummond's mind Ilbert's smile and nod had something amused, mocking in them. He had acknowledged the greeting with the curtest of nods.

Now he got up, shook hands awkwardly with Mrs. Ilbert, and made his farewells to Mary Gray. It was sheer ill-temper drove him out as soon as they had come. He had wanted to ask Mary if he might bring Nelly when she returned to town. He had wanted ... a good many other things. But now he stalked away from her presence with fury in his heart. If the Ilberts were going to take her up! — to exploit the book! The Ilberts belonged to the young Tory party which his soul detested, or he said so in his wrath; as a matter of fact, he had not many detestations, and in the matter of politics he had no personal rancours. Yet at the moment he thought he had, and fancied that a part of his indignation was because Mary Gray, who had learnt in the Radical school, was going to be made much of by advanced Tories. As he sat in his hansom, "stepping westward" into the heart of the sunset, he bit the ends of his moustache, and it was like chewing the cud of bitterness. Mary Gray had expanded to answer the genial warmth of Mrs. Ilbert's manner as a flower opens to the sun. It was not in her to be ungracious, and Mrs. Ilbert was a charming woman.

And now he asked himself what was he going to do for the next month or six weeks till his mother and Nelly came home? All the winter he had been in the habit of seeing Mary Gray two or three times a week. He had been home a week from Lugano, and he had kept away; and all the time something stronger than himself had seemed to be tugging at him to take the old familiar road. He had found it a hard struggle to keep away for those ten days. And how was he going to do it for all those weeks to come? He had always had so much to say to her — or, at least, there had always been things he wanted to say, for in his most intimate moments he was naturally rather silent.

For a second his thoughts escaped his control, and settled on the pleasantness that bare ugly work-a-day room had meant to him all the winter through. The sodden winter streets, swept by bitter winds, horrible in fog and snow, through which he had hurried on his way had had something heavenly about them. "Ah, le beau temps passé!"

He pulled himself together with a sharp shock of reproach. He was to marry Nelly in less than three months' time, and he was an honourable man. When Nelly was his wife he meant that every thought of his heart should belong to her. He must see Mary Gray no more. Yet as he pushed the thought of her away from him it came to him that another man might find the ugly gas-lit room, the wet winter streets with their bawling crowds and flaring lights, something of the same magical world that he had found them. Supposing that man were Ilbert? Well, supposing it were so, what business had he to resent it? But however he might ask himself rhetorical questions, the jealousy of the natural man swept over him in passion and fury. He said to himself that now he knew why he had always hated Ilbert. It was a prevision of this hour.

And at the moment the General was offering up his heartfelt thanks that Nelly's happiness was secure in the keeping of one so steady and reliable, if rather dull and slow, as Robin Drummond.

CHAPTER XXI

TWO WOMEN

The travellers came home the first week of June. During the weeks that had come and gone since Easter they had wandered about as the fancy took them. Rome, Florence, Genoa, Venice. They followed a path of wonders; but, somewhat to her father's dismay, Nelly did not prove the passionate pilgrim he had expected. She looked on listlessly at the wonder-world. Now that her first exaltation had died away it did not seem so simple a matter to make others happy. There was no royal road, she discovered, to the happiness of others any more than to her own.

Her father said to himself that Nell would be all right as soon as the wedding was over. He had not come to the point of thinking yet that marriage with Robin Drummond was not the way the Finger of God had pointed out to him. It was impossible not to notice Nelly's listless step and heavy eyes. The Dowager put down these things to ordinary delicacy, something the girl would outgrow.

"She wants a husband's care," she said. "To be sure, my dear Denis, you have done your best for her. But what, after all, could you know about girls?"

"As much as Robin Drummond, ma'am," the General said, with a growl; and was not placated by the Dowager's tolerant smile.

He was at once glad and sorry when the weeks were over. He dreaded, for one thing, going back to London where Nelly might hear news of Godfrey Langrishe. To be sure, he had acted entirely for her happiness, yet he had an idea that Nell might be angry with him for keeping things from her if she found out that Langrishe's regiment was engaged in the deadly frontier war. He had been so used to being perfectly frank with her that his reservation galled him.

He had studied with attentiveness the columns of such papers as had come his way, dreading to find Langrishe's name among the casualties. Hitherto it had not occurred, and for that he was deeply grateful. If there had been news he must have betrayed it to Nelly by his eyes and his voice.

"I wish we could have stayed longer," she said to him on the eve of their departure from Italy.

"And I, Nell."

"Oh," she looked at him in wonder. "I thought you were keen to be gone."

"Is it likely?" he asked with playful tenderness, "that I should be anxious to shorten the time in which you are mine and not Robin Drummond's?"

They were alone, and she turned and put her head on his shoulder.

"I shall always be yours," she said. "And I think marriage and giving in marriage a weariness of the spirit."

"Not really, Nell?" The General looked at her golden head in alarm, but already she was reproaching herself.

"Never mind, dear papa," she said. "I didn't altogether mean it. Poor, kind Robin! What a very ungrateful girl I am to you all!"

As soon as they got back the Dowager engaged her in a whirl of shops and dressmakers, and for that the General was grateful. He resorted to man[oe]uvres in those days to keep the newspapers out of Nelly's way that revealed to himself hitherto unsuspected depths of cunning. He opened the papers with a tremor. The orange and green and pink bills of the evening newspapers stuck up where Nelly could see them, laid on the pavement almost under her feet, brought his heart into his mouth. If they could only tide over the dangerous time, and Nelly be married and gone off on her leisurely honeymoon! Langrishe might almost fade out of her mind, become at least a gentle memory, before anything could happen to him: or the deadly little dragging war might be over and Langrishe have carried out a whole skin.

It was the height of the season and Nelly had her social engagements as well as the preparations for her wedding. As often as was possible Robin Drummond put in an appearance, but the House was sitting and much of his time was taken up. He looked rather more hatchet-faced than of old. Once, sitting in the Strangers' Gallery of the House, the General heard someone say as Robin was about to speak: "Who is that careworn-looking young man?" Careworn, indeed! The General fumed and fretted over it, the more because it fell in with a certain secret thought he had had once or twice. Robin had always been somewhat too much of an old head on young shoulders to please his uncle. To be sure, he had fed on Blue Books and slept on statistics, yet his engagement to a lovely girl like Nelly ought to have made him look happier. It was indecent in the circumstances, that's what it was, that anybody, with the remotest justification for the epithet, could call him careworn.

Once Robin on an afternoon when the House was not sitting called for his cousin and carried her off in a hansom without saying where he was taking her to. That was something of which the General heartily approved. If Robin had done it oftener his opinion of him would have gone up immensely. He rubbed his hands while he asked the Dowager what Mrs. Grundy would say to such doings. "Supposing they made a runaway match of it, ma'am, where should we be?" he asked cheerfully. To which the Dowager replied that Robin would never think of anything so silly. Why should he, when the wedding was fixed for the twenty-third and everything ordered, even the bridesmaids' dresses and the wedding-cake? "Perhaps for that reason," replied the General. But this was a dark saying to the Dowager.

The visit that afternoon was to Mary Gray. Even Nelly had heard of the book which Sir Michael Auberon had praised so highly, which the newspapers had declared to be more interesting than any novel. She had roused herself to be interested in the visit, to talk, to ask questions, to look about her, as they drove into the east, instead of gazing inwards with that introspective glance which had given her eyes of late the beauty of mystery, making them larger and darker than they had been in the old days.

She was exquisitely dressed, in a long cloak of cream lace over an Indian muslin frock, and an airy hat of chiffon and feathers. She had put on her best for her outing with Robin, her visit to Robin's friend. It was one of the sweet things she was always doing, with an intention in her own mind to make up for some lack or other which certainly her lover had not felt. When she alighted in the busy street people stared as though they had seen a white bird of Paradise; and coming into Mary Gray's room with a basket of roses in her hand she looked like a bride.

Now, at least, she wore the pilgrim air. She looked curiously about the unlikely place which housed the wonderful woman as she set down her roses, then back at Mary herself. Mary had come to meet her with outstretched hands. Her bright look at Robin Drummond was full of sympathetic admiration, of felicitation. She kissed Nelly warmly. She was not an effusive person, and nothing had been further from her thoughts than kissing, but her heart went out at once to this charming girl.

"*How* good of you to come to see me!" she said, pressing Nelly's hands in hers. "Into the east, too! And you must be so busy just now."

"I have been longing to see you," Nelly responded. "Robin has talked so much about you." At that moment Nelly had no doubt that he had talked. "And I wanted to see you here, in your ordinary life. Robin says you will not be here much longer — that there will be an official position found for you. And it was here that 'Creatures of Burden' was written!"

"Nearly all here," Mary said, smiling down at the young enthusiast.

Robin Drummond stood aside, in one of his characteristically awkward attitudes, his hat in his hand, watching them. He was not thinking sufficiently of himself to feel awkward, although he looked it. He was thinking of those two dear women, as he called them to himself, objurgating himself for his unworthiness to be the kinsman and lover of one, the friend of the other.

He had never seen Nelly look like that before. Her air of worship was charming. Now she let Mary Gray's hands fall while she went swiftly to the table on which she had deposited her beautiful red roses. "I brought them for you," she said, offering them to Mary Gray.

"How delicious! How sweet of you!"

The smell of the roses was in the room. It might have been the aura of the two exquisite women, he thought. Nelly had come in carrying a little whiff of scent that went with her, as much a part of her as the soft rustling of her garments. He closed his eyes and there came to his memory, sweet and sharp, the odour of wild thyme. Not a second of time had passed when he opened them again. Mary was still praising her roses. She was holding them to her face, leaning towards Nelly as she did so. Her expression was more than kind: it was tender. She put down her basket of roses and took Nelly's hands between hers. For a moment she held them against her breast before she relinquished them. She spoke with a little tremor in her voice. Why was it that Robin Drummond thought suddenly of the nightingale who leans his breast upon a thorn?

In an instant the thrill in the atmosphere had passed. She was bustling about to make them tea, if her soft, quiet movements could be called bustling. She brought a kettle from the unpainted deal cupboard which housed her utensils of every day. She disappeared for a few seconds and returned with the kettle full of water and set it on the gas-stove. She pushed the papers away from one end of the table and covered it with a dainty tea-cloth. She brought out cups and saucers of thin Japanese porcelain, some sugar, a loaf and butter, a box of biscuits. While she set her table she went on talking and smiling at them. The kettle began to sing on the fire.

"Ah!" she said, with a sudden thought. "The milkman will not call for an hour yet. What are we to do?"

"Let me go and forage," said Drummond eagerly.

"The nearest dairy is a good bit off."

"Trust me to find one."

When he had gone the two girls sat down and looked at each other. No wonder she was beloved, Mary thought to herself, gloating over Nelly's golden head, her blue eyes with the dark lashes, her lovely colouring, her innocent mouth. She had a poor opinion of her own beauty and rarely looked in a glass, but she was none the less generous to beauty in others.

"And you are very happy?" she asked.

She had an inclination to put her arms about Nelly Drummond as though she were a beautiful child. She was so glad Robin had remembered to bring her at last. It had been strange and lonely when he had ceased to come as he had been used to. It had been so pleasant to look up when his tap came at the door and to see his plain, pleasant face looking at her with a friendly smile. She had grown used to his visits all that winter through; and when they had ceased abruptly she had missed them more than she cared to acknowledge to herself. She had an impulse to take Nelly's hand to her breast and hold it there for comfort.

"And you are very happy?" she said again.

She was prepared for a happy girl's outpourings. What she was not prepared for was the sudden shadow that fell on Nelly's face, the weariness, as though she had been brought back to the thought of something disagreeable. A sudden wintriness went over her charming face. The eyes drooped, the lips trembled and were steadied with an effort.

"I ought to be very happy," she said. "Everyone is good to me. I have the dearest old father in the world and Robin is so kind and good. I ought to be very happy and to make other people happy."

But she was not happy! Mary stared at the golden head with incredulity. For the moment Nelly's mask — a transparent one enough at best — with which she faced the world was down. No happy girl had ever spoken so, looked so. And it wanted only a few weeks to her marriage!

Mary, no more logical than women less intellectual than she, felt as her first impulse a coldness, chilling her heart that had been so warm towards the girl Robin Drummond had chosen. The chill must have reached Nelly's delicate apprehension, for she looked up in a startled way.

"Robin promised me your friendship," she began.

"And, to be sure, it is yours," Mary Gray said, still wondering at the inexplicable thing that Robin Drummond's promised wife could have secret cause for unhappiness. She had no further inclination to caress the girl for whom she had been passed by. "We are going to be great friends," she said with a cold sweetness.

Then the kettle boiled over and created a diversion. While Mary was still mopping up the pool it had made on the floor Sir Robin returned. His voyage of discovery had not been in vain. He had indeed chartered a hansom to make it, and had brought back fascinating things in the way of cream and tea-cakes and other dainties. As he came in he glanced at the two whom he hoped to see friends. A shadow rested on Nelly's face. He saw nothing amiss with Mary Gray as she went to and fro, busy with the little meal, and had no fault to find with her words as they parted.

"We are going to be great friends, Miss Drummond and I," she said.

But the note of the nightingale that leans his breast on the thorn, the note of self-sacrifice and yearning tenderness had gone out of her voice.

CHAPTER XXII

LIGHT ON THE WAY

It wanted three weeks to her wedding when one day Nelly suddenly came upon Mrs. Rooke in one of the narrow, fashionable streets south of Oxford Street. Mrs. Rooke was coming out of a florist's shop, and she was carrying a sheaf of lilies in her hand. For one second she looked as though she would have turned aside and avoided Nelly. Then she came straight on with a little unfriendly uplifting of her white chin.

She might have passed with a bow if Nelly had not stopped straight in her path.

"How d'ye do?" she said coldly. "What a delightful day! I had no idea you were back. But to be sure ... I must congratulate you. It is next month, is it not?"

"Yes; it is next month," Nelly said with stiff lips. "The twenty-third of July, to be accurate. I have wondered about you. I hope Mr. Rooke is well and Cuckoo and Bunny."

Bunny was the youngest hope of the Rooke household, a wise, fat, golden-haired child, who had taken a huge fancy to Nelly. At the mention of his name his mother faltered. She had been used to swear by Bunny's sagacity. Bunny had been fond of Nelly Drummond; and there had been a time when Bunny's mother had referred to that fact as though it were Nelly's patent of nobility.

"Cuckoo is at school. Bunny hasn't been very well. Those east winds in May caught him. I had a horrible fright about him. Imagine Bunny — Bunny — choking with croup! I thought I should have gone mad!"

For the moment she had forgotten Nelly's offences, and only remembered that she had been Bunny's friend. Nelly looked back at her as aghast as herself.

"Croup! I never thought of such a thing," she responded. "He has never had it before, has he?"

"Never. That was why I was so terrified. I didn't know what to do. There, don't look so frightened about it! It is over — weeks ago. Indeed, the next day he was about, as well as ever. I should never be so frightened again. It was the horrible novelty of it."

That frightened look in Nelly's eyes had softened the little woman's not very hard heart.

"I wish I had known," said Nelly. "I have wanted to come to see Bunny. I brought him a toy from Paris — a lamb that walks about by itself."

"Ah! you were thinking of him!"

There was complete reconciliation now in the mother's voice and eyes. How could she hate the girl who loved Bunny and had remembered to bring him from Paris a lamb that walked about by itself? She put an impulsive hand on Nelly's arm.

"Come home with me and see him. You are not very busy? You can spare the time?"

Nelly was on her way to keep a dress-making appointment, but she felt that not for worlds would she have said so. She flushed up quite happily. That moment of hostility on Mrs. Rooke's part had chilled her sensitive soul.

"Might I call at Sherwood Square for the lamb, do you think?" she asked diffidently.

"To be sure you may. And I'll tell you what — stay to lunch with me. There'll be nobody but ourselves, of course. It comes to me now that I haven't seen you for centuries."

"Yes; I should like to stay for lunch, thank you."

Mrs. Rooke rather wondered at the pale determination which came over Nelly's soft face, succeeding the flush of a minute before. It did not occur to her that Nelly had been pushing away from her with both hands during the weeks since her return the temptation which at this moment was offered to her. Nelly was only too conscious of the strength of her desire to hear something of Godfrey Langrishe.

It was a feeling she did not dare look in the face. If she had had any idea at the time she agreed to marry Robin that she was going to be haunted by the thought of another man she would never have agreed. Even of late there had been moments when her common-sense had whispered in her ears, protesting against the folly of marrying one man when another had so taken possession of her thoughts. But day by day the net had been drawn closer about her feet. The wedding-clothes, the wedding-breakfast, the bridesmaids, the wedding-cake, the hundred and one arrangements for the wedding, had all been strands of the net that held her ever tighter and tighter. How could she, at this stage, contemplate the breaking of her engagement? How could she? The courage of her race had not risen to that.

Mrs. Rooke suggested a 'bus, and Nelly agreed. Now that she had done the thing against which her conscience protested she did not want to think over-much. She even wanted to postpone the hearing of the name which she had been hungry to hear for so long. The news she had desired too. How was she going to listen to his name, to talk of him calmly? She wanted time to gain courage. A 'bus did not give one opportunities for talking, hardly for thinking.

She knew perfectly well that she should find a clear coast at Sherwood Square. The General had come part of the journey into town with her on his way to the club. Poor Sir Denis! If he could only have seen his Nelly now he would not have been so easy in his mind. Lady Drummond was engaged during the morning hours; she had to lunch with an old friend. Nelly had been contemplating lunch in a quiet Regent Street restaurant rather than the going back to the lonely meal at home. She had known that a telegram to Robin would have brought him to her side, but she had not meditated sending that telegram. She had been glad, in her innermost guilty, repentant heart of her morning of freedom from mother and son.

The 'bus rumbled along as that vehicle of the middle ages does, making a prodigious screaming in the ears, filling one with horrible electric thrills as the brake was jammed down. Neither conversation nor thinking was possible. Nelly closed her eyes a little wearily in her corner. The other people in the 'bus had stared as she got in at the fresh daintiness of her attire, conspicuous in the dingy vehicle. Now, as she leant back with closed eyes, the tired lines came out in her face. Mrs. Rooke, from the other side of the 'bus, glanced at her with pitying wonder.

"Dear me!" she thought to herself. "It isn't the Nelly Drummond I knew. What has she been doing to herself? She must have been racketting a deal. She doesn't look in the least like a happy bride should. Poor child! I wonder if she is marrying against her will?"

Arrived at Sherwood Square the lamb was brought down and displayed to Bunny's delighted mother. Pat whistled for a hansom, and when the two ladies were in he carried out the animal and placed it in front of them, where it created some excitement in its passage through the street.

Behold Nelly, then, presently seated on the nursery floor, winding up the lamb for Bunny and forgetting all about her beautiful lavender muslin frock. The mother and nurse stood by as eager as Nelly herself. Bunny, indeed, was the least interested of the party. To be sure in the wonder-world of Bunny's mind baa-lambs that went of themselves and bleated were no great wonder, even though it was a pleasing novelty to find one in his nursery. He was more excited over the reappearance of Nelly herself and stood by her with one fat affectionate arm about her neck in a contented silence. In vain his mother asked him if he wasn't pleased.

"He is always like that," she said at last. "We took him to the Hippodrome and he only yawned, even when Seeth's lions came on. He didn't take the smallest interest."

"Begging your pardon, ma'am, that he did," the nurse interposed. "He were flinging 'imself on his precious 'ead twenty times a day for a week after. 'Twas a wonder he had any 'ead left, the precious lamb. Them there dratted clowns, I don't 'old with them nohow!"

The reconciliation between Bunny's mother and Bunny's friend and admirer was complete by the time they went down to lunch. Nelly had begged for Bunny's presence at the meal, and so the young monarch of all he surveyed was seated opposite to her in his high chair, with a napkin tucked under his chin, playing a fandango with a spoon and fork on the little table in front of him. Bunny filled the lunch-hour, Bunny's sayings and doings — there were not many of the former, but his mother managed to extract gems of wit and wisdom from his taciturnity — Bunny's likes and dislikes, Bunny's amazing development.

Only once was Langrishe's name mentioned. He had sent home a beautiful mug of beaten silver for Bunny. At the sound of his name Nelly's eyes were suddenly startled: she caught her breath; the colour swept over her face and ebbed away, leaving her paler than before.

Presently the luncheon-hour was over and Bunny had been carried off for his afternoon's outing. The half-hour or so in the drawing-room was over. Nelly was drawing on her gloves, standing by the window which over-looked the narrow slip of square, invisible now for the flowers on the balcony. The fateful visit was nearly at an end and Godfrey Langrishe's name had been mentioned only once.

She had a wild thought that her one opportunity was slipping out of her grasp. She had come here to have news of him. She must not come again. She must try and forget that he existed till such time at least as she could think of him calmly. Now she *must* know, she *must* hear, what was happening to him away there at the end of the world.

She glanced furtively around the pretty room, to which she would not come again. It was as though she said farewell to its comfort and pleasantness. She was not going to see Bunny and his mother again, not for a long time at least. Her gaze came back to the window, pausing ever so slightly on its way to glance at a portrait of Langrishe which hung on the wall, a portrait painted in the days when he had been his uncle's heir, by a great painter. She had been conscious all the time she had been in the room of the presence of the portrait although she had not looked its way. The picture had caught the quiet passion and intensity of Godfrey Langrishe's gaze, as though he looked on deeds of glory and fought his way towards them. The face was less stern than she remembered it; it had yet some of the bloom and bonniness of his boyhood; renunciation had not written its deeper meaning in lines about the lips and eyes.

She opened her mouth to speak of him, but at first no words would come. The fastening of her glove took all her attention it seemed. She had turned to the light for it, away from Mrs. Rooke's sympathetic glances.

She had almost controlled her voice to speak without trembling when the thing was taken out of her hands.

"I must not let you go," Mrs. Rooke said, "without giving you a message from Godfrey. A message and gift. It came a week ago. See — here it is. I was going to post it to you." She took up a packet from the side-table.

"How is he?"

At last it was said. Nelly's hand closed over the little packet. She would open it when she got home. To think that he remembered — that he had chosen a gift for her! Was there a word with it, perhaps? Her first letter — and her last letter — from him was lying perhaps in her hand.

But what was it Mrs. Rooke was saying? She bent her ears greedily to listen.

"He was well when he wrote, but the letter was written some time ago. Where he is, it is not easy to get letters carried in safety. One never knows what may be happening. It is, of course, a terrible anxiety."

The tears came into her eyes. There had been a little shadow over her brightness even while she had watched Bunny. Nelly had been aware of it dimly. What did she mean?

"Anxiety!" Nelly repeated falteringly. "Why should you be anxious? He is not ill, is he?"

Her heart had sunk, heavy as lead. Her soul cried out in fear.

"You know he is with the punitive expedition against the Wazees for the murder of Major Sayers and his companions? You never can tell what dreadful thing may be happening to him. It isn't possible you didn't know? And I had been thinking you hardhearted! Ah!"

Her arms went round Nelly.

"It isn't possible you didn't know? *Don't* look like that! Do you care so much as all that, Nelly? Why, then, why, in the name of Heaven, did you let him go? Why are you marrying your cousin? My poor Godfrey!"

She was conscious of a strident voice shouting the evening

papers in the street outside. Indeed, even while she spoke to Nelly, half her brain was listening in a strained way to that voice as it came nearer. What was it the creature was shouting? Before she could hear distinctly the voice died away again in the distance.

"Why did I let him go?" Nelly repeated after her. "Because, because, he would not stay. He knew that I loved him, but he would not stay. He never seemed to think of staying. When he had broken my heart it seemed that I might as well make others happy. My father, Lady Drummond, my cousin; they have been so good to me always."

"But you were engaged to your cousin, weren't you, when Godfrey left?"

Little Mrs. Rooke's dark eyes looked black in her frightened face.

"You were engaged to your cousin, were you not, just as you are today?"

"I never accepted my cousin till — till Captain Langrishe had gone. It was understood that when we grew up we should marry to please our parents if we saw nothing against it. No one would have wanted to bind me if I did not wish to be bound."

Mrs. Rooke flung up her hands with a dramatic gesture.

"Heaven forgive me, my poor Nelly, for it was I who sent Godfrey from you! I told him you were engaged to your cousin. I had been told so explicitly by Lady Drummond herself. How could I doubt that it was true?"

Nelly turned a white face towards her. Oddly enough, in spite of its pallor the face had a certain illumination.

"So he went away because of that. Only that stood between us. Do you think I am going to let that — a lie, a mistake — stand between us? I am going to break off my engagement, even at the eleventh hour."

The daughter of the Drummonds had found the courage of her race. She stared uncomprehendingly at the alarm in Mrs. Rooke's expression.

"Don't do anything rash," the little woman said, in a frightened voice. "Supposing Godfrey did not come back. Supposing —"

Again there sounded in the distance the voices of the vendors of evening papers. The voices came nearer, one, two, half a dozen of them. They were all shouting together.

"There must be some news," Mrs. Rooke said under her breath.

"I shall come and see you tomorrow," Nelly said. "Tomorrow I shall be free to come and go where I like. Do you know that I was bidding this room and you and Bunny a long good-bye five minutes ago? And if he never comes back — well, he will know I waited for him."

So preoccupied was she with her intention that she never noticed the newspaper boys and men fluttering their Stop Press editions like the wings of some birds of evil omen. As she sat in the hansom she drew the engagement ring off her finger and dropped it into her purse. Then she sighed, as though an immense burden had fallen from her.

CHAPTER XXIII

THE NEWS IN THE *WESTMINSTER*

As Nelly's hansom drew up at her own door another hansom was just turning away from it. She wondered with an impatient wonder who could have come. At the moment she could not have endured any hindrance between her and her project of telling her father that the engagement with Robin was to come to an end. She was not in the least afraid of what she had to do. The spirit of the Drummonds was thoroughly awake now.

Beyond her announcement to her father lay something vaguely painful which at the moment she did not consider. She would have to tell Lady Drummond and Robin, of course, and it would hurt them: they would be angry with her. She was going to make a scandal, a nine days' wonder. Her father would be grieved — angry, too, perhaps; but that could not be helped either.

And then — some resentment stirred in her heart against him for the first time during all the years in which they had been together. He had kept her in ignorance of her lover's peril. She was not a child that she should have been kept in ignorance. For the moment she had no tender excuses for him. If he had been candid with her, then all this trouble about Robin might have been spared, for she could never have promised herself as wife to another man while the one she loved was in daily and hourly danger.

She went into the house with a look of stern accusation on her young face. The dogs came shrieking down the stairs in vociferous welcome as usual, but she took no notice of them. Being old dogs and wise, they recognised a forbidding mood in her, and retired with deprecating wrigglings of their bodies.

She asked Pat if there were a visitor in the drawing-room.

"No, then, Miss, only the master. I can't make out what came over him at all to be comin' home in a hansom."

He was minded to tell her that the General was not looking himself, to give her an affectionate, intimate warning; but she passed him by. He stood watching her, holding the door open in his hand till she took the bend of the staircase that hid her from his sight.

"Bedad, the Dowager couldn't have done it better," he said, "shweepin' by me without a 'By your l'ave, Pat'; and the master, callin' me 'Murphy' to my face, what he's never done since he left the rig'ment. I wonder what's the matter with Pat. 'Twill be 'Corporal' next."

Nelly looked into the drawing-room. Her father was not there. She turned the handle of another door, the door of the General's own particular den, and going in she found him.

She never thought of asking herself how he came to be there at this hour of the day, he who lived by rule, the click of whose latch-key had sounded in the hall-door every evening at a quarter to seven as long as she could remember. The clock on the mantelpiece pointed to ten minutes to five.

The General was sitting in an armchair by the fireplace as though he had dropped into it on his entering the room. He was doing absolutely nothing, and that was an alarming thing enough, if but she had noticed it. A green evening paper was crumpled on his knee. If she had eyes to see it there was calamity in his attitude and his looks. But she had no eyes. She was too much absorbed in the thing she had to do.

"What, Nell!" he said, getting up as she entered. "We must have come home almost together. Where have you been, child?"

To his own ear his voice rang false, but she did not notice it. She did not meet his kiss. She did not see that he was looking at her with a fearful apprehension.

"What is the matter, Nell?" he stammered, noticing the alter-ation in her looks.

She came and stood beside him, seeming to tower above him.

"Father," she said, "I am not going to marry Robin. I want him to know at once."

"Not marry Robin!" This was something the General was un-prepared for. "Not marry Robin! God bless my soul, Nell! It's very late for you to say such a thing — within three weeks of your wed-ding! And all the arrangements made! What will people say? What will the Dowager say? You can't play fast and loose with a man like that, Nell. Why, it will be the talk of the town."

He tried to work himself up to the old fretting and fuming, but there was no heartiness in it. Under the projecting eyebrows his old frostily-blue eyes had a scared look. But if he had been in such a pas-sion as he had shown on a certain historic occasion when the regi-ment had nearly scattered before the approach of screaming Dervishes — a passion which had rallied the men and won Sir Denis his V.C. — it would have been all the same to Nelly.

"All that is perfectly immaterial," she said. "I am sorry for Robin and for Aunt Matilda. But all that will pass. I was mad to consent to the marriage. I am only glad that I came to my senses in time."

Was this Nelly? — this young, sure, inflexible creature! He stared at her in utter amazement.

"Supposing I were to say that you must go on now since you have gone so far, Nell?" he said, and felt at the same time the futility of the saying. "I never thought my girl would play so shabby a trick on Gerald's son. You know that people will laugh at Robin?"

"They won't. Robin is not the sort of person to be laughed at — at least, not for long. Besides, if it is any consolation to you, father, I may tell you that it will not hurt Robin much: Robin is not and never has been in love with me."

"What!" The General now was genuinely indignant. He had forgotten for the moment his other perturbation, whatever it might be. "What do you mean, Nell? Your cousin not in love with you! After all the years during which you have been meant for each other! Impossible, Nell! Robin *must* be in love with you."

"He is not; he never has been. That is my consolation, so far as he is concerned. Father, why did you keep from me the fact that Captain Langrishe was fighting the Wazees? Why did you?"

The General's colour deserted his cheeks once again.

"Poor Langrishe! What was the good of letting you know, Nell? You used to be — interested in the poor fellow."

"You shouldn't have kept it from me. I didn't read the newspapers, or I should have known. Do you know why I didn't read them? Because if I had I must have turned to the army news. I was fighting that as a temptation. I was trying to drive him from my mind. I kept away from his sister, although she had been kind to me; I went nowhere where I might hear his name. Then today I met her by accident. I went home with her. She told me — do you know what she told me?"

"What, Nell?"

"That her brother went away under the impression that I was engaged to Robin Drummond. Aunt Matilda had told her so and she had told him. So that is why he left me."

"I see," the General groaned. "A nice lot of trouble has come out of that scheme of your Aunt Matilda's for marrying you and Robin. I never would agree to it; I used to say: 'Let it be till the children are old enough to choose for themselves.' I wish I had taken a stronger stand. I only wished for your happiness, Nell. I always liked poor Langrishe, and felt I could trust him with even what I held dearest on earth. I did my best for you, Nell. If I kept his danger from you, it was only that I hoped to keep you from suffering like those other poor women."

She did not notice the haggardness of his face, nor the repetition of "Poor Langrishe." She was too much absorbed in getting to the root of things. She was determined to know everything.

"What happened when you went to Tilbury?"

Was this young inquisitor his Nell?

"I didn't see him. The boat had gone."

"And I thought you had offered me to him, and that he had rejected me! Oh, I know you would have done it in the most delicate way. There need not have been a word spoken. But it would have been the same thing in the end. I thought his love was not great enough to conquer his pride."

"My train broke down, Nell; I came ten minutes too late. I thought the hand of God was in it."

"It was a mere accident. God had nothing to do with it. I am only grateful that it has not ended worse. If I had married Robin and then discovered these things —"

"Don't say that you couldn't have forgiven me, Nell." The General took out a big white silk handkerchief and wiped his forehead with it. "Don't say that you couldn't have forgiven me! I meant it all for the best. My little Nell couldn't be hard with her old father."

She stooped suddenly and caught his hand to her lips. She noticed with a tender contraction of her heart that it was an old hand — knotted, with purple stains.

"I should be a brute if I could be angry with you," she said; and the tenseness of her face relaxed to its old softness.

"Ah, that's right, Nell — that's right. We couldn't do without each other. You've always your old father, you know — haven't you, dearie? — no matter what happens. I'll stand by you, Nell. I'll take you away. No one shall be angry with my Nell."

"You are too good to me," she said. "And I've been angry with you! What a wretch I was to be angry with you! On my way here I telegraphed to Robin to come this evening. I must get it over. You shall take me away if you will afterwards. I would stay and face it if it would do any good, but it wouldn't. After all, there is no great harm done. Robin's heart will not be broken."

"And afterwards, Nell?"

"Afterwards? Oh, you and I shall be together."

"Yes; we did very well when we were together. Listen, Nell." He put his arm about her. "I want you to be strong and brave. I came home to tell you, lest you should hear by accident. His poor sister did not know —"

The General's den looked out on the Square gardens. It was quite a long way across them to the road; yet through the quietness of the golden afternoon there came the shouting of the newsboys. It all flashed on Nelly with a blinding suddenness. To be sure, they had been calling the same thing while she stood with his sister and learned why he had left her, only she had not known.

"He is dead," she said, with an immense quietness. It was as though she had known it always.

"No; not dead, Nell — terribly wounded, but not dead. He is in English hands."

He stopped, shuddering. If he had been in those black devils' hands to be tortured to death! He had been only saved by a sudden rush of his men. Even his wounds would not have saved him from torture if God had not delivered him out of their hands.

"Show it to me."

All of a sudden she saw the newspaper which had been lying crumpled on his knee. That had contained the news all the time while they had been talking about things that mattered so much less.

He did not try to keep it from her. He turned over the paper and found the page of it which had the latest news. There it was, with its staring headlines. She seemed to have seen it just so, in another life.

She read it through to the end. It had been an ambush. The small detachment of troops had been led by the guide into the midst of a large body of the enemy — it had been surrounded. Captain Langrishe had fallen, as had a young lieutenant. The men had stood shoulder to shoulder, fighting desperately. By the most desperate courage they had rescued the bodies of their officers, which were being carried by the tribesmen into one of their towers among the hills. They had fought their way back with the bodies strapped to their horses. Lieutenant Foley proved to be dead. He had been hacked and hewed with knives. Captain Langrishe had been more fortunate; the life was still in him when the last intelligence had been sent down. There was very little hope of his recovery.

Nelly neither cried out nor fainted. When she had finished the reading she laid down the paper quietly. Her father watched her in mingled terror and relief. She was seeing it all — the rocky gorge with the inaccessible hills on either side, filled in with scrub and low trees; at the little neck of the gorge the dreadful tower; the small body of Britishers fighting their way step by step backward; the dazzling blue sky over all. Was Heaven empty that such things happened? She remembered in a kind of daze that she had been at a garden-party that very afternoon. She had worn for the first time her white silk frock with the roses on it and she had seen in many eyes how well it became her. That had happened in another world. A great gulf stretched between even the events of the afternoon and this time — this time, in which she knew that Godfrey Langrishe was dead or dying.

"I wish he might have known," she said quietly, "that after all I was not engaged to Robin."

CHAPTER XXIV

THE FRIEND

Robin Drummond had heard from his cousin's own lips his dismissal. Her father would have spared her, but Nelly would not hear of that and he let her have her way.

She told Robin everything in a dull, unmodulated voice, with a dead-tiredness in it which revealed her unhappiness more eloquently than words could have done. She stood by the mantel-shelf, holding one hand over her eyes while she told him. When she had finished there was a momentary silence.

"You are not angry with me?" she asked, turning about and looking at him with eyes of suffering.

"My poor child! Could I have the heart to be angry with you?"

"Ah! that is right. You were always kind, Robin. I shouldn't have liked you to be unkind now. You must win me your mother's forgiveness."

"She will come round in time."

He had an idea his mother would take it badly. But, of course, she would have to come round. The whole bad business had been her fault in a way; and if she was hard on Nelly, he felt like telling her so.

"I am glad to think I have done you no great harm, Robin. Indeed, the harm would have been in marrying you. I have realised for some time that I was not essential to your happiness."

He opened his mouth to speak and then closed it again. He was not a diplomatist.

"I am very fond of you, Nelly," he said, after a pause.

"Yes, I know you are. So am I fond of you. It was not enough, of course; I ought to have known better."

"And I. I can't forgive myself, Nell, for having been in a way the cause of the mischief. Take courage, dear. All may yet be well. God knows what happiness is in store for you."

"God knows," she echoed; but there was no assurance in her tone.

The General, lying in wait for him, drew him into his own den. He put his hand on Robin's shoulder, leaning heavily on it, like an old man with his son.

"I'm sorry for this, so far as it concerns you, my lad," he said. "But my great trouble is for my girl. She is taking it too quietly. I don't know what is happening — inside. One knows so little about women — how they take those things. She ought to have a woman with her."

"His sister. She is a good little woman, and she adores him. She would be good to Nelly."

"You can't go tearing off to people's houses at this hour of the evening" — it was nine o'clock — "and asking them to come with you. To be sure, the sister knows. I don't want Nell talked about."

"Nor I. Let him come home well and then they can talk of the nine-days' happy wonder. I'm going to the sister. If she fails, there is Miss Gray."

The General snatched at the idea.

"She came to see Nell the other day and I liked her. I began with a prejudice — I've no liking for women who take up the trade of politics. Writing books, too! I'm glad my Nell doesn't write books. I shouldn't like to see her name stuck up in the papers. But this Miss Gray of yours. She overcame my prejudice. She looks clean, my lad, clean outside and within. Nell's fond of her. The dogs pawed her as if they had known her all her life. I trust a dog's judgment. She didn't mind it either, though she was fresh as a daisy. What do you propose to do? To ask her to come round and see Nell tomorrow, if the sister fails? You can't very well ask her to come tonight."

He looked wistfully at Robin.

"Miss Gray often works late," the other said, consulting his watch. "If she is at home, why shouldn't she come back with me? She may be out, of course; the world has begun to run after her. She is not much attracted by the world, but she gives kindness for what she takes to be kindness. She is not conventional. If she feels she is wanted she won't mind coming in at ten o'clock."

"I believe Nell would talk to her," the father said eagerly. "If Nell would talk to someone my mind would be at rest. Poor Nell! The purpose of my life was to keep her from pain and sorrow."

He went back to his room shaking his old head, and Robin Drummond went out into the night. He drove first to Mrs. Rooke's house, and found the mistress absent. She had gone off to an old mother who had to be consoled.

Fortunately it was not far to Mary Gray's little flat, not more than ten minutes' hansom drive. He told the driver to wait while he ran up the stone steps. To his relief, when he had rung the bell at the white door he heard someone stirring within. Mary herself opened the door.

"Forgive my coming at this hour," he began apologetically. Even as he spoke he remembered that he had had a chance of seeing those little rooms that held Mary and had relinquished it on that bygone

Good Friday. He looked enviously beyond Mary herself to the glimpse of lamplit room. He could see a white wall with pictures on its panels, a bit of a dwarf bookcase, a chair drawn to a table heaped with books, a green-shaded reading-lamp. Against the lighted background Mary's cloudy hair stood out illumined.

"What is it?"

"It is my cousin. She is in great trouble. I will explain to you as we go along. Can you come to her? Her father is anxious about her."

She was a woman in ten thousand. She asked no questions, although it occurred to him that it must seem odd to her that she should be summoned, that Nelly should be in great trouble, seeing that he and her father were well.

"Shall I stay the night?" she asked. "Your cousin was so very anxious that I should come and stay with her. She showed me the room I should have — next to hers. Sir Denis seconded the invitation warmly. I said that I would try to come."

"It will be the best thing in the world. How long will you take to get ready? I have a hansom at the door."

"Five minutes."

She came down the stairs in four and a half minutes. Robin had been expeditious; it yet wanted twenty minutes to ten by his watch.

He helped her into the hansom, got in himself and placed her little bag at their feet. The hansom turned up the hill. She waited for him to speak.

"Nelly has found out that she made a mistake," he said quietly. "Her heart was not given to me, but to a Captain Langrishe of her father's old regiment. News has come that he has been badly wounded, so badly that in all probability he is dead by this time. He had exchanged into an Indian regiment, and almost as soon as he got out he was sent into the hills on the business of this wretched little war. Those conquests of ours, what they cost us! Why should we have all those thousands of miles of frontiers to defend? Why can't we stay at home and let the territories be for their own people?"

She smiled quietly to herself in the corner of the cab. The sudden excursion into politics was so characteristic of him.

The wind of the summer night came cool and friendly in their faces. The blue heaven was studded with stars. A little half-moon hung above the quiet shadows of the square through which they were passing. For the stillness they might have been miles away from London.

"What a Don Quixote you are!" she said. "I believe you would cede India if you had your way."

"I believe I should. Don't you wonder at me, Miss Gray? My forbears devoted their existence chiefly to extending the boundaries of the British Empire. Am I not their degenerate descendant?"

"Oh, you're a fighting man in other ways. You don't mind facing a hostile audience and saying unpalatable things to them. Mr. Ilbert says you'll have to fight for your seat at the next election."

"I wouldn't be bothered with a seat I hadn't to fight for. All the same, I'm obliged to Ilbert for his interest in my affairs. Do you know that he referred to me as a Little Englander the other night, as though there were only one way of loving one's country and that to rob other people of theirs?"

His tone was an offended one. The name of Ilbert seemed to have power to irritate him. He resented the idea that Ilbert had talked to Mary of him, disparaged him; he supposed she saw Ilbert often. The idea was exceedingly distasteful to him.

"He has the highest opinion of your honesty and capacity, your patriotism too," Mary said.

He did not want Ilbert's commendation; he hated that Mary should quote his opinions. He lay back in the hansom, staring before him, and his expression was one of unmixed gloom. Even her neighbourhood had no power to cheer him, although at first he had had a sensation of delight in her nearness to him, the perfume as of flowers that hung about her, the soft folds of her dress which he had touched in the darkness.

They were driving along Sherwood Square now. Across the square itself Robin could see the lit windows of the General's house. Their time together was short, he thought; and perhaps the same thought occurred to Mary, for she touched his sleeve with a gesture of sympathy.

"Will you let me say," she said, "how sorry I am for the pain and trouble this must be to you?"

"You mean, because Nelly has — has chucked me?"

"Yes; I mean that."

For a moment he looked down in silence. He wondered if he had any right to tell the truth. Would it not be like a disparagement of Nelly if he were to confess that he had never loved her? A memory floated into his mind. It was of Lady Agatha Chenevix and something she had said to him once at a dinner-party.

"When I must be indiscreet —" she had begun. "Yes?" he had answered laughingly. "When was your ladyship ever anything but indiscreet? and who has made indiscretion adorable like you?" Her ladyship had bidden him hold his tongue with frank camaraderie, and had finished the speech. "When I am indiscreet, I am indiscreet to Mary. She is like a little well, into which one drops one's indiscretions and puts the lid on." "A very clear, transparent, honest well," he had said.

After the momentary pause he lifted his head. The rest of the world might think him heartbroken if it would; he wanted Mary to know the truth.

"As a matter of fact, Miss Gray," he said, "Nelly has not broken my heart. She had always been very dear to me, like a dear little sister. There was a time when I felt that it would be quite easy to fall in with my mother's plan and marry Nelly. But I had come to the conclusion that my feeling for her was not enough for marriage, before that time in the spring when my mother intimated to me that Nelly was ready to fulfil her engagement. I never considered it an engagement. I was actually about to make things clear when that intimation was given to me. Then, I was led to believe that Nelly had taken it as binding. What could I do only go on? If Nelly cared for me — I confess that I ought to have known it to be an unlikely thing — then my great concern in life was that Nelly should not suffer. It was all a pretty bad mistake, but I am glad it has gone no further."

He heard something like a sigh, so faint that he could be hardly sure he heard it. It was, in reality, Mary's thanksgiving and great relief; a burden which had lain at her heart for months past taking wings to itself and flying away. She had not acknowledged to herself that cold doubt about Robin Drummond, who had seemed to come so near to her, while all the time he belonged to another woman. She had pushed away the doubt with loyal refusal to hear it; but it had been there all the time. Now it was gone for ever. There was no more need of excuses or explanations to her own heart.

"Thank you for telling me," she said.

They were at the house-door and the hansom had pulled up. They went up the steps between the couchant lions and before they could knock Pat had opened the door, as though he had been listening for them.

"Miss Nelly is in the drawing-room, sir," he said in his privileged Irish way; "but the master has just gone into the study."

They went up to the drawing-room. Nelly was sitting in a chair by the open window as Robin had left her, tearless, her unemployed hands lying in her lap. The circle of dogs about her watching her with anxious eyes would have been humorous in other circumstances. The lamps were lit behind her, but there was no light on her face, except the dying light in the pale western sky.

"I have brought you a visitor, Nelly," Robin said.

She looked up indifferently. Then something of interest stirred in her face.

"You have heard what has happened?" she said in a half-whisper.

Mary knelt down beside her and put her arms round the little frozen figure.

"Why, you are cold!" she said. "Come away from the window. I am going to ask for a fire, and then you will talk to me about it."

Robin Drummond left them together, and went down to tell Pat to light the fire in the drawing-room, because Miss Nelly was cold.

CHAPTER XXV

THE ONE WOMAN

Mary Gray's loving, capable care and sympathy carried Nelly through the worst days of her trouble. There were times when Mary had to hold the girl's hands, to fight with all her might against the acute suffering which menaced for a time her sanity and her health. The horrors into which Nelly fell when she thought upon the things which happened in such wars as this with cruel and cunning savages, were the worst things to fight. There were hours in which all the fears of the world seemed to be let loose on the unhappy child, when it seemed impossible to vanquish those powers of darkness with one poor woman's love and prayers. During these days Mary Gray hardly left Nelly's side. Fortunately she had ceased to direct the Bureau, and another capable, much more common-place, young woman had taken up her task. The official appointment was on its way, but had not yet arrived. So she was free to devote herself to her friend.

The doctor whom Sir Denis called in could do little for the patient except prescribe sleeping draughts to be taken at need. He understood that the girl had had a shock. He suggested a change, but Nelly would not hear of that. She must stay on in London where the first news would come. So stay on they did, through the torrid heats of July, when the dust was in arid drifts on the Square green gardens and blew in through the open windows, powdering everything with its faint grey.

"This young lady is better than my prescriptions," the doctor said handsomely of Mary Gray. And added, "Indeed, what can we do for sorrow except give the body a sedative?"

"If she could face her trouble clear-eyed," Mary said, "I should feel glad in spite of everything. It is these mists and shadows in her mind that it is so hard to fight against."

After a little while they were left pretty well to themselves in Sherwood Square. The Dowager was angry with Nelly as her son had anticipated; and, after a scene with Robin which prevented a scene with Sir Denis, she had gone off over the sea to the Court. Everybody went out of town: even Sherwood Square emptied itself away to the sea and the foreign spas. Only Robin Drummond stayed in town and came constantly. During the early days when Nelly kept the house and refused obstinately to go out of doors, he would leave Sir Denis in charge and carry Mary off for a walk in the Square.

The first sign of interest that Nelly showed in other things than her sorrow was when she indicated to her father the distant figures of Mary and Robin moving briskly along at the farther side of the Square.

"Do you notice anything there, papa?" she asked.

"What do you mean, my pet?"

Sir Denis was quite flurried at Nelly's suddenly coming out of her brooding silence.

"I mean Mary and Robin," she answered. "It has been borne in on me that that is why Robin was not in love with me. Poor Robin! He would have gone through it heroically. Never say again, papa, that he is not a true Drummond. And I should never have known if he could have helped it that I wasn't the only woman for him."

"You don't mean to say, Nell, that Robin is in love with Miss Gray?"

"That is it, papa."

The General turned very red. For a second his impulse was towards wrath; then he checked himself.

"To be sure, as you didn't want him, Nell, it would be the height of unreasonableness to expect poor Robin to be miserable for your sake. And Miss Gray is a fine creature — a fine, handsome, clever creature. Still, there is a great difference in their positions. It will be a blow to the Dowager."

"Mrs. Ilbert would not have minded."

"God bless my soul! You don't mean to say that Miss Gray could have had Ilbert?"

"She has refused him, but I don't think he has given up hope."

"God bless my soul! Why, the Ilberts are connected with half the peerage. We Drummonds are only country squires beside them. Such a handsome fellow too, and with such a reputation! Why should she refuse Ilbert? Is the girl mad?"

"Robin was first in the field. But I happen to know that Mary refused Mr. Ilbert while yet Robin and I were engaged. What do you think of that?"

"Madder and madder. I don't understand women, Nell. Such a fellow as Ilbert! Why, he might marry anybody. We must make it easy for them with the Dowager, Nell — as easy as we can. We owe a good deal to Miss Gray."

"Oh, she'll come round — she'll have to come round."

"Do you suppose they understand each other, Nell?"

"I don't think Robin has spoken. He seems to be waiting for something. I have only noticed the last day or two. Before that I was absorbed in my troubles — such a selfish daughter, papa."

"My darling, we have all felt with you. It is so good to see you more yourself, Nell."

"Ah!" She turned away her head. "I have a feeling — there is no reason for it at all — that good news is coming. I felt it when I awoke this morning."

Meanwhile Robin Drummond and Mary had the Square almost to themselves, except for a gardener or two. All around the Square were shuttered and silent houses. It was the most torrid of early August days, and presently the heat drove them to a sheltered seat beneath a tree. In the mist of heat around them the bedding-plants, the scarlet geraniums, the lobelia and bees, made a vivid glare. Only in the forest trees, too dense for the dust to penetrate, were there shadow and relief.

They were talking of Nelly.

"She will be all right now," Mary said. "She has come out of the darkness. Even if she has his death to bear I think she will bear it. She reproaches herself for the pain she has caused her father."

"Poor Uncle Denis! He lives in terror about Nelly. She is all he has had since her mother died."

"I think he may rest easy now. Nelly is not going to die — not even of grief. Now that she is better, Sir Robin, why don't you go away? I know your yacht is waiting for you, and you have got the London look; you want change."

"I shan't go till there is news one way or another."

"There ought to be news soon. It is hard on you waiting from day to day."

"I don't feel it hard. Perhaps if the good news came I might induce them to come away with me on the yacht. It would be the best thing in the world for them. For the matter of that, why don't you go away? You also have the London look."

"Oh, I shall go gladly when I may. I am really longing to be off. Do you know what I shall hear when I go over there? — a sound I am longing for."

"What?"

"The rain. I close my eyes now and fancy I hear it pattering on the leaves. Oh, the music of it! One is never long without it at home. We've had six weeks without rain here. Can't you imagine the soft, delicious downpour of it? The music of the rain — my ears hunger for it."

"Oh, now indeed I see that it is time you went. You will probably have enough of the rain."

He spoke gloomily, and she laughed.

"It will probably rain all the time I am there. And I shall be able to forgive it because of its first delicious moments."

"What are you going to do?" He asked the question almost roughly.

"I am going to be with my father, in a mean, little two-storied house of six rooms. At least, it is mean outwardly; but no house could be mean inside where he lived and spread his light. He will have to be at his work every day till he gets his fortnight's holiday in September. If I get away in, say, a fortnight's time, I shall help my stepmother about the house while he is at business all day; I shall have a thousand things to do. They have only one servant; and my stepmother and sisters do the greater part of the work. They would treat me like a queen when I go over there, if I would let them; but I never do let them. I love dusting, and cooking, and mending, and helping the little ones with their lessons. Then as soon as my father is free I am going to carry them off to a hotel I know between the mountains and the sea. It is a big, old-fashioned house, and there is a lovely garden, full of roses and lilies, and phlox and stocks and holly-hocks and mignonette and sweet peas. I stayed there once with dear Lady Anne. We shall all have a lovely time. There is a trout-stream at the end of the garden and the trout sail by in it. There are hundreds of little streams running down from the mountains. They make golden pools in the road and they hang like gold and silver fringes from the crags that edge the road."

There had been a deliberation in what she told him about the little house. But she was mistaken if she thought to surprise him. He was picturing her there at her domestic duties and thinking that no small or mean surroundings could dwarf her soul's stature. Hadn't the hideous official room that held her been heaven to him? — the singing of the naked gas-jets the music of the spheres?

"It will be a great change from London," he said.

"I am going back to the old days. I have refused to see any of my fine new friends. The Ilberts will be staying over there with the Lord Lieutenant at the same time. I have forbidden Mr. Ilbert to call."

Again his mood changed to one of unreasonable irritation. What had she to do with the Ilberts, or they with her?

"If I find myself over there I shall certainly call," he said, with an air of doggedness.

"Oh, very well, then, you shall," she said merrily. "*You* won't embarrass us, not even if we have to ask you to dinner."

An hour or two later the good news came, brought by Mrs. Rooke in person. Captain Langrishe could hardly yet be considered out of danger, but he lived; he had been sent down in a litter to the nearest station, where there were appliances and comforts and white people all about him, outside the sights and sounds of war, beyond the danger of recapture by the enemy.

Nelly bore the better news well: she had been prepared for it, she said. Seeing her so quiet, Mrs. Rooke brought out a scrap of blue ribbon cut through and blood-stained. It was in a little case which had been hacked through by knives. It had been sent home to her at the first when there was no hope, when, practically, Godfrey Langrishe was a dead man.

"It is not mine, my dear," she said to Nelly, "and I think it must be yours. I did not dare show it to you before."

Nelly went pale and red. Yes, it was her ribbon, which had fallen from her hair that morning more than a year ago when Captain Langrishe had ridden by with the regiment and the wind had carried off her ribbon.

She received it with a trembling eagerness.

"Yes, it is mine," she said. "I knew he had it. He showed it to me before he went away."

"How furious Godfrey will be when he misses it!" Mrs. Rooke said. "Somebody will be having a bad quarter of an hour. And now, Nelly, when are you going to be well enough to come to see my mother? She longs to know you. She is the dearest old soul. She wanted me to bring you to her while yet we were in suspense. But I waited for news, one way or another."

"I should love to go," Nelly said.

"She has a room in a gable fitted up for you; the windows open on roses. The place is full of sweet sounds and sights. All through this trouble her thoughts have been with you. Will you come?"

"If papa can spare me."

"Then I shall ask him, and we can go down on Saturday. Won't he come for the day? When you know my mother I am going to leave you there with her. Poor Cyprian is off to Marienbad and I must go with him. He's dreadfully afraid of losing his figure. A fat lawyer, he says, is the one unpardonable thing. Will you look after my mother?"

The General was only too glad to give his consent to the plan which had brought the colour to Nelly's cheek and the light to her eye. After leaving Nelly in Sussex he and Robin would go down to Southampton, get out the yacht and cruise about the coast till Nelly felt inclined for a longer run.

So Mary Gray was free to go. She went out in the afternoon, leaving Robin to look after his cousin. The General had gone off to the club with a lighter heart than he had known for many a month. Robin had suggested a drive, but Nelly would not hear of that. She was going to save up her pleasure, she said, for Sussex and Saturday.

She consented to walk in the Square, where she had not been for quite a long time. He noticed that she looked delicate and languid and his manner to her was very tender. In fact, a new under-gardener in the Square, who was very susceptible to romance, put quite an erroneous interpretation on Robin's manner to his cousin, and hovered in their vicinity with eager curiosity till he was pulled up sharply by one of his superior officers.

"So we are all going to scatter, Nell," Drummond said, half regretfully.

She glanced at him.

"Poor Robin! It was too bad, keeping you in town."

"I haven't minded it at all, I assure you, Nell. Indeed, I couldn't have gone happily while you were in suspense."

"Robin," she said suddenly, "what are you waiting for?"

He started. "Waiting for?" he repeated. "What do you mean, Nell?"

"You're not going to let Mary go without speaking to her?" Under her light shawl her hand felt for and held the locket which contained the blood-stained blue ribbon. "Haven't you waited long enough? I believe she would wait an eternity for you, but don't try her. Speak now."

"My dear Nell," he stammered, "it is only a fortnight or so from the day that should have been our wedding day."

"I was thinking as much. What have you had in your mind? Some foolish Quixotic notion. What were you waiting for?"

"To tell the truth, Nell, till you should be happy."

"Don't take the chances of letting her go away without telling her. Do you think I haven't known that you were in love with her all the time? Why, that first day I saw her I said to myself in amazement, 'Where were his eyes that he could have chosen you before her?'"

"Nelly, how do I know that she will look at me?"

"She will never look at anyone else. Speak now, if only in fairness to the men who might be in love with her, who are in love with her and may have false hopes."

"She won't look at me, Nell."

"She has sent Mr. Ilbert about his business, but he will not let her be. He says that so long as she is not anybody else's she may yet be his. I didn't want to betray him, but I must make you understand."

Poor Ilbert! For a moment Drummond's mind was filled with a lordly compassion towards him. Ilbert rejected! And for him! To be sure, he knew Mary cared for him. She was not the girl to have admitted him to the intimacy of last winter unless she cared. She had borne with him exquisitely. She had even taken her successful rival to her breast. He had made her suffer, the magnanimous woman.

Suddenly he took fire. He had been a slow, dull fellow, he said to himself, and quaked at the thought that Ilbert might have robbed him of his jewel. Now, he felt as though he must follow her, and make her his without even the possible mischances of a few hours of absence.

"She comes back to dinner?" he asked.

"She comes back to tea," his cousin answered, "and you have made me tired, Robin. I am going to rest till tea-time."

They went back to the house and Nelly left him in the drawing-room while she went away to her own room. He knew that she was giving him his opportunity and was grateful for it. How could he have been so mad as to think of letting Mary go away with nothing settled between them?

He walked up and down restlessly, while the dogs watched him in amazement from their cushions. It was a topsy-turvy world in which the dogs found themselves of late. They had almost reached the point of being surprised at nothing. It was lucky the carpet was so faded and shabby, for of late the General had worn a path in it with his restless movements; and now here was his nephew behaving as though he were an untamed creature in a cage and not a sober, serious legislator.

At last he heard her knock, and her light foot ascending the stairs. She looked surprised to find him alone and asked rather anxiously for Nelly.

"You didn't let her get over-tired?" she asked, apprehensively.

"No; we walked very little. She said she would rest till tea-time. Well, have you packed?"

"I have put my things together. I am going to ask to be allowed off tomorrow. I shall sleep at the flat tomorrow night, if they can spare me, and be off the next morning."

"You are glad to be free?"

"Very glad. I was also glad to stay. And you?"

He rose up to his awkward length from the chair into which he had dropped on hearing her knock and went close to her.

"I shall never be free again in this world," he said. And then, with a change of tone: "Do you suppose I am going to let you go over there a free woman?"

He drew her almost roughly to him.

"I have always loved you," he said.

"And I," she answered, "I have loved you since I was sixteen."

"My one woman!" he cried in a rapture.

CHAPTER XXVI

GOLDEN DAYS

The time went peacefully with Nelly and the mother in the little house among the Sussex woods. And presently, since Nelly showed no indication of wishing to join them, and could not be spared indeed, and since Robin was plainly ill at ease yachting up and down the coast, the General declared his intention of going off to a grouse-moor in Scotland, rented by an old friend, over which he had shot year after year for many years back.

On hearing of this sudden change of plans Robin expressed a polite regretfulness, but the General looked at him with twinkling eyes — he and Robin had come to be on the best of terms of late — and bade him be off to Dublin without any confounded hypocrisy about it.

"You've been wishing me anywhere, my lad, this last week or two except aboard the *Seagull*," he said. "Not but what you've borne with me — oh, yes, you've borne with me; a lad of my own couldn't have done more: and now you've earned your reward."

So the General went off northward for what was left of the grouse season. Later, he was to go into Sussex for the partridge and pheasant shooting, not so far from where Nelly was living in a state of blissful peace, with excellent reports of Langrishe's recovery coming by every mail.

And be sure, the *Seagull* spread her white wings and flew, as fast as wind and wave could carry her, across the Irish Sea.

Sir Robin presented himself unannounced at the little house in Wistaria Terrace, where the youngest but two of the Miss Grays opened the door half-way to him, and was visibly alarmed at the sound of his title.

The little house smelt of cookery, perhaps of washing, although doors and windows were open. But little Robin Drummond cared for that. Beyond the demure child who had admitted him he caught sight of Mary sitting on the shabby little grass-plot, in a wicker-chair, with a Japanese umbrella over her head. And roses could not have been sweeter than the atmosphere.

The simplicity which belonged to his character came out in his dealings with Mary's family. Walter Gray came home to find his daughter's grand lover stretching his long figure on the grass at her feet, while the smaller Grays, their shyness quite departed, rolled and tumbled over him as confident as puppies. To be sure Walter

Gray, with his disbelief in distinctions of rank as otherwise than accidental, was not unduly elated by the fine company in which he found himself. He looked hard and long at Robin Drummond as hand met hand. Then a bright look of reassurance came over his face. He could trust even Mary to the owner of those eyes.

They discovered a deal in common later on as they walked, with Mary for a third, in the long twilight and early moonlight. Walter Gray imparted his secret thoughts as to a spiritual brother. His dreams, his aspirations, his Utopia of a world as he would have made it, he laid bare to Robin Drummond in his slow, easy talk, with a hand through his arm.

"He was born to be a great man," Robin Drummond said to Mary later, in a generous enthusiasm, "and he shall not miss his vocation. He must have leisure and ease. When we are married he shall have a corner of the Court to himself, and he shall put his dreams into black and white. I know the room; it looks into an elm-tree, and the owner of the room has the key to the birds' secrets. There is an oriel window, and in the room is a little old organ, yet wonderfully sweet. You shall play to him when he lacks inspiration."

"He could do better with the young ones about him and the mother grumbling placidly in his ear," said Mary.

"Then they shall have the Cottage. It is within the walls and looks to the mountains. It is a roomy old place and has a big over-grown garden of its own."

"I wonder if he will take it from you?"

"He will have to," said the lover.

Then they went back to supper: and he was introduced to Gerald, the young bank-clerk, whose mind was not yet cured of the fever for the sea, who had a roving eye in his smooth young face; and Marcella, the eldest one of the young Grays, who was a typist in the same employment as her father. And though at first the young people were shy of Mary's lover they were quickly at home with him. The fine breeding of Walter Gray had passed on, to some extent, to every one of his children.

"It will be my privilege to look after them," Robin Drummond said to Mary. "As for the lad, he will never be a financier. He is too old for the Navy, but why should he not learn the seaman's trade on the yacht? He has a pining look which I don't altogether like."

"It will be said that you are marrying all my people," Mary said uneasily.

"We shall not hear it said," her lover answered placidly. "We shall be out of hearing of that sort of thing."

When their friendship had the ratification of weeks upon it he broached the matter of the cottage to Walter Gray. They were walking together as they usually did of evenings; and Walter Gray walked with a stick, leaning on him, with the other hand thrust through his arm. He had a groping way of walking, which Drummond had noticed and ascribed to his abstraction from the things about him. After Drummond had unfolded his plans there was a silence, during which he watched Walter Gray curiously. Was he going to refuse, as Mary had suggested?

They were near a lamp on the suburban road which stood up in the boughs of a lime, making a green flame of the tree. Walter Gray pulled up suddenly and lifted his eyes to the light.

"Do you notice anything?" he asked.

Drummond peered down into the eyes. Yes, there was a slight film upon the pupil of one.

"Cataract," said Walter Gray cheerfully. "I shall never be fit for my work any more, even if an operation should be successful. Marcella knows. Good girl, she has kept her own counsel. I have not been working for some time at the watches. Mr. Gordon, kind soul, continues my salary. I have been learning type-writing against the days that are to come. I confess I have a desire to write a book. I have saved nothing, Sir Robin Drummond. How is it possible, with fifty shillings a week and eight children? I have no pride about accepting your offer. If my scrip is empty and yours is full I don't object to receiving from a fellow-pilgrim what I should give if our cases were reversed."

"Ah! that is right," said Robin Drummond. "As for cataract, in its early stages it is easily curable. Sir George Osborne —"

"I will do whatever you and Mary wish. But I anticipate blindness. I shall not mind very much if I have the light within. There will be the book to solace my age; and after a time I shall not be so helpless."

The Dowager came round after all sooner than was expected. The reconciliation was hastened by a letter she received from Mrs. Ilbert congratulating her on her prospective daughter-in-law. "My poor Maurice," she wrote. "I don't mind telling you, dear Lady Drummond, that Maurice was head-over-ears in love with your charming and distinguished daughter-in-law that is to be. The boy takes it very well, says that the better man has won, which is exactly like Maurice. Since your son has chosen a political career I congratulate him on having such a woman as Miss Gray by his side. She will be a force in political life, so says Maurice. And she will be the noblest inspiration. Though I am grieved that she is to be your son's Egeria and not mine yet I offer you and Sir Robin my heartiest congratulations. I may add that I also congratulate the party to which your son belongs."

Lady Drummond had rubbed her eyes over this letter. Congratulate *her* — was it possible? — on being the prospective mother-in-law of Mary Gray, the daughter of a man who worked for his living at repairing the insides of watches! She, the widow of a hero, a rich woman of social importance! Congratulate *her* and Robin and Robin's party! And not one word of congratulating Mary Gray! Was Caroline Ilbert mad?

However, the thing impressed her. It worked by slow degrees into her mind. She had listened often to such foolish heresies as that which declared brains more important than rank or wealth. In a general way she had not dissented. Brains were very important. Gerald had thought a good deal of brains. If he had lived he had meditated a book on Napoleon's Wars. She had often met writing and painting and musical people in her friends' drawing-rooms. They had not appealed to her nor she to them. But she had grown accustomed to their presence there and to meeting them on an equality to which in her heart she had never subscribed.

However, she had the wisdom to see that there was no use in holding out against her son and to console herself with the idea that Mary was going to be a personage, even apart from the incredible social promotion of marrying Sir Robin Drummond. So she actually reached the point of coming in person to Wistaria Terrace to make a formal recantation of her opposition to the marriage, and to take Mary to her imposing, black-bugled breast.

To be sure the little house had almost driven her back from its threshold. She filled the small shabby hall, she fell over the brushes left by the general servant who had been scrubbing the oilcloth, not expecting her ladyship; she sat uncomfortably on the green rep chairs of the drawing-room staring at a Berlin-wool banner-screen which represented a poodle with beads for his eyes, at the silver shavings in the grate, and the school drawings, finished by the nuns, of the younger Misses Gray. There were certain aspects of that drawing-room dear to Mrs. Gray which Mary had been too tenderhearted to try to alter.

There Mary had found her and had been moved in her innermost humorous sense; but she had been glad to be friends with Robin's mother, and so had done her best to advance the reconciliation.

Lady Drummond had a surprising proposal to make. It seemed that her friend, Lady Iniscrone, had placed at Miss Gray's disposal for the wedding the big house on the Mall formerly occupied by

Lady Anne Hamilton. Lady Iniscrone wrote that they had heard of Miss Gray from a friend of Lady Agatha Chenevix, and had felt interested in her progress ever since. Of course, remembering the tie which had existed between Lord Iniscrone's aunt and Miss Gray, Lord and Lady Iniscrone could never be without interest in Miss Gray's progress.

Mary smiled a smile of fine humour over the reading of the letter. At first she was in the mood to refuse. But, being her father's daughter, and so endowed with that sense of the comedy as well as the tragedy of life which makes it easy to regard things and persons equably, she consented at last. She would have preferred to be married from Wistaria Terrace, but she had no difficulty in making a concession to Robin's mother.

So the wedding-breakfast was spread in the dining-room where she and Lady Anne used to have their meals together. Mrs. Gray held a terrified reception of the few fine folk whom Lady Drummond had declared it necessary to ask in the long drawing-room with the three windows where Lady Anne used to sit with little Fifine in her lap.

Mary had wished to be married from the poor little house where she had grown up, but on her wedding day she felt that she had done as Lady Anne would have wished. There was nothing changed in the house: the old-fashioned substantial furniture, the faded carpets and curtains, were just the same. There were one or two familiar faces among the servants. After all, Lord and Lady Iniscrone had used the house little, since Lord Iniscrone had developed a chest affection which kept him following the sun round the world for three-fourths of the year.

The marriage had taken place earlier at the big, dim old church behind which Wistaria Terrace hid itself away, and the few fine folk were not bidden to the wedding but to the reception. A great many glittering things were spread out on the tables in the long drawing-room. It was surprising how many well-wishers the new Lady Drummond seemed to have in the great world. Sir Denis Drummond had come over for the wedding, and Nelly was a bridesmaid, with Mary's type-writing sister, Marcella. She was a different Nelly from her of a couple of months earlier, her delicacy gone, her old pretty bloom come back, her eyes bright as of old.

"Mrs. Langrishe wants me to return to her!" she confided to Mary, "but we are going to Sherwood Square. You know, *he* is on his way home. In a week or two he will be on the sea. He must come to me, not find me there waiting for him. Do you know, Mary, that though his mother and sister have taken me to their hearts, he has not written me a line? You don't suppose, Mary, that he could be going to keep silence *now*?"

"Of course not," said Mary. "Seeing what you have suffered for him —"

"He must never know that," Nelly said, with gentle dignity, "until he has spoken. What should I do, Mary, if he never spoke? But I think everyone would keep my secret, even his sister and mother. I asked them not to speak of me in their letters. I am in suspense, Mary."

"It will not be for long," the happy bride assured her. As though she were wiser than another in knowing the way of any particular man with any particular maid!

CHAPTER XXVII

THE INTERMEDIARY

Some time in December Captain Langrishe came home.

Nelly knew the day and the hour that he was expected, but she was as terrified of meeting him as though she had not had so much assurance of his love for her. She knew the events of the day as though she had been present at their happening. Cyprian Rooke's brother, a young, distinguished doctor well on his way to Harley Street although only a few discriminating people had found him out, had gone down to Southampton with Mrs. Rooke and her mother to meet the invalid, who even yet must bear traces of the terrible illness through which he had passed. Nelly could see it all, from the moment the big boat came into Southampton Docks till the arrival in London. Captain Langrishe was going down to his sister's cottage in Sussex. The mother and sister, who already claimed Nelly as their own, had been eager for her to be there on their arrival, or to come later. But Nelly was adamant.

"He must come to me," she said. "And I think the one thing I could not forgive is that anyone should interfere: *anyone*, even you two whom I dearly love. Promise me that you will not."

They had promised her. They were women of discretion; and they felt that now he was come back to them things might safely be left to take their own course. To be sure, as soon as he could he would go to Nelly as to his mate, naturally, joyfully. In an early letter, written before Nelly's embargo, Mrs. Rooke had told him that Nelly's engagement had been broken off. Later, she had conveyed the news that Robin Drummond had consoled himself with rapidity, and was to be married to the Miss Gray whose book on the conditions of women's labour among the poor had made such a stir, and not only in political circles. Godfrey Langrishe in his letters had not commented on these communications.

"Let Godfrey be!" said the sister, who knew him with the thoroughness of a nursery companion. "He will do his own wooing. He would not thank us for doing it for him."

All next day Nelly waited. After the very early morning she did not dare go outdoors lest he should come in her absence. The General went off to his club to be out of the way. At a quarter to seven he opened the door with his latch-key and came in, more than half-expecting to find an overcoat which did not belong to him in the hall. There was none; and he went on to the drawing-room with a vague sense of disappointment. Langrishe must have been and gone.

In the drawing-room he found Nelly alone.

"Well, papa," she said, as he came in, and offered no further remark.

"No one been, Nell?" he asked, with a little foreboding.

"No one."

"Ah, well, to be sure the boat must have arrived late. They may not have got back to town till today."

The next day passed in the same way, and the next day. The fourth day Nelly went out and did her Christmas shopping. She held her head high now, in a spirited way which hurt her father to see, for her face was very pale. That evening she put on a little scarlet silk dinner-jacket, in which the General declared that she looked every inch a soldier's daughter. But the brilliant colour only made her look paler by contrast.

On the fifth day the General, instead of going to his club, went to see Mrs. Rooke and fortunately found her at home. He hardly knew the little woman, but she was a friend of Nell's and had been good to her. Besides, he was so bent upon getting to the root of the business about Langrishe and Nell that he felt no embarrassment on the subject of his errand.

"My dear," he said, bowing over Mrs. Rooke's pretty hand — he had a charming way with women — "I have come without my daughter knowing. Perhaps she would never forgive me if she knew. Tell me: what is the mystery about your brother? Why has he not been to see us?"

"I am so glad you came to ask me, Sir Denis," Mrs. Rooke replied. "I was just about to go to Nelly. Godfrey is so obstinate. The doctors cannot say yet if he is going to be a cripple or not. His sword-arm was almost slashed through. Jerome Rooke, my brother-in-law, says it will be all right. On the other hand, Sir Simon Gresham shakes his head over it. Godfrey is to see him again in a few weeks' time. He is waiting for his verdict before he speaks to Nelly. My opinion is that if the verdict is adverse he will never speak at all."

"Why, God bless my soul, then!" shouted the General in his most thunderous voice, "he must speak before! he must speak before! Everything must be settled. They shall hear Sir Simon's verdict together."

Those people had been right who had called Sir Denis unworldly. Mrs. Rooke blinked her pretty eyes before his outburst.

"You know, of course, Sir Denis, that his profession will be closed to him in case his arm doesn't get well. Godfrey has always felt that he had too little to offer your daughter. But now — it will be a maimed life if the worst happens. Both my mother and I appreciated Godfrey's reasons. We could not say that he was not right. Poor Godfrey! I don't know what he will do if he loses his profession. You know he was devoted to his work."

"I know, ma'am." The old soldier's eye lit up with a sudden spark. "In any case, with the help of God, he will have Nell to comfort him. Your brother's address is —"

"You are going to him?"

"It seems the one thing to do. I've no pride about offering my girl where I know she is deeply loved."

"You are a trump, General!" Mrs. Rooke said, with sparkling eyes.

"Thank you, ma'am," the General answered, blushing like a school-boy. "I was never one to sit with folded hands. The Lord didn't make me like it. And I've asked His direction, ma'am; I've asked His direction humbly, and I hope humbly that He is granting it to me."

"Well, God speed you!" Mrs. Rooke said. "Godfrey will be good to Nelly, Sir Denis. He has always been so trustworthy. And he has had so many hard knocks. He deserves happiness in the end."

"He shall have it, with the help of God."

The General never made any forecast without the latter proviso, although that was often said only in the silence of his heart.

The railway journey, unlike the last made in the cause of Nelly's happiness, went without a hitch. The day was a beautiful, bright, sunshiny one, with clear skies overhead. The General had the carriage to himself, so that he was able to sit with both windows open as he liked it. He felt the winter air quite invigorating as the train rushed through the pale golden landscape. Robins were singing in the bare trees, which showed their every twig outlined delicately against the pale sky. The brown coppices and hedges by which the train hurried were bright with the scarlet of many berries.

The General, sitting up spare and erect — he had never lolled in his life, and held all such soft ways only suitable for ladies — contrasted the journey with the last; and took the radiant day like a good omen. He wished Nell could have been with him to have the roses blown in her cheeks by the delicious fresh wind. However, he was going to bring her home roses, pink roses; the white rose in his Nelly's cheek did not at all please him.

The little house was quite near the railway, a gabled, two-storied cottage with diamond-paned windows, and creepers and roses all over its walls. Even yet on the sheltered side there was a monthly rose or two on the leafless bushes. The house basked in the sun; and Mrs.

Langrishe's red-and-white collie came to meet the General, wagging his tail with a friendly greeting.

The maid who opened the door smiled on him. She knew him for Miss Nelly's father; and Nelly had a way of making herself beloved by servants wherever she went, and not only because she was ready always to empty her little purse among them.

Mrs. Langrishe? Mrs. Langrishe was out, but was expected in to lunch. The Captain had just come in. Would Sir Denis see him?

Sir Denis would see the Captain. He followed the maid through the clean, orderly little house, every inch of it shining with the perfection of cleanliness, to the study at the back which opened on the garden. Captain Langrishe was sitting in a chair in a dejected attitude at the moment the General first caught sight of him. He sprang to his feet, turning red and pale when he saw who his visitor was.

"Well, my lad," the General said, taking the uninjured left hand in a cordial grip. "And how do you feel?"

Langrishe looked up at him with shy eyes.

"To tell the truth, Sir Denis, not very cheerful. I have been, in fact, keeping company with the blue devils pretty well since I came home. You know —"

"Yes, I know. We must hope for the best. But, if you can't carry a sword any longer, why it must mean that the Master of us all has another post for you. And now, why didn't you come to Sherwood Square?"

"I couldn't, with this in suspense," Langrishe stammered. "It is most kind of you to come to see me."

"My dear boy," the General put his hand on Langrishe's shoulder, "you must come, with this in suspense. Do you know that my girl has looked for you day after day?"

The young man flushed and stared at the General's kind face in bewilderment.

"I would rather die than cause her a minute's pain," he said, with quiet fervour.

"You have caused her a good many," the General said grimly. "Not willingly, I am sure of that, or I wouldn't be here. Haven't you heard how she suffered? Why, God bless my soul, I was afraid at one time that I might be going to lose her; and all through you, young man — all through you. Now I'll have no more shilly-shally. If Nell is fond of you and you are fond of Nell —"

"God knows how I love her!" Langrishe cried out, a glow of passion lighting up his worn, dark face. "But you don't understand, Sir Denis. I feel sure you don't understand. I have nothing in the world but my sword. My uncle, Sir Peter, gave me that. He gave me nothing else. Lady Langrishe, who nursed my uncle through an attack of the gout before he married her, has just presented him with an heir. I have no hopes from my uncle. If I lose my sword-arm I lose everything. I am likely to lose my sword-arm, Sir Denis."

"Whether you do or whether you do not is in the hands of God," the General said. "I don't think Nell will mind very much if your sword-arm is ineffectual or not. You've done enough for honour, anyhow. And I'm not going to betray any more of the child's secrets. You'd better come and hear them yourself. I'll tell you what: come on Christmas Day. Come to lunch and bring your bag with you. I daresay you won't want to cut your visit short?"

"You really mean it, Sir Denis?"

"Mean it, my lad? I've meant it for a long time. I've watched your career, Langrishe. I know pretty well all about you. You'd never give me credit for half the cunning I've got." The General rubbed his hands softly together and tried to look Machiavellian, failing ludicrously in the attempt. "There's no man I would more willingly trust my girl to. Why, I went after you to Tilbury when you were going out — to find out what you meant. I'll tell you about it."

For the moment the General forgot completely how he had man[oe]uvred in the second place to marry Nelly to Robin Drummond. In fact, he didn't remember about it till he was going home, and then, after a momentary shamefacedness about his unintentional disingenuousness, he decided, like a sensible man, that there was no use talking about that now.

Before that time, however, he had lunched with Mrs. Langrishe and her son after a talk with the latter. Now that he had succeeded in breaking down the lover's scruples, Godfrey Langrishe was only too anxious to fling himself into the next train and be carried off to his love. But the General would not have it so, though he was pleased at the young man's impatience.

"It wants but five days to Christmas Day," he said. "Come then. You can spare him, ma'am?" to Mrs. Langrishe.

"I have had to spare him for less happy things," the mother responded cheerfully.

There was no happier old soldier in all his Majesty's dominions than was Sir Denis Drummond on his homeward journey. In fact, he found himself several times displaying his gratification so evidently in his face that people smiled and looked significantly at each other. One lady whispered to another of the Christmas spirit.

It was by a stern effort of his will that he composed his face as he went up the stairs of his own house. He didn't deceive Pat, who had admitted him — for once the General had forgotten his latch-key.

Pat reported to Bridget:

"Sorra wan o' me knows what's come to the master; he's gone up the stairs, and the heart of him that light that his foot is only touchin' the ground in an odd place."

"'Twill be somethin' good for Miss Nelly then," Bridget replied sagely.

The General schooled his face to wear an absurdly transparent look of gloom as he entered the drawing-room, but it was quite wasted on Nelly, who didn't look at him. She had a screen between her face and the fire as she sat in her fireside chair, and her little pale, hurt, haughty profile showed up clearly against the peacock's feathers of the screen.

The General had meant to have some play with Nell, but that forlorn look of hers went to his heart.

"I saw Langrishe today, Nell," he said. "He's coming for Christmas. We can put him up — hey?"

"Papa!"

He heard the incredulously joyful half-whisper, and he felt the pang that comes to all fathers at such a moment. Nell was not going to be only his ever again. He had been enough for her once on a time; yet, here she was, come to womanhood, breaking her heart for a stranger.

"If I were you, Nell," he said gently, "I'd be seeing about my wedding-clothes."

CHAPTER XXVIII

NOEL! NOEL!

Captain Langrishe arrived only just in time for lunch on the Christmas Day. By the time he had been shown his room and had deposited his bag and returned to the drawing-room it was time for the luncheon-bell.

The meeting between Nelly and himself would have seemed to outsiders a cold one. To be sure, it took place under the General's eye. One might have supposed that the General would have absented himself from that lovers' meeting, but as a matter of fact he did not. Nelly's flush, the shy, burning look which Langrishe sent her from his dark eyes, were enough for the two principals. For the rest, all seemed to be of the most ordinary. No one could have supposed that for the two persons mainly concerned this was the most wonderful Christmas Day there ever had been since the beginning.

During lunch Langrishe talked mainly to the General. They had plenty to talk about. The General found it necessary to apologise to Nelly for "talking shop," an apology which was tendered in a whimsical spirit and received in the same. Pat, waiting at table, quite forgot that he was Sir Denis Drummond's manservant, listening to the stirring tale; and was once again Corporal Murphy, back in "th' ould rig'mint." In fact, he once almost forgot himself so far as to put in an eager comment, but fortunately pulled himself up in time. He mentioned afterwards to Bridget that the Captain's talk had nearly brought him to the point of "joinin'" again. "Only that I remembered that at last you'd consinted to my spakin' to Sir Denis I couldn't have held myself in, Bridget, my jewel," he said. "But the thought of gettin' kilt before ever I'd made you Mrs. Murphy was too much for me."

There was considerable excitement in the servants' hall over Captain Langrishe's presence. Pat, of course, knew all about him since he belonged to "th' ould rig'mint"; but it was through Bridget's feminine perspicacity that it broke on the amazed couple that it was for him Miss Nelly had been breaking her heart all the time.

"It 'ud do you good," said Pat, "to see the way she carries her little sojer's jacket, and the holly berries on her pretty head like a crown."

To be sure, the younger ones of the servants' hall were talking too, and they even approached Pat, who outside the duties of his office was not awesome, for the satisfaction of their curiosity.

"Just wait," said Pat oracularly. "an' ye'll see what ye'll see."

The speech meant nothing to Pat's own mind except that they would be all wiser later on. However, it went nearer the mark than he had intended.

The afternoon of Christmas Day was always the occasion for a Christmas Tree. Everyone in the house was remembered in the distribution of presents, even the dogs. The tree was set up in the servants' hall and the General had never omitted to distribute the presents himself in all the years they had been at Sherwood Square. He had mentioned the tree to Langrishe at lunch, apologising for asking his assistance at so homely an occasion. His eye twinkled as he said it; and rather to Nelly's bewilderment the young man blushed like a girl. Apparently he had heard of the Christmas Tree before, for he made no comment.

After lunch the lovers were a little while alone. Sir Denis had his secrecies about the Tree, gifts which had to go on at the last moment and to be placed there by himself. When he came back to the drawing-room he was aware from the looks of the young couple that everything had been satisfactorily arranged between them. He looked as cheerful himself as anyone could desire. While he put those last touches to the Tree he had been thinking how good it was that he was going to have his children to himself, no troublesome Dowager with her claims and exactions to come between them. For a long time to come, anyhow, Langrishe must be off active service; and they would all be together in the kind, spacious old house. And presently there would be Nelly's children. Please God he would live to deck the Tree for the delight of Nelly's children! It was the thought of the golden heads of the little lads and lasses yet to be dancing about the Tree that brought the dimness to his eyes, the look of happy dreams to his face.

The Tree was far from being a perfunctory, haphazard affair. Everything had been thought out and planned beforehand. The servants sat in a circle with eager, expectant faces. In front of them was a circle of dogs. The dogs' presents were not much of a novelty. A new collar for one, a new basket for another, a medal for the oldest of the dogs; the possible gifts were very soon exhausted, but they made hilarity, and the dogs barked as they received their gifts as though they understood and enjoyed it all, as no doubt they did.

There was a delightful sensation for the servants' hall when the gold watch which had been hanging near the top of the tree was handed down, and its inscription proved to be: "To Bridget Burke, on the occasion of her marriage to Patrick Murphy, with the affection and esteem of the master and Miss Nelly." The servants' hall broke into cheers. They had all known that there was something between Bridget and Pat, but the thing had hung fire so long that it might well have hung fire for ever. Pat's present was a ten-pound note for the honeymoon. Mr. and Mrs. Murphy were to have a fortnight together after their marriage in some seaside place, before settling down to their old duties. Sir Denis had made Pat the offer of a cottage in the country, but this Pat had refused, to his master's great relief. "Sure, what would you do without me?" he said. "I was thinking the same myself," responded the General.

The General had it in his mind that presently, when those children came, it might be necessary to give up Sherwood Square and live in the country for their sakes. A little place in Ireland now, the General thought, where there was always plenty of sport and good-fellowship. However, that might wait. But the thought was a sweet one, to be turned over in the old man's mind.

Sometimes the present took odd shapes. There was a young housemaid whose eyes were ringed about with black circles, eyes pale with much weeping. Her mother was ill among the Essex marshes, and the only chance for her life, said the doctors, was to get her away to a mild, bracing place for some months. Bournemouth would do very well. Bournemouth? Why, Heaven was much more accessible, it seemed, than Bournemouth for the poor mother of many children.

"Emma Brooks," said the General. "I wonder what's in this envelope for Emma Brooks."

Poor Emma came up, smiling a wavering smile that was on the edge of tears. She took the envelope, peered within it, and then cried out, "Oh, God bless you, sir!" It contained a letter of admission to a convalescent home at Bournemouth for six months, and the money for the expenses of getting there. "It's my mother's life, sir," cried Emma. "You shall go home tomorrow, my girl, and take her there," said the General. "I'll pay whatever is necessary."

At last the Tree was stripped of nearly everything but its candles and its bright dingle-dangles. There was a little basket at the foot of the Tree addressed to the General, which had been moving about in a peculiar way during the proceedings, and had been a source of much fascinated interest to the dogs. On its being opened a fat, waddling, brindle bull-dog puppy sidled himself out of a warm bed, and made straight for the General's feet. A puppy was something Sir Denis never could resist, and though there were already several dogs at Sherwood Square, all desperately jealous at the moment and being held in by the servants, he discovered that he had wanted a brindled bull-dog all his life.

"But what is that," he asked, "up there at the top of the Tree? Why, I was near forgetting it. Come here, Pat, you rascal, and hand it down to me. It's a pretty, shining thing for my Nelly, as bright as her eyes. Hand it down to me, Pat. I want to put it on her pretty neck."

The gift was a beautiful flexible snake of opals in gold, with diamonds for its eyes and its forked tongue, such a jewel as the heart of woman could not resist. The General himself clasped the ornament on Nelly's neck, where it lay emitting soft fires of milky rose and emerald.

There was a little pause. The Tree seemed to be finished. The women-folk began to clear their throats for the *Adeste Fideles* with which the festivity concluded. Afterwards there was to be a glass of champagne all round.

The pause, however, was a device of the General's to give more effect to what was to follow. Captain Langrishe had been standing apart, his shy and modest air commending him the more to the women who thought him so handsome and the men who knew him for heroic; for had not Pat sung his praises? And to be sure, the women's hearts swelled at beholding a hero taking part in their own particular festivity of the year, a hero that is to say with his heroism brand-new upon him and from the outside world, so to speak. They were so accustomed to a hero for a master all the year round, that in that particular connection they hardly thought upon him.

"I believe, after all," said Sir Denis, as though he were talking to children — it was his way with women and children and dependents and animals — "I believe there's something for my girl which she'll think more of than anything else. It's hidden just down here at the foot of the Tree, and might very easily be over-looked if one didn't know beforehand that it was there. Captain Langrishe, will you give this little packet to my Nelly? It's your gift. She'll like it from you."

Langrishe came forward, looking radiantly happy and handsome, and wearing withal that look of becoming shyness. He extracted from somewhere near the roots of the Tree a white paper-covered packet, very tiny and tied with blue ribbon, which he undid with quick, nervous fingers. When he had laid the covering aside it revealed itself as a little ring-case. Opening it, he took out a beautiful old-fashioned ring, a large pearl surrounded by diamonds. He held it for a second between his fingers; and turning round he went to Nelly's side and taking her hand lifted it to his lips. Then he slipped the ring on to her third finger.

"My dear friends," said the General in an agitated voice, "I am very happy to announce to you the engagement of my daughter to Captain Langrishe."

At that the cheering broke out, led by Pat. As the dogs joined in, and even the brindle puppy added his shrill note, there was the happiest, merriest uproar lasting over several minutes, during which the General stood, looking proudly from the shy and smiling lovers to those dependants whom he had really made his friends.

And at last, when the pause came, the General spoke:

"And now, my friends," he said, "to show that God is not forgotten in our happiness and in our grateful hearts, we will sing the *Adeste Fideles*."

THE END